TO PLUCK A CROW

D1521201

BOOK TWO:
DEATH STALKS THE HOUSE OF
HERBERT

BY

SUE TAYLOR DAVIDSON

Renaissance
Diverse Canadian Voices

This is a work of fiction. Any similarity to any events, institutions, or persons, living or dead, is purely coincidental and unintentional.

Cover art by Nathan Fréchette. Typesetting and interior design by Nathan Fréchette. Edited by Joel Balkovec, Myryam Ladouceur, and Evan McKinley.
Legal deposit, Library and Archives Canada, 2020.
Paperback ISBN: 978-1-987963-77-9
Ebook ISBN: 978-1-987963-84-7
Renaissance Press
pressesrenaissancepress.ca

TO PLUCK A CROW

BOOK TWO:
DEATH STALKS THE HOUSE OF
HERBERT

To Pluck a Crow

Book One: The Hands Behind Shakespeare's Pen
Book Two: Death Stalks the House of Herbert

This book is dedicated to my beautiful, kind and honest Mom, who is now with the angels I am sure.
Mom, I miss you so much, we all do, and you and Dad continue to influence each of us in ways that are "just right" for each one

and

To this beautiful world, with all its peoples, its animals, its shocking beauty, as we struggle together to be hopeful and kind during the Pandemic of 2020. We will survive and we will do so by caring for each little flower, each single person being important.
Never let fear overcome.

and

finally, when all is said and done, to The Great Spirit Who holds each one of us in very gentle hands... Miigwech, if I may borrow from my long-suffering, brave and truly inspiring Aboriginal friends, the leaders of tomorrow...Thank You...

PROLOGUE

When you last read about Janek, Sarah, Philip Sidney and Mary Sidney Herbert in Book One: The Hands Behind Shakespeare's Pen of the series, I must admit I left you, gentle reader, high and dry. Yet I hope you will be eager to hear more about the protagonists, and the villains, of this work of historical fiction.

Mary and Philip had constructed their play, Romeo and Juliet, and had decided to cast Philip and his lover, Penelope Devereux, in the title roles. Mary had played the part of Juliet's nurse. They had hoped their aunt Katherine would carry the script back to Queen Elizabeth, who liked nothing better than a new drama. No one was to know that Mary and Philip had authored the work. They had counted on Elizabeth's curiosity and hoped she would have the Queen's Men, her troupe of players, stage it before the proposed wedding of Penelope — against her will — to Robert Rich, a man of wealth and title, and an infamous drinker and spendthrift. Through the influence of the play's tragic message, the siblings had hoped the Queen would change her mind and disapprove of the wedding. Then Philip Sidney and Penelope Devereux would be free to wed, because he was desperately in love with her. His poem, Astrophel and Stella, was a tribute to her. The ploy was a long shot, to say the least. The Queen despised Penelope's mother, Lettice Knollys, for marrying her beloved courtier, "Robin", Sir Robert Dudley, the Earl of Leicester. Mary and Philip believed the Queen was using the unwanted wedding to get back at Lettice.

Did their attempt make a difference?

Sadly, no.

The desperate Penelope was married months later to Lord Rich, and Philip was bereft. He had, as a student in Europe, experienced melancholia, which today we call depression. His sister, Mary Sidney Herbert, wanted to prevent a recurrence. She set about writing another play, calling it *Love's Labour's Lost*, which she hoped would rouse him to action. The play illustrates the winding paths love can take, the insincerities and manipulations of people to get what they want. It does not end in fulfillment for the main characters, but rather poses a challenge, just as *Romeo and Juliet* does.

As you know, in the previous book, the chapters alternated between the past and present day. When we last set eyes on Janek, he was sitting beside Sarah's hospital bed, stroking her hand. She had been hit on the head by the knavish Irishman, Colin O'Hara, a colleague of Janek's at the British Library, who, with an unknown accomplice, had followed our heroes all over southern England to the Isle of Wight. At Carisbrooke Castle, in their pursuit of the missing papers and wills of Mary Sidney and other members of the Herbert family, Sarah had stumbled upon a key hidden in the stony ramparts. By sleight of hand, she had duped Colin, who had then been arrested, while his shadowy accomplice had escaped. Janek and Sarah were now in possession of an antique unusually shaped key.

Though Janek had long been involved romantically with the beautiful, but at times distant, Sybil Merryweather, he had recently realised his feelings had changed. He and Sarah had fallen in love over the course of their adventures. Sarah had professed to Janek that she wanted to continue this quest for clues about Mary and Philip Sidney's lives and the possibility that they had co-authored some of the works attributed to William Shakespeare.

Will you accompany all of us on this mission of mystery?

CHAPTER ONE

Somewhere in the back streets of London, tucked away in a shadowy alley, there is a small coffee shop, frequented by locals but little-known to Londoners in general. The windows are darkened with anti-glare glass. If by chance you had been there yesterday, you would have seen two people talking, huddled together, yet if you were the least bit observant, their body language would have told you the couple was anything but close.

One was a man in his mid-fifties, wearing a dark navy coat and looking for all the world very respectable. The other was the woman who had bicycled onto the ferry the morning before and escaped to the mainland from the Isle of Wight.

That woman was Poppy, accomplice to the now-imprisoned Colin, Janek's colleague, who had betrayed him by attacking Sarah on the ramparts of Carisbrooke Castle. Poppy had befriended Sarah at her London hotel, tricking her into revealing how she and Janek planned to search for clues to the authorship of Shakespeare's works.

"I told you from the beginning he was an incompetent eejit!" Poppy hissed.

"Who are you to tell me anything?" he responded haughtily. "You are well-paid to do your work and keep your opinions to yourself. Now, let's get back to our plan, shall we?"

His icy stare froze her thoughts in their tracks. This man was more dangerous than she had imagined. Their contract had initially seemed so civilised, almost an intellectual assignment, if she had to put a name on it. She knew there was always the potential for some roughhousing but had not expected it this time. Why would anyone hurt someone else for antiquated information? It had given her a new insight into the scholarly profession. These people were no better than the petty criminals she had been raised with. In fact, they were far worse, because with their money they bought anonymity, which made them more dodgy. Of course, it would be she and Colin who would take the fall for the Boss and his cohorts, should anything go wrong.

Her voice betrayed her nervousness as she asked, "Will Colin get off then?"

"Again, that's none of your business. Does it matter to you? Are you two involved in some way?"

"No, never!" Poppy vigorously shook her head.

"Fine, then. Back to the business at hand. My sources tell me that Janek and Sarah are an item," he scoffed. "It was to be expected. On the positive side, they will be easier to follow now. She will likely stay in England, as his dutiful lady, shall we say? Colin has informed me that she found something in the ramparts of Carisbrooke Castle. We always knew evidence was hidden there, but were unable to find it. It was only a matter of time. Unfortunately for us, she found something before we did. It is now your job to find out what. The sooner the better. I trust you have some leads?"

"Don't worry, I have my methods and contacts," Poppy declared with more confidence than she felt. *It is too dangerous to tell him the truth.* He could fire her or do worse.

He rose to leave, and threw a five pound note on the table.

"In the future, we will not meet in person. Email and cell phone will more than suffice. Oh, and please stop worrying your pretty little head about this business. You are in my capable hands. Do you understand?"

He tipped her chin up and nailed her with a venomous stare. Then he was off and out the door, whistling as he went.

Poppy shivered and felt bile rise in her throat. She wanted to wash her face to remove any trace of his touch. He was a creep, but not of the kind she was used to. She could deal with those men. This one was way over her head. She was in too deep. What had once seemed an almost innocent assignment, if any of them could be called that, now felt ominous. But she couldn't run. He would find her and that was a risk she could not take.

The waitress came with the bill, and she pulled herself together. *I am tough*, she thought. Maybe after this job, she would settle down and get a respectable position, even a little cottage. If she played her cards right, she could make him pay. The money would give her the freedom she desperately desired.

Poppy made her way down the winding streets, heading for her hotel room. Once she got there and was alone, she pulled out her phone. The woman on the other end answered on the second ring. Poppy had never heard her so upset.

"I can't believe *he* dumped *me*! I mean, anyone could see we weren't compatible at all! But it should have been me who did the deed. I carried him for almost three years! And they were long, let me tell you. Always sneaking about, hoping he never found out about the other men in my life. But any idiot would have known! All those excuses I gave him— he was far, far too trusting!"

Sybil Merryweather barely stopped for breath.

"Our friends were always asking me why I was with him. Well, you and I know the real reason. No one understood what I saw in him. I mean he *is* good-looking, I'll give him that. And he was always *so nice*, you know. Nothing like the men I usually hang out with. And so intellectual. It bored me to tears and it was all I could do to listen to him go on and on about his bloody Mary Sidney and all his other stupid ideas. And then he turned around and dumped me! No one, I repeat, no one has *ever* done that to me!"

"Are you regretting it then? The break-up?" Poppy asked.

"Of course not! How could you even think that? I don't *need* him in any way. I won't even miss him. In fact it will be a big relief not to have to lie to him anymore. I hated that! He was such an innocent type and he never questioned me once..." her voice faltered and the sudden tears surprised her. "Oh my God, I have never cried over anyone, so why am I doing it now?"

Yes, precisely. Why? Poppy thought at the other end of the phone. *Good question, that. Methinks the woman doth protest too much.* She let silence work its magic. Sybil was now sobbing at the other end of the line. Something in Poppy's gut twisted. She really felt sorry for this woman, for the first time.

"Listen, Syb, I'll be right over. You stay where you are. I'll pick us up a nice bottle of a wine you like and some crisps and we'll have a girls' heart-to-heart. How about it? Don't go anywhere. Cry it all out and you'll feel much better, I guarantee it."

So, Sybil was not the hard-hearted rich girl she had appeared to be at first. Somehow, Janek had managed to get to her, with his trusting ways and his nerdy enthusiasms. It was true he was no match for Sybil, but it was odd that the woman seemed to care so much. *People are never what they seem,* Poppy thought, not for the first time, and this realization scared her. *You always have to have your guard up, girl,* she warned herself. *Look at you! You're starting to care about Sybil's feelings, and this is a job to you. Stop it now, or you'll get soft.*

She knew she needed information from Sybil, details that would help her determine Janek's next move. Her life might depend upon it. If truth be told, she had very little idea of what to do next, or how to follow Janek and Sarah, his new girlfriend, without the help of Colin. He had been on scene, working side by side with Janek, and always knew what was going on. Janek had been an easy mark. But now there was no Colin and possibly no Sybil, unless - *maybe* she could get Sybil to go after Janek again, to seduce him and try to win him back. It would be in her best interests to do that. Maybe they could work together to keep him in hand.

Or maybe not. Sybil was far too busy with her socialite lifestyle to be cruising around England on someone's tail. What was she thinking? *These people aren't your own, missy. You are nowhere near their class, nor will you ever be,* Poppy admitted to herself. Yet, that depended on how deeply Syb was hurt. She'd wait and see.

A few hours later, they were on their second bottle of wine. Sybil had consumed far more than Poppy, which had been the plan: get her drunk, obtain her help to get information from Janek, and leave.

Syb had cried the whole time and it was becoming tiresome. The woman really did care for Janek. It was as if she had just awakened to her feelings for him. Unbelievable, really! All she could talk about were the little things they had done together that had brought her joy, something she hadn't realized was missing from her life. It was like talking to the newly converted. Peace and light everywhere! Sybil even looked more human, with her hair unwashed, wearing fuzzy bedroom slippers, her face streaked and her eyes swollen from crying. Gone, at least for the moment, was the sophisticated woman with the perfect makeup, the enchanting smile and the slight air of aloofness. This was the real Sybil here, and her heart was broken.

Now what to do? Would Janek take her back? Was that what Sybil really wanted or would she grow tired of him as quickly as they settled back in together? The situation was difficult. Poppy really couldn't see them as a happy couple and yet she needed them to be an item again so that her information source would not disappear.

"OK, Syb, have you talked to anyone but me about the breakup? No, so do you want him back, really....?"

"I don't know," Sybil said, drying her eyes and sitting up straight for the first time. "It's all so new to me. I never expected to feel this way, you know? If someone had told me I'd cry over him one day I would have laughed in her face. Me, the strong one! No way. And look at me now!" She was about to start whimpering all over again. The girl sitting beside her abruptly stood up.

"So, what can we do to get him back? Have you tried talking to him?"

"No, I don't do that. At least I never have before. And I don't know if I want to. What if he says *no?*"

"What if he doesn't? Maybe all he needs is for you to show you really want him after all this and he'll come running back. You have a lot more to offer him than that other girl from what I've heard. She's nerdy like him. They're too alike those two and it can't last. Maybe he needs a challenge?"

Sybil looked sideways at her friend and started for the first time to smile. "Do you really think so?"

Oh, it's worse than I thought! Poppy admitted to herself. She's smitten, at least when she's drinking. I really don't know how to deal with this. Way over my head. I don't know this new person in front of me.

"Listen. Where do you think Janek would go next? I mean, I've just been told that Sarah girl found something in the walls of the castle. It could be linked to Janek's search for the missing papers from Mary Sidney Herbert's estate. It's very important to keep them in our sights, you, for your sake, and me, for my work. After all we both know why I'm involved in this business. So anything you can tell me will help both of us."

"Oh, let me think." Sybil closed her eyes and after a long time her body began to tilt to the left as if she wanted to lie down and fall asleep right there. Her friend propped her upright and raised her voice.

"*Sybil*, where would Janek go next?"

Startling awake, Sybil blurted out, "Go next? Janek? Yes, what was it he said? We had a long talk about us, and he said he couldn't stay in the relationship anymore. He had met someone who made him see that we were fooling ourselves. That it was fairer to both of us for him to let me go, so I would find the right person too!" And she began to wail again.

"Oh please! Stop!" the words were out before Poppy could check herself. "If you really want him back, let's find a way, OK? So what else did he say about his plans— his plans mind you, not your relationship. We know all that already."

"Something about he and Sarah staying at Carisbrooke Castle. But he said we could talk in person if I felt I needed to when he returned to London."

"And that is when..." Poppy prompted.

"He didn't say. He didn't know. It would depend on what they found."

"OK, let me help you to bed and we'll talk in the morning. Do you mind if I crash here for the night?"

After Sybil was settled, Poppy returned to the sofa and poured herself a big glass of red wine. Her thoughts were becoming clearer: *I'll return to Carisbrooke early tomorrow and follow them by car. But I'll go alone. Sybil won't be up to the trip after all the wine she's consumed. I'll encourage her to give herself a few days' rest and re-think whether she indeed wants to pursue him. If she does, I'll definitely encourage it, because she'll be my info source. If not, I'll encourage a head to head with Janek, to see what it was they found in the castle ramparts. If they don't reunite, so be it. It may be best for both of us. She's softer than I thought and I can't carry her.*

With that she laid her head down on the sofa cushion and was asleep almost instantly. It had been a long and crazy day.

"Janek, it's been wonderful having a whole day to ourselves here at Carisbrooke. I'm feeling a whole lot better since I've been able to sleep and not worry about Colin, now that he's in jail." Sarah was sitting in a lawn chair, her feet resting on Janek's legs.

"Glad to hear it!" Janek's smile was quickly replaced by a look of concern. "But you're not out of the woods yet. Remember, you have to keep getting plenty of rest, no lifting, no stress. Concussions don't heal overnight, even if we want them to."

"It's too bad we didn't find a place that key would fit," Sarah replied. "The key might be meant for the box of Herbert and Sidney family papers that

Philip Herbert asked his solicitor to hide here just before the Civil War erupted. Now, we have an opportunity to research why the box was hastily removed from Carisbrooke, and where it was stored when they were returned to him. Perhaps the papers never reached Philip, but were handed down to Herbert family members or others close to the Sidneys after Mary's death. We don't know when, or even *if*, they left this castle but we have searched everywhere, and they are not here! It's frustrating and exciting at the same time."

"Here's the thing that's niggling in my brain," Janek answered. "We still don't know if all of Mary's writings were included with the family papers. If our research doesn't lead anywhere, we must consider the impact of Mary's realization, before she died, that her sons, William and Philip, were embarrassed by the fact that she wrote plays and by her second marriage to someone they considered below her station. She just may have, as has been suggested in the past, commissioned her new husband, Doctor Matthew Lister, to safeguard all that she wrote."

"Then we must make the trip north to the Matthew's last home, where we've been told about a secret passage that needs to be explored. I am sorry that I'm not yet up to rattling around the British countryside in the Mini, lovely as it is," Sarah looked sadly at the man beside her.

Janek moved closer and kissed her on the nose, missing her lips as he leaned over in his chair in an awkward balancing act. They laughed. *Truly,* he thought, *it would be so much nicer to be able to stay at the castle a few more days, to let Sarah really recuperate.* Since neither of them was independently wealthy, they had no option but to return to London the next day and continue their research there.

Sarah had asked her Master's thesis advisor for an extension to remain in England to continue her research. Today was the day he would inform her of his decision. He had not been happy when she had related that yet another accident had occurred. She hadn't even mentioned that she had been attacked by her new boyfriend's colleague, Colin, while in the process of discovering a hidden key in the walls of the castle's fortress. That would have tipped the scales against her. She had tried to convince the professor that she could gain so much more by allowing Janek to guide her around England, since he was researching the same two people as she: Mary Sidney Herbert and her brother Philip. Had she mentioned that Janek was trying to find proof that Mary and Philip had written some, if not all, of the works attributed to William Shakespeare, her fate would have been sealed. There was little sympathy for the Shakespearean authorship debate at the University.

"Why do you think people are so threatened by the suggestion that Shakespeare may not be the true author?" Sarah asked.

"I've wondered about that a long while now, and haven't come up with anything but speculation," Janek replied, his brow furrowed. "There are entire industries, academic, tourist, and theatrical, built up around the myth of William Shakespeare. Many people have a lot invested in this man. Years of study, the commercialisation of Stratford-upon-Avon, the Globe Theatre, and other Shakespearean venues around the world, not to mention schools of academic thought, and the development of the entire English language as we know it today. I think scholars are afraid of losing credibility and that if it were discovered that there was another author behind Shakespeare's pen, then this whole industry, and perhaps even the works themselves, would be denigrated. There is a huge group who are proud of the fact that an 'ordinary' man, not a particularly highly educated or wealthy one, achieved such heights and wrote so well. William was not a poor man, nor was he particularly 'ordinary.' He was a member of the higher middle class in his village. His family had money and a lovely home and he was considered well educated. That being said, it is curious that when he died there was not a book among his belongings, which were all listed in his will!"

"So, if someone were to find conclusive evidence that there was indeed another author, or even more than one, would that person be seen as a hero or villain?" Sarah mused. "Perhaps if the evidence was well presented and without a doubt, that person would gain quite a reputation, not to mention quite a lot of money, if he or she played their cards right. That, or their lives could be in danger!"

She was sitting upright now. Her eyes widened as she gripped Janek's arm.

"Could that be why we are being followed and threatened? Someone doesn't want us to find anything, either because they are threatened or because they want to be first to discover the truth?"

"Anything is possible Sarah. I am inclined to think that there is someone quite powerful, either politically or academically, behind the threats, and that he or she may have hired people like Colin to keep an eye on us. The fact that your laptop was stolen makes me lean towards the idea that this powerful person is on the same quest as we are."

"The person behind this knows he or she could never hope to make anyone change their beliefs, unless irrefutable proof is found. No one can control another person's thoughts. At the same time, it's uncanny how different people all over the world seem to be on the same wavelength at the same time, sometimes unaware that others share their questions. It's like new theories are floating in the ether!"

For a moment he hung his head, looking very discouraged. Sarah leaned in and brushed his cheek with her fingers.

"Dear, sweet Janek, I am with you in this. I'm on your side. I can't yet say I am convinced that William Shakespeare did not write the Folio works, but I want to join you more than anything. I hope you won't try to stop me just because it could get a little dangerous. I won't be stopped any more than you will!"

CHAPTER TWO

"Love sought is good, but given unsought is better"
Twelfth Night - Act III, Scene 1

The twenty-first of September, 1583 dawned bright and blue as Frances Walsingham stood gazing from her high window, the faintest of smiles softening her fine features.

It is a lovely day for a wedding, she thought, and then frowned. Why I am not happier?

Her heart knew the answer right enough. Philip Sidney, perhaps the realm's most sought-after bachelor, was to become her husband. But his heart beat for another. Frances had known it all along but these were common things in the world she inhabited. She knew of few marriages which began with love. The question was, could theirs *end* in love?

She believed her own heart could be true. For some time now she had felt it stir whenever Philip was near. Their paths often crossed at Court and he was always sweet with her, but he treated her more like a little sister than a grown woman. Truth be told, their marriage arrangement had both surprised and delighted her, especially since Philip had not been forced into it like other courtiers in Elizabeth's court, who had secretly becomes fathers. If a lady-in-waiting was found pregnant, she and her lover were first expelled from the Queen's presence, often to the Tower, and after an acceptable period of time living under such 'encouragement', were usually properly married.

Philip had never touched, nor even approached, Frances in a romantic way, nor had any of the other courtiers. They were all afraid of the influence which her father, Sir Francis Walsingham, the Queen's spymaster, could have on their lives, if not their heads. Again a faint smile lit her face. She was her father's only surviving child, a daughter he loved unconditionally, even while he was fully committed to the Queen's business. Frances knew his softer side, the side her mother had known, for he had doted on her as well. Yes, he could be very severe, harsh even, when crises surrounded the Queen, and he was one of the few who managed to assert his opinion even when it disagreed with Elizabeth's. He thought only of Her Majesty's safety, above even his own family's. Despite this, Frances had grown secure in his love for her, just as she had trusted in the love of her mother, Ursula. But Walsingham had always been a faithful man.

Frances's thoughts returned to Philip. What could he be thinking at this very moment? Would he regret that he would not be taking the hand of his beloved Penelope Devereux, now the married Lady Rich? And what of her, that lovely golden-haired mistress of many? For at Court it was often gossiped that Penelope's marriage was in name only, that she had several lovers, perhaps the most devoted being Philip Sidney. Would these dalliances continue after his marriage today, he who was thought of as the very model of virtue and courage by the others at Court?

Closing her eyes and standing very still by the window, she sent up a desperate prayer that theirs would be a happy and fruitful union, and that love would grow. It was all she could do now.

Not far away, Philip was sitting alone on a garden bench gazing out, an abstracted expression on his face. He could not really admit to happiness at this marriage, but he thought he could possibly be content. Frances was so young, with thirteen years between them. She was truly beautiful in a fragile way, her mouth tiny and heart-shaped and her long hair as dark as a moonless midnight sky. He liked the quiet of her presence whenever she was near and felt she had depths that had never been tapped. Her father was another matter, harsh and business-like in his duties, but very excited for his daughter's union. Lord Walsingham loved Philip as a son, and always had, ever since the year when Philip visited him, his wife and their tiny five-year-old daughter, while Sir Francis was posted in Paris as the Queen's ambassador. The eighteen-year-old Philip had held little Frances, and she had hidden her face in his shoulder as screams erupted below their balcony, the sound of the first death cries of the Huguenots at the horrific, barbaric, St. Bartholomew's Day Massacre. The persecuted Calvinist Huguenots, had let down their guard, mistakenly believing that they could allow themselves to trust the Catholic people of Paris.

It happened during the public celebrations of the marriage of the Catholic daughter of the French King Charles IX, to the Huguenot Henri III of Navarre, the independent kingdom in the northern Iberian peninsula. Even as they had celebrated, the helpless Huguenots had been slaughtered. Philip's horrified reaction, sincere concern for all present, and bravery in that instance, had endeared him forever to Sir Francis, as equally as had the young man's religious fervour and highly philosophical intelligence. Frances's soon-to-be husband, in his own right, admired his future father-in-law's extreme dedication to the Queen, England, and the Protestant faith.

Philip's face coloured as he thought about the generous dowry Francis Walsingham had lavished on his daughter, not to mention the great sums Philip's uncle, Robert Leicester, had himself furnished. Theirs was to be the wedding of the year, with an elaborate reception, and the Queen present. It was all wonderful, except for Philip's ruined pride, in bringing very little but himself to the marriage, and indeed only a mere part of himself at that. He was quite impoverished, and still dependant on the Queen for his welfare. Elizabeth had not yet assigned him to a role which merited recompense, dangling him like a plaything between one position and the next. He had been knighted earlier in the year, yet this was only in order to represent John Casimir from Germany, his good friend and correspondent, who was to have been made a member of the Queen's Order of the Garter, but had been unable to attend the ceremony. Unfortunately for Philip, none were paid positions. But military service would be remunerated, if only Elizabeth would grant him leave to serve overseas.

One who would not be invited to this wedding was Penelope, his dear mistress. He had agonised over what to do about her, until the day Lady Rich herself had laughed at his confusion. As they lay together at her country home, where by now she was living mostly without the presence of her drunken husband, who preferred the city, she herself had broached the difficult topic.

"Of course I will not attend! I do have *some* pride left! Poor Frances would be mortified, and she is a very sweet young thing whom I have no intention of hurting!"

"You must not refuse me, after I am married, Penelope, please. You know how my heart beats only for you. Yes, I am to be married — but reluctantly. The heart has laws of its own."

Penelope had turned to face him, looking deeply into his eyes. She had seen his sadness, felt it every time they were together. How could she have told him that she no longer felt as deeply as he did? She had neither wanted to hurt him, nor lie to him. Surely he must have known how she felt after all these years? Her body could not have lied to him. Why had he not perceived it?

Jumping up quickly, she had informed him in soft tones that she must see to her servants in the kitchen, as her husband would arrive before the dinner hour, and that Philip must be off as quickly as possible.

Philip had been crestfallen. He had said nothing as he rose to sit up in the large rumpled bed.

Penelope had sighed heavily, beginning to feel annoyed.

"Your new wife will give you a child before long, the child you wish for, just let it be. And you will be a sweet and gentle father, like yours was to you. Open your eyes wide, Philip! Life has something precious to offer you, if only you will reach for it!"

"I wish only that in reaching, my hand would grasp yours, and for life." His voice had been bitter. "My life feels wasted without you."

"Then you must leave for good! I will not have you moaning about like this. My life is hard enough as it is without you making it more miserable. If our every reunion is to be this way, then I must end it once and for all, Philip! I cannot bear these pitiful conversations any longer!"

Philip had been taken aback, seeing her eyes blazing. As she had left the room abruptly, he had thrown himself back on the pillow and pounded his fist into the feather mattress. For months now, the melancholia that had plagued him as a young man had returned with a vengeance. He had carried himself through his days by sheer willpower, falling into bed after drinking too much, night after night. His life had needed to change. That was why he had finally succumbed to pressures from his uncle and his sister to marry. When an image of Frances came to his mind, his eyes filled for a moment with tears. He no more wanted to hurt the young woman than he did to marry her, but his was an indecision that had somehow ended in the cards being laid on his table anyway.

There was no turning back.

Mary Sidney Herbert lifted the veil from Frances's eyes and kissed her on the cheek. "It will all be well, you'll see," she whispered and lowered the veil again. She gave the girl her most reassuring smile and took her husband's arm, following him into the cathedral. Her true thoughts were not so confident. She and her uncle, Robert Sidney, had orchestrated this event, trying desperately to lift Philip from his gloom, but she knew it had not succeeded. She was beginning to learn, through her young married years, that nothing could be forced, and a part of her had lately deeply regretted interfering in her brother's life. Thank God Penelope had had the sense to persuade him that her presence at the wedding would be unwanted. How could he have thought otherwise? She knew Philip was not cruel, but he was definitely a dreamer, living in a world divided. His inner needs and wants were in constant conflict, leading him to make the most unwise decisions. She did not dare fool herself that he would fall in love with Frances one day, she merely hoped he would. But that was indeed out of all of their hands. Mary wished for the day that he would leave Penelope for good and try to build a new life with Frances. The girl's eyes shone with love and respect whenever she looked at Philip. *Surely there was a possibility that might count for something someday.*

They had now reached their designated pew. She sat contentedly beside Henry and looked sidelong at him. Yes, he was aging, but how she loved the creases by his eyes, that had occurred quite naturally through the years they had lived together. He had laughed much, smiled often, and even cried at the births of their three children, William, Katherine and the very new baby, Anne. What a beautiful life hers was, and how her heart had warmed and swelled with Henry's many loving kindnesses. She was truly happy, a rare occurrence for most women of her generation, she realised. She stood with a thankful heart and prayed silently, that Philip and Frances would be graced as she and Henry had been, and gazed in hope as Philip gently lifted the veil from the clear eyes of his young lady.

CHAPTER THREE

Sarah read the email a second time: her thesis advisor was upset but he granted her six-month extension. There was a funding reserve in the department which he had transferred to her project This was welcomed with a whoop that brought Janek to her side. He picked her up and twirled her around, kissing her.

"Shall we make our way back to London, Sarah, so I can introduce you to my apartment?" His smile was a little tentative when he asked, "Or are you feeling a little unsteady with all the quick changes?"

Sarah smiled back and hugged him.

"It *is* all very new, and more has happened to me in three weeks than probably ever before in my life. But I know I am happy with you, I trust you and wouldn't want to be anywhere else."

They held each other. Then, with a look back at their castle apartment, they made their way past Carisbrooke Castle's ancient gate, packed suitcases into the Mini and drove away.

Neither one noticed the small grey rental car that pulled out a second later, keeping their car in its sight.

"Thankfully, I have lots of vacation days left! So, what lead should we follow next, Sarah?" Janek asked.

"Tell me again all you know about Mary Sidney Herbert's second marriage?" she replied.

"Henry, her first husband, died in 1601. There were reports of a chronic illness which had taken hold six years earlier and had caused him grief. He seems to have had good periods and bad ones but early in the seventeenth century, he succumbed to the illness and died at Wilton House. Mary was bereft, by all accounts. Theirs seems to have been a happy marriage."

"Henry was buried at Salisbury Cathedral. Their oldest son William, of course, became the Third Earl of Pembroke, inheriting Wilton House and all other country estates which had been managed by his father and mother. But because William was involved in Elizabeth I's Court, until her death in 1603, and later in building his Court career under James I, he had little time for Wilton House. He asked his mother to remain in Wiltshire at their family home, overseeing all William's properties, as she had in the latter years of her husband's life. Not much changed as she had always been an astute business woman."

"About two years after Henry died, Doctor Matthew Lister graduated in London, and by 1605 he was employed as Mary's physician. He later became the royal doctor to King James I and his family. Matthew was supposedly ten years younger than Mary, and because of their age difference and his lower status, their relationship and the prospect of a future marriage, would have been frowned upon. But there are reports of their ongoing love, and even a suspicion of a secret marriage, which flaunted the norms of their society. It was known that Mary's two sons, William and Philip, were not in favour of their liaison."

"Nevertheless, Mary and Matthew travelled together, entertained and attended society functions. They even built homes together. Mary had always been interested in medicine, healing, and pharmacology, having her own chemistry lab in Wilton House. It was a match of shared passions."

"It is known that when Mary died at Aldersgate House in London, Matthew was with her. After her death, he moved north to Bedfordshire. There are two interesting historical accounts which speak of Matthew's home there. One is by his nephew, after his death, in which a Lord Alsbury informed the nephew that Matthew's lodgings were designed by himself, with reference to the description of the Pleasure House in Philip Sidney's

Arcadia."

"The other is the tale of a secret passage to his house, which led underground to a small church nearby. At that time, there was a budding rebellion of the Parliamentarian Roundheads against the Royalist Cavaliers of Charles I and II. Many believed the passage was constructed to hide the rebel Roundheads. The passage still exists, but it has been boarded up. No one has been allowed access for centuries. It is considered unsafe. Not to mention, that its current position happens to be underneath a graveyard. It is considered sacrilegious to disturb burial grounds. But wouldn't it be a great place to hide documents?"

"Sarah, if Mary's sons were ashamed of their mother's love for Matthew Lister, do you think she would leave her private papers or her written works to them?" I believe she would rather have trusted them to Matthew, in secret."

Sarah nodded in agreement as Janek continued.

"Another wedge between Mary and her sons occurred because of the attitude towards women writers at the time. We know that many of her writings were kept from being published during her lifetime, by her sons. Unfortunately, most of Mary's extensive body of literature has disappeared, including all the shared works which passed between herself and Philip, which history has proven existed by the accounts of others. All the writing she shared within her famous 'Wilton Circle' of writers is also missing."

Sarah sat, deep in thought for a few minutes before replying.

"I am trying to put myself in Mary's shoes. I would have chosen Matthew as the one to guard my works, especially those written with the brother I had loved and whom I had always admired. I would have been saddened by my sons' lack of understanding of the importance of my life's work, with its dedication to the honour of Philip's memory. You are right. I would not let those sons know that I had asked Matthew to safeguard the writings...maybe even to have them published. And another thing, Mary and Matthew, being so versed in medicine, would have realised she was dying. Was it smallpox, the same disease that had plagued, but not taken the life of, her mother?"

Janek nodded and commented, "So, I think that would make Mary even more determined to keep her writings hidden for the time being. Matthew likely would have been her choice of person to guard them. Do you think we should first travel to Matthew's village and investigate the passage, Sarah?"

"It sounds like a logical step and it would be exciting!"

There was a long silence in the car. They reached the ferry and waited in a lineup of cars quite a distance from the wharf. The two sat very still, each lost in their own thoughts.

CHAPTER FOUR

"Wherever sorrow is, relief would be:
If you do sorrow at my grief in love,
By giving love, your sorrow and my grief
Were both extermin'd."

As You Like It - Act III, Scene 5

Philip Sidney sat opposite his new wife Frances at the dining table of his father-in-law, Sir Francis Walsingham. Sconces circled the room, the walls were festively decorated with willow boughs, and a hush had come over the fifteen guests at table.

"A toast to my lovely daughter, Frances, and her illustrious husband, the newly knighted *Sir* Philip Sidney, who hopes to soon be elected Member of Parliament representing Kent."

The guests raised their goblets. Over his, Philip observed how the candlelight shone in the eyes of his young wife. She had a soft, child-like face and as their eyes met, hers filled with tears. *She is so proud of me,* he thought with a pang of guilt. *And I cannot rid my heart of its pining for another.* He turned to his left, stood, and proposed a toast to the man seated beside him.

"A toast to our distinguished guest, Mr. Giordano Bruno, once a Dominican, but of late he has left his religious brothers on the continent, to serve as professor in England's Oxford University. The Catholic Church's loss is our gain! May his scientific, astrological and philosophical works continue to inspire us all! After dinner you are invited to a session in the parlour where Giordano will entertain us with his memory games."

Again the guests toasted. Philip glanced around the table, his eyes meeting those of his sister as she sat across from her husband Henry, his best friend. Mary appeared radiant, being four months pregnant with her fourth child. William, her first, was now four and baby Katherine, already two-and-a-half, and there was also little baby Anne. His sister smiled back and bowed her head.

Servants bustled about with plates of meats and vegetables, breads and cheeses, bowls of soup and servings of expensive wine.

Frances watched from her place near the head of the table. Her father and her new husband were in their element, entertaining and confidently discussing matters of state. She did not feel out of her depth. She was proud of her father's status and his loyalty to the Queen, and from a very young age, she had been schooled in all things political. Her father had recognised her keen mind and had encouraged her education as well as her understanding of the intrigues of court. He did this because he felt it would protect her when he was gone. She was their only remaining child and he knew that the dangerous position he held as Elizabeth's principal secretary and protector, put his family in jeopardy. It was essential that his daughter would know how to tell the faithful from the traitors.

But this night Frances was happy to remain silent, to listen and delight in watching Philip. She rarely saw her husband. Between the Queen's demands at Court, entertaining dignitaries with her father, visits to his sister's estate at Wilton House, and his recent attempts to enter the political arena, they had but one day or one evening a week together. Tomorrow, Philip would accompany Giordano to Oxford, where he would remain for a fortnight. Tonight all she wanted was to gaze on him, to take him and all his enthusiasms into her own heart, for she was very much in love.

Her father noticed her stillness and it made him happy. *Yes, this match has been the right one for her,* he thought. *And perhaps her great love will touch Philip's heart, even yet.* Walsingham knew everything there was to know about those

24

who hovered about his Queen and it was no secret to him that Philip was still in love with, and even visited, Lady Penelope Rich. She was no lady in Walsingham's eyes. He knew about each man who courted the married woman, and while he pitied her union with the arrogant drunkard Lord Rich, he could not excuse her behavior. His own first wife, Anne Barne, had been faithful to her death and he had been fortunate to find the same commitment with his second wife, Ursula, Frances' mother, who now sat beside him. He turned to her and grasped her hand. She squeezed his and smiled back. This dinner was one of their most pleasant to date in the early months of the year 1584.

With the meal over and the guests sated, Walsingham rose and asked them to proceed to the parlour for the evening's entertainment. There would be plenty of time after the party ended to entertain Giordano privately. After all, he was here as a guest only so that the Queen's protector could attempt to allure him to the task of spying on Catholics, for the better education of the Protestant government. Giordano's friendship with his son-in-law made this plan all the more possible.

True to Walsingham's prophecy and surely due to his influence, August of the year 1584 found Philip and Frances living in Kent, where Philip had been elected First Member of Parliament, and his friend Edward Wotton the Second Member.

Frances was then six months pregnant. She was a little more philosophical about her marriage by this time, having repeatedly learned through her father that Philip was unable to give up his Lady friend. She dearly hoped their child would solidify their marriage vows.

Philip had been a representative to Parliament in the past, more than ten years previously, for Shrewsbury. He had been in his late teens then, and had hated the position. There was no one happier than he, at that time, when the Queen demanded he travel with a delegation to France to arrange the possibility of her marriage to the Duke of Alençon. The mission had ended in failure, but Philip had been replaced in Parliament, to his great relief.

He felt even more ambivalent about this new position. Endless parliamentary meetings about trivialities stifled his true political interests. He loved to be involved in the government of his day, especially when the issues discussed were crucial to England and excited his adventurous mind. The daily haranguing over routine county problems wore down his spirit. He wanted action. By September, Philip had reverted to pestering Elizabeth and his father-in-law for a military position overseas.

The small family had twice visited, for lengthy periods, his sister Mary and Henry at Wilton House. Those had been pleasant, peaceful times. Frances had come to appreciate the close relationship Philip and Mary had, as something she had always wanted herself, but had never known, as she had only one sister who had been six years younger than her and who had died at seven years of age. Thus, she had had no siblings with whom to share her growing intellectual capacities. Mary and Philip had even allowed her to write a small play with them! In fact, their play was due to be performed in front of the servants at Wilton House, in three weeks' time. She had been practicing her lines, and felt that all her years in Court as a lady-in-waiting had come to fulfillment, for there was dancing and merriment in the roles, just as there had been when the Queen commissioned a play in one of her royal residences. Each of the Sidney siblings, herself, even her father and mother, along with members of the Herbert family, had been assigned roles in their production of *A Midsummer Night's Dream*. The weeks spent at Wilton had been the best of her married life to date, and she had been privy to other sides of her husband which gave her great delight. She hoped Philip would not withdraw from the play and she planned to ask him as soon as he returned home.

As it turned out, a letter arrived from Mary the very next day, inviting the family to Wilton House:

Dear Philip and Frances,

We insist that you and all your family come to visit us and stay at Wilton for some days. We must double our efforts so as to stage this play before I deliver my baby in October. Whether we all know our lines or not, you simply cannot refuse us. It will be a great celebration and I expect you all in two days' time. Two very pregnant ladies need much cheering!

Philip agreed, himself also much in need of a diversion, which caused a great stir of happiness in his relations, and the entire family found itself at Wilton House before they knew it.

Mary could hardly contain her joy at seeing her brother so happy. She found herself quite emotional around the married couple, remembering the first wonderful years of her own marriage, and knowing that Philip was still struggling with his feelings for another. Her heart went out to Frances, who now carried this child. She supposed her mood swings were related to her impending delivery date. She had been the same way before all her births, with William, Katherine, and little Anne. Because of this, Mary decided to direct their little play and not act in it.

For the two days before the play was staged, she, Philip and Frances locked themselves into her library and re-wrote parts, laughing at times and at others, very intent on getting the words "just right" as Frances would say.

Philip and Mary had both witnessed the glorious and much-hailed fete their uncle Robert had organized in the year 1575 at his castle at Kenilworth. What a time that had been! The play they were working on was entitled *A Midsummer Night's Dream* and was largely inspired by the fantastic theatrical productions, the games and the fairy kingdom atmosphere of that party. Mary and Philip regaled Frances with tales of all they had witnessed, the long year and a half of preparations that built up to the event, the incredible gala itself and the tragic aftermath.

Robert Dudley had spent himself and almost all his fortune, in improvements to Kenilworth, building a new wing for Elizabeth and her

Court, constructing lovely paths, a lake full of colourful fish, and in its centre, a large fountain surrounded by elaborate gardens— everything a woman could want for her pleasure and honour. Then he had hired actors, playwrights, entertainers of all kinds, and commissioned lavish meals to be prepared for the nineteen days of entertainment, hospitality, and merriment.

"Through this superfluity, he was in truth making a final heroic effort to woo Elizabeth and tempt the Queen to marriage," Mary stated, shaking her head sadly.

The siblings described their feelings, the sights, sounds and scents of those heady days, until Frances's thoughts were swimming with images. She had been there, with her father Francis and her mother Ursula, but she had been only seven at the time. The family had lived with Elizabeth and the rest of the Court in the newly fashioned wing of the palace. She remembered large ceilings and huge open windows with vista views of colourful gardens. Her memories of the evening festivities were few, as she had usually been put to bed after the supper hour and attended by her governess. The one night she had been allowed to stay up late was the evening of the amazing fireworks display. People from surrounding towns lined the castle gate, and the noise could be heard for miles about. Her parents knew she would not be able to sleep through it and had allowed her to join them. Never before had there been such a display! But poor Frances had wailed at the noise made with the initial explosive firework, for it had elicited in her traumatic memories of the sounds of the first gunshots at the St. Bartholomew's Day Massacre in Paris when she, as a five-year-old girl, had clung to Philip's neck. And now he was her husband. *Life is indeed a mystery*, she reflected.

Mary was fourteen at the time, and living at Court, where her own mother was also in service. Twenty-one-year-old Philip, as a courtier to the Queen, had been deeply involved in all the preparations and plans, alongside his mother, father and uncle. With vivid memories put to paper by Frances,

28

acting as scribe, the three constructed imaginative scenes of wood nymphs, fairies and ancient characters, palaces and potions. It had truly been a magical time for all, and this play revolved around magic and the pursuit of romantic love, with all the pitfalls and elations of love's quest. Complications similar to those witnessed by anyone who had ever lived at Court ensued, and parts of the play described actual scenes the three had experienced.

"We must include the Lady of the Lake and her nymphs!" Mary clapped her hands in delight.

"The very long bridge from the castle gate all the way to the close, over the lake, the many fragrant fruit trees, and beautiful flowers!" Frances cried excitedly.

"And Triton aback the mermaid!" Philip's eyes twinkled.

Finally the day of the pageant arrived. Their play was witnessed by family members and servants and was a huge success! Elaborate costumes and scenery had been constructed, but it was the words which conveyed best the sheer enchantment of those days.

But all good and great things, someday come to their end. By September 28, Philip and Frances were back in their home and Mary was swiftly approaching her delivery date.

On October 14, Mary's labour started in earnest and by four o'clock that day, she held her new son in her arms. She and Henry lay together in their large bed, discussing the child's name. "Of course he will be a Philip, after his long-suffering but much-loved uncle!" she declared, and Philip it was.

She asked Henry to bring William, Katherine and Anne to see their new little brother. Henry left quickly, returning with William and Anne, one in each arm.

"Where is Katherine?" Mary asked, alarmed.

"She is being attended by the nurse. She has been unwell all day. I didn't want to distress you, dear," her husband stated, but his eyes looked worried.

Mary tried to rise but he hastened to lay her back on the pillow. "You should not see her now, especially after your mighty struggle today. Katherine will be fine, and she has asked me herself to give you a kiss on the cheek."

Mary sighed and lay against the pillows. Her daughter was often unwell, her constitution weak, and she hoped it was the excitement over a new baby that had caused the latest bout of illness.

At shortly after ten that evening, she awoke to a long wail, which in her sleepy state she thought was little Philip. Turning in the bed, she felt at once that Henry was not nearby. The door burst open and he entered, tears filling his eyes as he approached the bedside.

Mary's heart did a twist and she felt a strong pain grabbing her left side. "Where is little Philip?" she cried out.

"Philip is fine, he is with his nurse. It is Katherine, Mary!"

"No, no, no!" she screamed and scrambled up, throwing the covers to the side and racing to the door, her feet bare on the stone floor.

Her husband grabbed her by the shoulders and turned her to him. He held her for a long time as she sobbed into his shoulder. "Let me go to her!"

"It is too late, my dear. She has slipped away from us." His sobs echoed in the somberly lit room as Mary fainted in his arms.

November dawned miserably as cold and bereft as Mary herself. She cried every hour and was unable to nurse poor Philip. When he was brought to her, she clung to him, her eyes frenzied, her thoughts frightened. *Was he feverish? What was that spot on his neck? Why did he shiver in the mornings?* "Are you, too, only here for a short time with us?" she asked the little man, but he only gazed back at her, his eyes seeming troubled and his body tense. She then would hand him back to the nurse and retreat to her bed for the day.

One morning there was a knock at her little library, and her brother entered the room, quietly and with much concern etched across his brow.

"How are you today, my dear sister?" he asked gently, noticing that she was wrapped up tightly in a large blanket. *She is so unwell,* he thought seeing her pallor and the spark that had once lit her eyes all but gone now.

Mary looked at him for a long time, and burst into tears. She cried uncontrollably as he crouched down to her level and held her around the shoulders.

After about ten minutes, she pulled herself away and covered her face with her hands.

"I was not with her! I let her die alone! I cannot forgive myself for that!" she wailed. "I am tortured by what she must have gone through in the end!"

"Mary, your guilt is misplaced, but your sorrow is not. Give to your grief words, so that your heart may not shatter, but mend. Let words lead you back to yourself and your life, here, in this place, at this time. Little Philip needs his mother *now*. Let your words be a bridge to him."

She looked up, seeing his eyes as if for the first time that day. Something he had said was working its magic. What was it? *Words, words, give to your grief, words...that was it!* She was grasping at a thread, trying to trace her way back to the moment right here, right now. For so long she had been inside herself, trapped there, unable to come up for the air she needed to continue to live.

That night she began, filling papers with words, writing down her ugly, bitter feelings, the new fury and anger, the cloying sadness, the overriding guilt. She wrote it all, everything she thought, felt, hated and feared. The fire burned low, the room became darker and more somber. At nearly six in the morning, the fire was out and she sat, spent and shivering, the blanket about her shoulders in a tight knot. The sun broke over the horizon and she turned to see its rays creep like golden fingers across the window sill. Light came ever so slowly but she sat very still and watched it reach out for her, first warming her toes and then her legs, her stomach, her shoulders. Finally it touched her face, and leaning back, she waited for the warmth to reach her hair. By the time it had haloed her head, Mary was asleep in the chair, papers strewn about the floor and the quill pen resting in her open hand, the page on her lap reading:

Give sorrow words; the grief that does not speak

Whispers the o-er wrought heart and bids it break.

February 12, 1585, was a joyous day for the Sidneys. Frances gave birth to a lovely, delicate baby girl, and together she and Philip chose to call her Elizabeth after the Queen, who insisted on being her godmother, as she was to so many others at court.

Philip visited his wife's chamber later that evening. "Mary and Henry send their happy congratulations to you Frances. You look exhausted, my dear." He sat on the bed and stroked Frances's head gently. She closed her eyes and opened them quickly.

"You are not going away, are you, Philip?" she asked fearfully.

"No my dear. No. You must rest. I will come to lie beside you and our little girl. Lie back and close your eyes. Do not worry. I am not about to leave you!"

Frances sighed and began to cry softly. "What is it, Frances?" he asked, tipping up her delicate chin.

"Oh Philip, I know your heart would prefer another wife and children with her." Her weak state made her very vulnerable. "But you are to me my knight... my best one. Our little Elizabeth has your features and she may make you happy yet, even if I cannot." She sobbed into his sleeve.

For a long time Philip held her tightly, tears filling his eyes too. He was so torn. He knew his actions towards her were always dutiful, that he had tried to be a serious, upright provider for his wife, but he had to admit his heart was elsewhere. His many infidelities haunted him, sickening his stomach. He had not been aware until now how perceptive this young wife had been. In her love, and he knew she loved him with her life, she had all these months been tortured by what she felt she could not have, him.

For a long time, husband and wife sat holding each other, both desperately sad. Then Philip drew away, and looked into her eyes. "I am no knight errant, only one in error, and you deserve so much more, Frances. Will you let me make a new promise, tonight, only to you, to guard faithfully your loving heart and to no more venture to another's arms?" He was crying with her.

She slowly nodded her acceptance, still searching his eyes, hoping against all hope that he would one day come to love her as completely as she did him.

He lay her head against the pillow as their little girl began to cry. Lifting her from her cradle beside the bed, he carried her gently to Frances and then climbed beside the two into bed. As he held Frances who held Elizabeth, he gazed at his wife's beautiful pixyish face, with its long thin nose, high forehead, tiny rosebud mouth and large soulful brown eyes, as if seeing her for the first time. Innocence, intelligence and an overwhelming, faithful love shone out of that face. Their daughter was more a Sidney than a Walsingham. In her he saw his sister's visage and that of Mary and Henry's third child, Anne, staring back at him. *I am a father now!* The thought hit him from somewhere far away, coming forcefully from he knew not where. It was truly somewhat of a fearful thing. Like his new commitment to his wife, he felt his life was about to change, to draw from him things he had never known he had to give, to open up parts of himself he could only now hope were real. By the world at large, he was known for his courage, but in this moment he realised he had only just begun to understand what courage meant.

Months later, on August 15, 1585, a letter came, addressed to Philip

Sidney. He tore open the sealed envelope and quickly read the contents, a broad smile forming on his lips. "Frances!" his voice rang throughout the foyer. "Frances! It has arrived!"

His wife looked over the banister, down the long staircase. She saw the surprised joy on her husband's face, but pain shot across her own heart. As he ran towards her, she saw the royal seal, a deep red blot on the letter he waved at her. Her pulse quickened.

"I am finally, *finally*, granted my wish! Elizabeth has assigned me to military action in Vlissingen, where I am to be Governor, fighting alongside my uncle Robert on behalf of the Dutch against the Spanish!"

Frances tried to smile, forcing her lips upward and opening her eyes wider, feigning surprised delight. Had Philip looked into those eyes, he would have seen fear and disappointment.

When he reached her, Philip swung her in the air and she felt as light as a feather in his arms. He hugged her close. She tried to meet his eyes with some enthusiasm, but tears betrayed her. Philip, taking them to be tears of joy for him, wiped them away gently with his hand. "I shall miss you and Elisabeth, I truly will," but the smile had not left his eyes.

"How long until you leave, Philip?" she almost whispered, bringing forth all the courage she could.

"Twelve days, my dear! How short a time to prepare! I must discharge my Parliamentary duties to a new representative and then I shall be free to leave!" He spun her again, lightly set her down and asked her to summon their servants and muster a plan of preparation. And then he was off up the remaining stairs, racing to grab his heavy coat. As he again passed her, immobile on the first landing, he took her shoulders and looked into her eyes.

"I will count on you to write to me and keep my spirits up, while I am away. You must believe me when I say I shall miss you. You do believe me, do you not?" His face became anxious.

"I do, Philip," was all she could muster. "And I will write you, every day." With a smile, he was gone.

Frances did not move right away. In truth, she was shocked. Everything had happened too quickly for her. She had believed Elizabeth would continue to refuse Philip's requests for military action, especially since his uncle had recently displeased the Queen by assuming the title of Governor-General of the provinces of the Netherlands, where he was stationed.

The troubles had started when King Philip II of Spain united with the Catholic League of France, the Spanish Netherlands, Belgium, and other surrounding states, through the Treaty of Joinville of 1584. Frances remembered the many heated meetings held in her home, between Dudley, her father, Philip, and other courtiers, in hopes of convincing the Queen to support the Dutch Protestants against the Spanish Catholics. Frances had been both relieved and proud, when they had finally persuaded Elizabeth to financially and militarily aid the Dutch in their many skirmishes with the Spanish and the Catholic League on Dutch soil, especially at Antwerp. But the wily Queen responded, on August 10, 1585, with a treaty of her own. The Treaty of Nonsuch stipulated that in return for royal support, two major cities, Vlissingen and Brielle, and Fort Rammekens on the small island of Walcheren, would come under Her Majesty's rule, and be named "cautionary towns." This would allow the Queen two British representatives on the Councils of State of the provinces.

When Robert Dudley acted against Elizabeth's wishes and allowed himself to be named Governor-General, the Queen had been furious with him for overstepping his authority on her behalf. At the time, Philip and Frances, through her father, had borne the brunt of the Queen's angry accusations. Frances had been sure that Philip would suffer the stormy wrath of the Queen for quite some time, and that all his hopes for military action overseas would be thwarted.

She now stood in shock on the landing of her home, wondering at the

Queen's change of heart. Frances had been secretly delighted to have Philip at home these last months, as he had conducted many meetings from their house. Philip had been excited again about politics, and had been so happy and faithful! Faithful as he had promised! Every day she felt their love growing, and most nights he was home, he was with her, in their bed. He seemed to see her in a new way, just as she had hoped so many months ago when he had renewed his commitment to her at the birth of their daughter. And how he doted on little Elizabeth! Now all of that was about to change, and her dear husband would be again absent, this time for a long period. Not to mention the dangerous conditions he would be subjected to. Her hands began to shake and she felt faint. Steadying herself against the banister, she closed her eyes and offered up a silent prayer on his behalf. She wanted to cry out *Not now!* but her frustration had to be pushed to the side to prepare for this separation.

CHAPTER FIVE

Janek pulled the car behind a white three-storey building, and parked in a space off the lane which ran close to a streetscape of light pastel-painted apartments of similar age and architecture. "This is it, Sarah," he smiled at her, "my humble abode."

She followed him up two flights to *No. 4*. He opened the door, and gestured for her to enter, his hand on the small of her back.

She gazed on a welcoming space, full of bright primary colours vying for attention, crowded with bookshelves, and with sunlight spilling in. They stood at the end of a short hallway leading to the living room, where she could see two overstuffed brown leather couches, facing each other and a fireplace against the wall with a mantel full of pictures and a ceramic clock in the centre. There were handknitted red and black throws on each couch, and matching large pillows. The rug under the couches was an intricate red, black and gold design. To the right of the living room, was a wooden table with mismatched chairs and a deep blue tablecloth. Large, beveled stained glass windows on the far left reflected the afternoon sunlight and threw tiny rainbows across the room.

"I love it here. So homey!" Sarah smiled. Janek took her hand and led her further into the room, took her jacket and hung it on a coat stand. Two small open doors with arches led to the kitchen, which was large and rustically decorated. The cupboards were white, the gas stove black, and the floor was tiled in black and white 1950s-style squares. Here, again, were lots of red accents, mixed with blue and gold.

Down the hall to the left of the kitchen, was a small bathroom with a claw-footed tub and shower, and then at the end, the bedroom.

Sarah smiled up at Janek. The walls were a soft blue, the bed covered in a duvet with a midnight blue duvet coverlet decorated with stars. A large bay window looked out on the alley below. On the wall beside the bed, there hung an oversized painting of an old railway station at night, with several people on the platform, boarding and saying goodbye as the snow fell about them. The scene was softly lit from lamps on the platform and the overall effect was serene and sad.

"My grandfather painted this picture after leaving Poland, in 1940, a year after World War II erupted. He and my grandmother settled first in northern France, on his cousin's farm, and that is where my father was born. I think he was very sad to leave his native land."

Sarah gave him a hug. "I love it here Janek. I love all of it. Your home is like you!"

He turned her to face him and held her very close. "Sarah, I hope you will be happy here. It is our home now." They kissed and tumbled onto the large bed.

Unknown to them, in the street below their living room window, Poppy sat in her grey rental car and pulled out a cell phone.

"The two are back in London, cozying up at his digs. Yes, I've spent time with Sybil. No, she's a basket case. Confused and sort of regretting the breakup. I've got plans for tailing them– hey, don't get your knickers in a knot! Let's meet for breakfast tomorrow morning. We can get to know each other and I'll fill you in then."

Later that evening, Janek lit a fire and he and Sarah sipped wine and ate crisps as they made plans for the week ahead.

"Janek, let's again put ourselves in the shoes of Mary Sidney Herbert. We know that at the end she had smallpox, so she knew she was likely to die. The legacy she had built with her writings and those of her brother would surely have been on her mind.

"Could there be others in her life that she might have willed these manuscripts to? Think of it: she would have had all she had written, plus all of Philip's notes, letters and unfinished works, the ones he had given her many years before. They were always exchanging their writings, asking for each other's opinion and we know she would never have destroyed his work."

"Interesting you should say that, Sarah. History tells us that, as he lay dying, Philip did indeed ask that all he had written be destroyed! But his wife, Frances, passed everything she found to Mary. These notes, combined with those Mary and Philip had exchanged over the years, were safeguarded by her. She refused to destroy them, and instead began in earnest to complete unfinished works he had left with her. That is how his famous *Arcadia* came to be published and then became so popular. Philip had originally written it for Mary when she was newly married, but he always considered it an inferior work. After he died, leaving it unfinished, it was revised and later published in two formats; the first time by his best friends Fulke Greville, Matthew Gwinne, and John Florio, in 1590. Then in 1593, Mary, not appreciating the friends' work, revised it again and published it under the name *The Countess of Pembroke's Arcadia*, which became the most popular and well-known version."

"Janek, how do you remember all these details, names, dates?" Sarah was astounded.

"It's how my mind works. Sarah, I've been investigating the Sidneys for over five years, they've become my second family!" he joked.

Sarah looked at him, the flames from the fire dancing in his eyes, his blond hair hanging forward over his forehead. In Janek she felt a kindred spirit, in his ardent search for truth, she saw innocence, and she admired his courage, going against the grain of the intellectual establishment that surrounded him at the British Library.

She was in love for sure. Unaware of her scrutiny, Janek, head bent over his laptop, continued:

"So, let's make a list of potential people she might have trusted with that information," he suggested. "We know that her two sons, Philip and William, were certainly not interested in publishing these works before she died. They would have been socially embarrassed had they published a woman's literary works. As you know, there wasn't any love lost between her children and her lover Dr. Matthew Lister so they would not have listened to him, had he pleaded their mother's cause. Philip and William were ambitious politicians, courtiers to King James. We know they both wrote as well, but not for their living. That being said, there is no record that they published Mary's works after she died."

"So Matthew is first on the list" Sarah scribbled his name on a chart she had made. "As her husband or lover, I think we can surmise that he could be trusted to do what she asked with the papers and plays. What happened to him immediately after she died Janek?"

"I know he continued to work for James I and Queen Anne, and when they died, he was royal physician to Charles I and his family. Eventually he returned to his home in northern England, where he bought a country estate in Burwell and Calceby, Lincolnshire, and remarried. The estate was beautiful, with lots of land surrounding it, beside St. Mary's Church. The house is now in ruins, but the church is still standing and is actually an active parish today."

"Did Matthew own any other properties?" Sarah asked.

"Several. He had been knighted by King Charles in 1636, and was very rich. He had no children, but left almost everything, including his properties, to his nephew, Martin Lister, another doctor of medicine and natural science. Matthew's second wife, Lady Anne, received revenues from some lands and an ermine-lined dress! Martin received all properties including one in London, a lodge later named 'Hudson's Lodge.' King James I had made Matthew Keeper of the Paddock Walk in Windsor Park, and the lodge came with this responsibility. Matthew and his brother, another

Martin, also co-owned several properties in Leicestershire and Yorkshire. After Matthew's death, at the age of 92, Martin settled in Friarshead, a beautiful estate that still exists, originally owned jointly by him and Matthew."

"Could we visit Friarshead?"

"Not without the owner's permission. It is not open to public visits."

"OK. So we can visit the ruins of Burwell House and St. Mary's Church. We'll leave Friarshead as a question mark." Sarah noted everything on her chart. "I think it's important, that we understand Mary and Matthew in the days leading up to her death. If I were going to entrust my life's work to Matthew, I would want to know what he planned to do with this treasure in the future. I would want to be sure my wishes were honoured. But what do you think Mary would have wanted with regard to her writings?"

"I am not sure, Sarah. Though Matthew was likely guardian of the works she and Philip had completed together, there may be another possibility. Mary was the godmother of her niece, Mary Wroth, the daughter of her brother, Robert. The two were known to have been close and to have lived together at Wilton House for a time, Mary Wroth being in her Aunt Mary's care when she was a child." He paused with a laugh.

"There are too many Mary's!" Sarah nodded.

"Yes! Mary Wroth was also a writer and became the very first woman to publish a work of fiction in Britain. This she accomplished in 1621, three months before her godmother's death. Her first published book was entitled *The Countess of Montgomery's Urania*, and though she acknowledged writing it, she denied having published it, but this can be disputed. The young Mary Sidney Wroth had fallen completely in love with her older cousin, William Herbert, Mary Sidney Herbert's son. And it seems he with her. They had two illegitimate children together— Katherine and William— despite the fact that they were each married to someone else."

"Here it gets interesting. Many of us Shakespeare "alternative believers—

" and his eyes twinkled as he looked over at Sarah, "consider that Mary Wroth could have been the Dark Lady of the Shakespearean sonnets. She was a beauty, with dark hair and eyes, and a wealth of talents, including music and dancing. There was even a tumultuous time in the relationship between Mary Sidney Herbert and Mary Wroth, when the aunt believed the niece was having an affair with her husband, Matthew!"

"Aha! A love triangle, complete with jealousy!" Sarah exclaimed.

"Exactly! Mary Wroth knew she was suspected of this affair, and she tried to make things right between the three of them through constantly referring in her writings to her lifelong commitment to true love... her chastity, as she saw it. But her true love was for her first cousin, William Herbert, and her children with him were born after her own husband had died, and after William had married, late in life, to Mary Talbot— *another* Mary! Though William would not acknowledge these children, many years later we have proof of William's paternity, because his cousin, Thomas, entered the information about them into the Herbert family history book entitled *Herbertorum Prosapia*.

"Wroth wrote herself and William into the characters of Pamphilia and Amphilanthus in *The Countess of Montgomery's Urania*. The theme of all her writings was her obsessive call to William to be as faithful to her, as she was to him. In that sense she was one of the first writers to challenge men to a new, human virtue, that of chastity in love...of devotion to only one woman. Women in her day were expected to be chaste to their husbands only. Men were never expected to be. Her call was revolutionary at the time and she suffered for it. She was in fact asked to stop publishing and *The Countess of Montgomery's Urania* was not republished after the first print run. She was shunned by society and rarely left her home. Unfortunately, the book finally destroyed her reputation, or what was left of it, and Wroth moved out of London, remaining in seclusion from the society and the Court in which she had grown up. She continued to write, more power to her!" Janek's voice was full of admiration.

"But Sarah, I think that at the time of Mary's death, she could not have foreseen the effect her niece's book would have on women writers in England. Men were very critical of Mary Wroth and her name was mud at Court and society. Queen Anne was in direct competition with Mary over her favoured courtier, William, which further added to the shaming of Wroth. Women, though, were much more receptive to her work, as history has proven.

"Her children by William were kept secret by the entire family over centuries. She continued throughout her life to protest her love for William, but he never publicly acknowledged his children nor did he support them in his will. Mary Wroth literally faded from history after a time and if it weren't for biographers such as Margaret P. Hannay, we would know very little of her brave struggles to assert her truth.

"Sarah, can you imagine Mary's feelings when it was finally revealed to her by Mary Wroth that the affair was not with Matthew, but with her son, William?"

Sarah was lost in thought for a few moments. She finally spoke:

"Given Mary's commitment to her family, I think she would have been angry at first, and then disappointed in her son, while at the same time she must have been relieved to know her lover was not unfaithful, especially with her own niece! Though cousins married in their day, in my own research I have learned it was rarely encouraged and was frowned upon for first cousins to marry. The Fourth Lateran Council in 1215 declared that a couple could not have the same great-great grandparent, or the marriage would be prohibited on the grounds of incest. Then Henry the VIII changed this law through his Marriage Act of 1540, so that he could wed Catherine Howard, who was actually first cousin to his former wife, Anne Boleyn. Before that time, the cousin of a wife was automatically considered the cousin of her husband, thus making marriage to a wife's cousin illegal. So, by the time

William and Mary Wroth got together in the early part of the seventeenth century, though it was definitely not common and was seen mostly in royal weddings, it could not be declared illegal.

"But to get back to Mary Sidney Herbert's knowledge of her impending death... I think she must have asked someone, perhaps Matthew or Mary Wroth, to hide all evidence of herself in connection with the plays and sonnets, but to publish them under another person's name until society was ready to acknowledge women authors of great talent. She wouldn't have had any idea how far in the future that would be. To that end, would she not have chosen a younger person to carry out this task, to insure its longevity?"

"I agree," Janek said. "So, let's start with Matthew. We have more leads surrounding him. I think she could have asked Matthew to pass the knowledge of her authorship on to a family member she would have named, upon his impending death, to guarantee her works would one day be found and acknowledged. Remember, the First Folio of Shakespeare was only published in 1623, which was two years after Mary's death, and *seven* years after William Shaksper's. If Mary in fact had written most of the plays, who could have financed the publication at that time? The Folio was dedicated *To the most noble and incomparable paire of brethren, William, Earl of Pembroke and Philip Earl of Montgomery*, Mary's sons. *That* has got to count for something."

"Had the Herbert family known William Shakespeare?" Sarah asked.

"There's no evidence of that," Janek replied.

"Intriguing," was all Sarah could say.

"Because Matthew was rich, he was more likely to have lent financial backing to the publication of the First Folio. Mary Wroth, married to a gambling man, was reduced to poverty during her marriage. When Lord Wroth, and then, tragically, their only son died, her husband's estate was willed to his brother. That was the way things were done in Mary's day. She was then impoverished and could not have afforded to publish her aunt's work, even though in her admiration of Mary Sidney Herbert, she would have wanted to."

"So, another reason to start with Matthew," Sarah stated. "You said he left a will?"

Janek typed quickly, looked up from his laptop and said, "Here it is— can you make a note, Sarah— please note this reference to the book *Web of Nature: Martin Lister (1639-1712), the First Arachnologist*, by Anna Marie Roos, which states that Matthew's will is to be found at the National Archives, Kew, under document *PROB 11/261, sig.9.* We can investigate this Kew link."

"Janek, I've been wondering about whether something could have been hidden at one of Mary Herbert's former residences, if they still exist. When I search for 'Mary Sidney residences' it shows me Houghton House, in Bedfordshire. Building commenced by Mary and Matthew in 1615, six years before she died. It was fit for living in by 1617, but was finally completed in 1621, the year of her death," Sarah said excitedly, and read further. "Matthew basically built it to resemble the architecture described in Philip Sidney's *Arcadia*. Much later, the home was abandoned, all furnishings and roofs removed and it was left to nature. So it is a ruin now, but can be visited by the public. I'll add that to our list as well."

As they planned their visits to trace Mary and Matthew's homes, Poppy sat across from Sybil Merryweather, Janek's former girlfriend. Sybil was not happy.

"When will you meet with him to discuss your breakup?" Poppy's tone was guarded. *I hate all this dancing around, walking on eggshells*, she thought.

There were fresh tears in Sybil's eyes. "I'm so disappointed in him, you know? I couldn't have seen it coming. He was always the faithful one."

"Yes, but we've been over all that already. It's not helping you to dwell on it. Be positive! Get a backbone, girl! Act like you don't care about it! Talk about moving on! Then watch him come running back!" Poppy asserted, though she had misgivings. *Best not to mention them, if I need to track Janek and Sarah's movements,* she thought. "OK, so pick up your phone now and call him. Make sure you see him ASAP! No time to lose!"

Sybil sighed, grabbed her cell phone and speed dialed Janek's number. The phone rang three times and then she heard the click.

"Hello, Sybil," Janek's voice was tentative.

"Am I calling at a bad time?" she asked.

"No, not at all. How are you doing?" the kindness was back in his voice.

"Not too bad," a tear rolled down her cheek. Poppy kicked her under the table. "Umm... can we meet for a little while to talk, Janek? I think that would help."

"Sure, Sybil. Is tomorrow a good day? Why don't we meet at Cosmo's around the corner at ten in the morning?"

"See you then," she clicked off and sat crying softly while Poppy looked on.

"See, that went pretty well!" Poppy said with forced cheerfulness. "Now let's work on getting your backbone up, shall we? I'll get you a glass of wine." Perhaps she was pushing Sybil to act too quickly. But time was of the essence and her own hand was forced as well.

Sybil sat slumped in the chair, looking forlorn. She kept asking herself why she felt so sad. It was not as if she had foreseen a future with Janek. He wasn't her type at all. *What is my type?* she wondered. Immediately a man came to mind, a tall man with black hair who she had been seeing on and off for the last six months. The skier, Marc Comtois. She had met him on a business trip to Switzerland and the fireworks between them had nearly knocked her off her feet. He called every three days from one spot or the other around the globe. They had met again when he was in France before a competition in January. She remembered guiltily cancelling her weekend away with Janek to fly to Pointe Percée in the Aravis Mountains to spend a sizzling weekend with Marc. In fact, she was to see him in London next week. He seemed really eager. *Well, at least I won't have to dodge around Janek, pulling the wool over his eyes!* she thought, but still felt miserable. Funny that. Feeling miserable about not lying. *What has my life come to? What kind of person have I become?* and the thought terrified her. It was going to be hard to be real.

Meanwhile, Janek had put down the phone and turned to Sarah.

"That was Syb. She wants to meet." His eyes searched Sarah's for her reaction. He wanted to reassure her that she needn't worry about his "feelings" for Sybil. They were gone. It was surprising and disturbing that everything had happened so quickly and in truth, he suddenly wondered if he was a shallow person.

Sarah saw his brow crease and felt a rush of tenderness for him.

"Of course, you must meet and talk with her, it's the best thing to do. Take your time. There are bound to be feelings left that have to be faced."

"No, Sarah! That's just the thing, there aren't, at least on my part. And I know that means it must have been a very superficial relationship. What must you think of me? Ever since I met you, I've been pulled in two directions. I have never felt for anyone the way I've come to for you! I never want to hurt you Sarah! You are so much more to me already than Syb ever was, ever! I hope you believe me?" He looked desperate.

She rose from the sofa and hugged him tightly. A small part of her still worried that he would choose Sybil again, over her. She felt she could never compete with Sybil, from what she had heard of her life and the circles she moved in. Janek was so wonderful and she felt like she would not be able to let him go. The tears glistened in her eyes as she whispered, "I believe you." *This is all new to me*, she thought and admitted that if she were being honest she should have said "I *want* to believe you." But instead she put her head on his shoulder as he softly stroked her hair.

CHAPTER SIX

"There came to my remembrance a vanity wherein I had taken delight, whereof I had not rid myself. It was the Lady Rich. But I rid myself of it, and presently my joy and comfort returned."

Philip Sidney, overheard at Arnhem, the Netherlands

Mary Sidney Herbert sat alone in the Pembroke family pew, her tears spent. There was finally silence all around her. Gone were the peals of the organ, the sounds of the choral voices, the tolling bell, the shuffling of feet on stone. It was over.

She welcomed the hush. It wrapped itself around her like a cocoon and she felt a blessed moment's peace.

For others, 1586 had dawned bright and full of promise. Philip and Frances had a new life in their midst. But for the remaining Herbert and Sidney families, the year had not progressed in a happy fashion. Mary's dear father, Henry Sidney, had become increasingly weak and none of her medicinal herbal preparations, nor those of the family doctor, had been of any use. By springtime, on May 5, he had died.

The funeral had been exhausting and intense, the Queen insisting upon honouring her loyal servant with a grand ceremony, procession, posthumous accolades and a memorable reception. Of course Mary had been assigned the planning and financing of the preparations. The Queen could laud, but she herself did not lavish. Mary's poor mother, Lady Mary Sidney, had been so bereft that many commented that her days, too, were numbered.

They were right. In early August, her weakened condition led the doctor to confine her to bed. By August 15, she too was dead.

Mary's emotions had ranged wildly during those months. At times hopeful, then defeated, then again full of energy, she insisted on being beside her mother throughout, and after her father's death, moved her to Wilton House. In the end her overwrought sadness literally felled her, and she suffered her own collapse in late July, only to rally herself in the first week of August for her mother's sake. "All for naught," she whispered to herself.

She had stumbled from one death to the other, all the while longing to again hold, if even only for a moment, her little Katherine, taken from her so cruelly the previous autumn. At times her arms ached to wrap themselves around the tiny three-year-old who, though sometimes fragile and thin, had always had a smile and arms outstretched to be cuddled.

That last hour of her father's life, he had spoken quietly to his wife, Mary and Philip, newly returned from the Netherlands to be with his father. Henry Sidney repeated many times the words "Release yourselves. Too much struggle." His family questioned him, not understanding the implications. Only his devastated wife understood. She said nothing, shedding silent tears and lying across his chest, as he held her for the last time.

Theirs had been a mutual devotion, an unfaltering love and a shared struggle. Friends had believed Lady Mary would die first, completely worn out as she had been by years of undaunted service to her Queen's every whim. But they had not foreseen how stoical the Sidneys would be in the line of service. They never complained openly about Elizabeth's impoverishing demands; instead their way was to bear all in loyalty and supreme effort.

Today, after a much smaller funeral at Salisbury Cathedral near Wilton, she, Henry, and their relatives would soon begin the long trek by carriage to Penshurst Place, their parent's marriage home in Kent. There they would lay to rest the matriarch, Lady Mary, beside the much-loved patriarch, in the family plot. The sheep would keep them company while their adult children went about their own lives. *A fittingly peaceful rest for two who had spent their lives giving too much,* she thought.

Mary looked about her. *How much time had passed?* she wondered. She remembered asking Henry and Philip to give her a few moments alone in the church, where she had been married and which she and her small growing family attended most Sundays. It was time to leave.

Underneath her overwhelming grief she sensed a great insecurity. *I am orphaned!* The thought jolted her from the hazy melancholy that had wrapped her in its protective folds. She began to shiver. Pulling herself to her feet, she made her way swiftly across the stone floors, well aware that buried beneath them were many ancients, whose long forgotten names, once carved deeply into the floor, were daily worn down by the faithful of the present day.

At the entrance to the cathedral, as she sped blindly past him, Henry caught her, and held her fast. "Mary, I am here." And he did not let her go until her breathing was back to normal and her shoulders slumped against him.

Days later, Philip departed again for Europe, returning enthusiastically to the battlefield. Frances wrote to him every day, as she had promised. He had been so happy to be at home with her and Elizabeth. This past year of marriage had been their happiest, even with him gone for long periods. Frances realized she was finally able to trust that his love for her was real and it was growing. This knowledge shored her spirit against worries for his safety and it was with great and sudden anxiety that she read the letter delivered late September by special courier from the Queen herself.

Dearest Frances,

You must leave immediately for London, in the carriage I have sent. Your dear husband has been wounded on the battlefield of Zutphen, and your father and I have arranged for you to be taken there by boat, departing this evening. We have been told the wound is in his upper left leg, and it is refusing to heal. He has been calling for you in his delirium. I am excessively saddened to have to inform you of this news, but your pending visit is most important to Sir Philip and to ourselves. You can trust that the Court will be praying for his continual healing while you are on your way.

In faith,
Elizabeth I
This day, the twenty-ninth of September, 1586.

Her heart lurching, she screamed for the servants and within the hour, arrangements were made and instructions given for the care of little Elizabeth. Two bags were packed and she was on the doorstep holding her daughter tightly in her arms one last time. With a quick kiss and a whispered promise to return with her father, she descended the stairs and soon disappeared into the coach. Elisabeth began to wail.

Within three days' time, Frances was at her husband's bedside. Upon arrival, she was told the story of Philip's misfortune. Before leaving for the battlefield, he noticed that the Dutch captain leading the charge had removed his tasset, the leg armour worn by soldiers, in order to ride with less encumbrance. In solidarity, Philip had removed his own armour. During the ensuing strife, he was shot in his left thigh. While being carried from the battlefield, he noticed another wounded officer, and had offered his water to the soldier, declaring that the man looked more in need of it than him. Three days later, Philip was in a feverish state, the wound festering and the military doctors unable to stifle the infection, which daily grew until it was out of control. By the time Frances arrived, gangrene had set in.

She ran to kneel beside Philip's sickbed. He was sleeping fitfully, but at her touch he awoke and took her two hands in his. "You are here my love! Now I will improve!" She bathed him all that evening, hoping to reduce his fever, administered the herbal remedies and medicines the doctors had prescribed, and by midnight had fallen asleep in the chair beside him. He cried out several times in the night. They both slept fitfully, but in the morning she refused to take her rest.

This went on for several days, with no respite in sight. The gangrene grew worse and spread further.

"Draw the curtains and lie beside me Frances," he pleaded one evening. She quietly did as he bid. He held her very close. "I think I am not long for the world my dear, and I have prepared words to be sung at my funeral service."

She placed two fingers over his lips. "Shhh. I will not hear talk of this!" But his eyes were pleading.

"Frances, you have been to me a wife like no other could have been. I have been an ass and the worst kind of rogue and you must forgive me. You know of my past feelings for the Lady Penelope Rich. You know of my many transgressions with her. But since I renewed my commitment to you alone at the birth of our Elisabeth, I promise you I have remained true. Penelope was a vanity, a terrible vanity in the true sense of the word, for our dalliances blinded me to your love and to the possible growth of love for you in my own feeble heart. I did not deserve you Frances..."

She again covered his lips with her fingers, but he would not be dissuaded.

"Please, I must finish, or I will have no peace! Hold me now for I am growing cold. Frances, my entire life has been a vanity, I see that plainly now. If only it was willed that I would heal and return with you to England!

How I would change! But I fear that will not be. No, hear me out my dear, dear wife. The pursuit of fame and recognition for military heroics— all has been vanity. Life at Court, the constant pandering, the rumour mongering, the scraping for every little bit of attention from a Queen who plays us all like fiddles, has all been vainglory! It now sickens my heart more than this wound sickens my mortal body. But Frances, our love has grown, has it not? Only our love has not been subject to the vanity that had me in its grip for all these years of life. And I say now that this realization gives me great, immeasurable solace, as does your being here at my parting. Remember me as one who loved you more than life itself at the end, but be open to the love of a good man to care for you and our daughter when I am gone. For go I must, I sense, though it not be my will. Even this death will have been caused by my vainglory, Frances!"

His eyes grew desperate and he shivered so much that she wrapped her whole body around him and pulled the bedclothes tightly about them, in the hope of keeping him warm. But it was to no avail. Within an hour's time, he had passed again into delirium, alternately hot and bitterly cold.

In the early morning of October 17, he slipped away.

A full month later, his body arrived on home shores and was transported to London. Perhaps the largest funeral ever held in that city to date, was his. The Queen and Walsingham had arranged his to be the celebration of the death of one of their greatest military heroes, the stories of his selfless bravery preceding his body's arrival in England.

His young widow was inconsolable for many weeks upon her return to London. She refused to take part in the planning of the great ceremony, remembering his heated words about vanity and its pitfalls. Instead, she and

Elisabeth, soon to turn two, stayed at Wilton House with her sister-in-law and her family, until the day they left for the "horrific display of a funeral" as Frances called it.

Mary was in a state of profound shock by the time Frances left. The three deaths of the last year, and now her beloved brother's death, without any chance to say goodbye to the one who felt like her spiritual twin, were too much for her. She had been told that the Queen had forbade women other than Frances, to attend the funeral. Nor were they allowed to offer a written eulogy to be read at the service. Her spirit, her heart, and her intellect were crushed.

Being with Frances and Elizabeth had been exhausting but at the same time there was nowhere in the whole world that she would rather have been. The two women cried together and from dawn to dusk, walking endlessly on the Wilton estate. As they walked they were in turns silent, then talkative, distraught, then consoled by each other's presence, unspoken understanding and love of Philip. Neither could see beyond the present moment, nor did they want to go there.

Little Elizabeth helped them both through those days. In her innocent baby chatter and tentative running ramblings, she even managed to draw laughter from the aunt and the mother, and somehow made them realize that life must go forward, if only for the child's sake. She became their focal point, their reason for being. Mary, experienced in the ways of death, was painfully and yes, gratefully, aware that her own children had helped her back into life. Their needs had soon become her need to rise each morning and slowly, tentatively face the new challenges and the fresh little joys that would inevitably come each day. There was no escaping life, other than perhaps through death and that possibility was far too morbid to even entertain. Death was a fearful thing! Mary convinced her sister-in-law that she had to choose life, one moment at a time.

But when Frances and Elizabeth left, Mary sunk into a deep pit of despair, longing, and ill health. Little did she know then that it would be two tormented years before she was able to pull herself out of its mire.

CHAPTER SEVEN

"How are you, Janek?" Sybil rose awkwardly from her chair, and tentatively embraced him. She had chosen a seat at the back corner of the coffee shop, even though it had been nearly deserted when she walked in.

Janek looked at her and realized she had been crying, though he could see she had tried to conceal it with makeup. He felt miserable. He had not meant to hurt Syb and in truth he himself had been overcome with the suddenness of his change of heart towards Sarah. Everything had happened so fast, but even in this moment he could not deny that his new feelings for Sarah were much stronger and more real than his for Sybil had ever been.

"Oh, Syb, I am so sorry!"

He reached for her hand but she pulled back. "No, Janek!" She was beginning to feel uncomfortable herself. If he had known how she had cheated on him, without a moment's thought of it hurting him! She reminded herself once again that she had entered into relationship with him, initially, under false pretenses. She hoped he would never learn about that. All these thoughts were crashing through her head as she looked at him.

Perhaps for the first time, Sybil appreciated what she saw: innocent and caring eyes and the nerdy old fashioned way he wore his hair, flopping over his forehead. Something about his sincerity had finally gotten to her. In her world of high flyers, one never really knew who to trust. People often weren't what they presented to the outside world. There was a look they cultivated, a suaveness and brash confidence they portrayed in order to survive and attract attention. Across from her sat a man to whom none of that mattered. Janek had not changed through their relationship. She had. Now that it was all over, she realized with a start, that he had worked his magic on her and this, more than anything, unnerved her. *Am I in love with him?* She didn't know. *What is love, anyway? If this is it, I've blown it for sure!*

He looked helplessly at her now and she saw a difference in his eyes. He really had fallen in love with someone else. What a quick turnaround! She shook herself mentally and thought, *No contest! Sarah is probably as nerdy as him and I can't and won't compete! I'd have to throw away everything I have gained to be with him, and then who would I be? I don't even know!*

Janek saw her distress and again reached for her hand but it was too much for her. She said angrily, "You could at least have told me earlier, while you were gallivanting around the countryside, in my car I might add. She must be some girl, this Sarah!" Her eyes blazed.

"Syb, it wasn't like that! I didn't even realize I was falling in love until the evening we were searching the ramparts at Carisbrooke! Nothing happened before that, before I phoned you and admitted I couldn't continue with our relationship! Please believe me!"

"Oh I believe you, Janek! I really do! Anyone else no— but you, oh yes, Mister Perfect!" she lashed back.

He looked like she had struck him. But it's the truth. He was always so annoyingly kind, faithful, making her look like the guilty one, not even intentionally. This whole thing is crazy! I am in an alternate universe, here! The thoughts tumbled around her head until she felt she would scream.

And then he said the one thing that did it for good. "I only did what you would have done for me, Syb." She began to sob, big loud sobs. He got up from his chair and knelt beside her, his arm about her shoulders.

"Give me a moment!" she said, pulling a tissue from her purse and rushing to the washroom.

Janek returned to his chair, feeling more miserable than he ever remembered feeling. His heart ached for her sadness but he knew he could not go back on his decision to end things with Sybil.

It felt like he had matured overnight. Sarah and he were right for each other, he felt in every bone of his body. He could no more turn from that, than return to Sybil.

She marched back from the washroom, her makeup repaired and her back straight, with a blaze again in her eyes. She had given herself a good talking to. She didn't appreciate or want Janek's lifestyle and, though she would miss his kindness, it really could get tedious. No, she would bow out. There was just that nagging feeling of desire for what he offered, sincerity and a guilelessness that she had never seen before. But she would find another person, more for her in the ways she needed him to be, than this naïve guy who sat across from her. She just hoped she could forget him over time, and that is what made her angry.

"Janek, I am fine! I will get on with my life and let you get on with yours. And speaking of that, what will you and Sarah do as a couple? I mean, can she even stay in England? Will you be jaunting about the countryside looking for your *clues?*" She made quotation marks in the air. Poppy had convinced her if he was unbendable, to settle for friendship with Janek for now, whatever that meant and to keep him "tied to your apron strings, so to speak, because you just never know." Fat chance of that, and anyway, after today she intended to move on big time.

Poppy's adamant demand to know what Sarah had found at Carisbrooke Castle nagged at Sybil. She'd have to broach the topic soon, and ask him to drop a postcard from his travels from time to time, so she could keep Poppy informed.

"Sarah has a six month extension and is doing the paper work now to allow her to stay in the UK. And yes, we will be following the trail of Mary Sidney's life, both to benefit Sarah's thesis and for my own book. Sarah found a key lodged in the walls of the castle, Syb, but she was assaulted by Colin—you know, the guy I work alongside at the library! It was shocking! I know you never believed me that someone was interested in stealing my research, but it was all true!"

Sybil feigned surprise. "That's unbelievable! Why ever would Colin do that?"

Janek sighed. Syb could see his concern for Sarah and it made her heart lurch again.

"Will your dodgy car get you around England?" Sybil asked incredulously.

"I have a new, well I should say a used, car from my uncle. It sat in a garage most of its life, so it will be great for visiting Mary's different homes or the ruins of some of them. We plan to leave tomorrow for Houghton House in Bedfordshire to examine the ruins of the last country home Mary lived in."

"Janek, whatever drives you to do this research, tramping around England, looking for *what*? Risking your life and now Sarah's too? Shouldn't you be trying to move up the ladder at the Library?" She was both upset and, as before throughout their relationship, truly baffled by his interests.

"There's nothing I want to do more than this research Syb, you must know that by now. That is what divided us in the first place, don't you see? We lived and moved in different worlds and we both discovered over time that those worlds were tearing us apart."

Oh, if you only knew how much, Sybil thought as she sat staring at him with wide eyes. And if you ever were to discover how your research was the very thing that also brought us together. There is so much you are innocent about in this relationship. But the time for truth telling has passed. It is far too late for that now! In the end, she merely nodded sadly.

"Before you go, Syb, I want to write a cheque to your father to cover the damages on your car from our accident outside of Salisbury. Do you know the amount?"

"I'll talk to Dad about it and get back to you, how about that? Anyway, Dad has plenty of money and his insurance will cover most of the damages. You don't mind me calling you once in a while just to see how you are? Or perhaps you will text me about your journeys? We're not enemies after all."

"If you are sure, Sybil. Yes, call or text me whenever you like."

It was time to go. They hugged briefly and she walked off to her car, heels clicking along the sidewalk, her head held high. Janek watched for a while, then turned and, letting out a pent up sigh, made his way home, thinking how happy he would be to see Sarah when he returned.

Sybil punched in Poppy's number. It went to voicemail, so she briefly reported on her talk with Janek, stating that the discovery Sarah had made was an old key, that the two were going tomorrow to Houghton House in the first leg of their cross country trip to discover Mary Sidney's homes. "As if anything could be more boring!" she declared as she hung up. Then, with wheels spinning, she raced away.

Poppy saw Sybil's call come in and let it go to voicemail. *I have no patience to wipe away her tears this time!* she thought as she listened to the message. A smile lit up her face. *Time to call the Boss! I'm going on a road trip! Hope he'll be pleased and get off my back for a while,* she thought and then made a quick call home to her parent's house to inquire about her daughter. The sooner this job ended, the quicker she'd be back with Samantha. She really missed her little face!

Sarah had been watching from an upstairs window. She spied Janek rounding the corner and sighed. His steps looked jaunty enough and there was a smile on his face.

When he entered the apartment, she was waiting by the door. He smiled so broadly and looked so happy to see her that it melted her heart. Then he picked her up and twirled her around, coming to rest with her on the sofa. "I am so glad that's over!" was all he could say.

"It went well, then?" Sarah asked. "I mean as well as can be expected?"

"Yes, it did," he replied thoughtfully. "She was upset at first but we both realize that we live separate lives and it could not work, I think. At least, I think she is coming to realize it too. Sarah, there really weren't any 'feelings' left when I saw her. I only felt bad for her."

Sarah said nothing. There wasn't anything *to* say. He would have to sort out these feelings himself in time, just as she had done in Canada when her earlier relationships had ended for the very same reason. Time would mend Sybil's heart too, just as it had done for hers.

Sarah got up to make tea, leaving him on the sofa to think, while she prepared everything. Twenty minutes later she re-entered the room with a tray of cups and their tea. He was fast asleep on the sofa and looked very peaceful. But he stirred awake as she set the tray on the coffee table.

They drank in silence for a while. Then she said,

"Janek, while you were out, I followed your lead on Aldersgate Street. I know you told me that in the early 1600s, after Henry died, Mary moved there. And also that in the 1800s, someone had attached a board above No. 134, Aldersgate which stated it had been Shakespeare's house. I found a reference in a book by an N. Robinson, called *Shakespeare's London*, published in 1881, which says there is no evidence that Shakespeare ever lived there. Instead, he proves that a 1593 Subsidy Roll only says that someone named *William Shakespeare* bought a house in Bishopsgate in St. Helen's Parish, but may never have lived there, as well as one in Blackfriars. I had to look up what a Subsidy Roll actually was, and I discovered it was a financial record dealing with housing taxes. From the 1300s to the late 1600s, there were Subsidy Rolls recorded across Britain, and from 1662 on, these seem to have been replaced by what were called Hearth Taxes.

"So I started to look into what was the exact address of the house Mary lived in, on Aldersgate. So far, I have not found anything, but all the Subsidy Roll information gathered over the centuries is now housed at Kew, in the National Archives." She looked at Janek, who was smiling broadly. Her face coloured. "Of course you know all of this!" she exclaimed and playfully punched his arm.

"I do, Sarah, but it was so much fun watching you get all excited. We really are two peas in a pod!"

"So have you already found evidence that Mary lived at Number 134?" she asked.

He shook his head. "Not yet, though it is on my agenda to go to Kew. Should we do that before leaving for Houghton House tomorrow?"

They discussed the idea but decided to keep to their original plan. Both wanted a road trip adventure and they reasoned there would be time when they returned to London to research further at the National Archives.

"The first thing we have to do is retrieve the copy of the key we found in the walls of Carisbrooke Castle. I brought the mold of the original key— the one we had made at the castle— to the best historical locksmith I could find, this morning before you got up, Sarah. We should have a couple of copies of it by tomorrow at ten o'clock. Luckily, working at the British Library holds some weight, and old Mr. Culver himself, of Culver's Antiquarian Locks and Keys is going to make our keys. He was so fascinated with the mold that I told him our story and he promised to keep it confidential. He said he had several keys from the fifteenth to seventeenth centuries which looked quite similar and then he showed me his treasure collection. I think we have a new friend in him, Sarah."

A mile away, Poppy prepared herself for the next day's road trip too. She had researched Houghton House and at first she had laughed when she discovered that a popular British TV program about ghost hunting had an excerpt on the internet about that very house. A crew had spent the night at the mansion ruins trying to contact Mary Herbert's ghost, of all things! This Mary was more popular than she had first imagined.

Very soon, though, she had realized that she would not be able to follow them right up to the ruins. Even if she disguised herself, Sarah could recognize her, as they had met previously when Poppy was assigned by her Boss to befriend Sarah at her London bed and breakfast

Also, the ruins were an open, public site, which was not huge. There was no place you could lose yourself as it was open to the air, the roof having been removed. She supposed Janek and Sarah might visit by night, but there was no way she could risk being at the site before or after they arrived, without Sarah possibly seeing her. She made a quick call to the Boss, but discovered he had already arranged that she have assistance. She was to pick up the other new watcher, a young man named Crik. "Yes, I spoke with him on the phone last night," the Boss said.

"What a name! Is it 'Crick, like a pain in the neck?'" she had joked, but that had been met by a stony silence. The man at the other end had coughed and spelled it very slowly, "C-r-i-k for your information, and do not be impudent!" *Probably some hoodlum from a London street gang*, she thought to herself. Crik could be at the site, hidden nearby and would be equipped with binoculars and a long range camera. As the Boss stated, this Crik would be more capable than she, of watching them and even of ambushing the two should the need arise.

"Wouldn't want you to break a nail, would I?" As usual, the Boss made her skin crawl. *I really can't wait to get out of this job!* she thought as he slammed the phone in her ear. And then she shouted out loud, "Piss off, you bloody wanker!"

The next morning the sky was a bright blue, with white clouds scudding across it. The wind was up. Sarah and Janek loaded the Mini with suitcases, snacks, their laptops and good rain gear. As they pulled out of the lane, a grey car a block away pulled out too.

"Janek, do you think there will be any chance that someone might start following us again, like the last time?" Sarah asked him as they left the apartment.

"I don't think so Sarah, because I checked this morning and Colin is still in jail, here in London. He was the only one who seemed out to get me, I should say 'us', as it was you who suffered most from his assault at Carisbrooke. I think all the other incidents related to my research, like the theft of your laptop and my memory sticks and the missing library books, must have been perpetrated by him. After all, he had direct access to my locker and all the books, as an employee of the British Library. He threw his entire career into jeopardy simply to get at the information we now have. What an idiot! I can't read his motives. Was it from jealousy, real interest, or something else? I am not quite sure."

"You know, Janek, I once wondered if he had an interest in Sybil. He kept mentioning her whenever he had the chance. Did he know her well?"

"Not really. Other than meeting her at parties at the library. Once or twice we all went out for drinks. He could be a real flirt but that was how he was with all the women. He was a good looking guy and he used it!" There was bitterness in his voice.

Sarah sat back in her seat and looked sideways at Janek. Now here was a good-looking guy, though he didn't seem aware of it. He was considerate, smart, and kind too. This brought her to thoughts of her father and with a pang of guilt, she realized she hadn't phoned home in two days. Normally she would have immediately given her parents her new address, but in her present state of bliss she had completely forgotten. *Must call tonight and fill them in, especially as we'll be on the road for over a week.*

A stretch behind them, Poppy and Crik were getting acquainted. On first meeting him, Poppy had thought to herself, *long dark streak of misery!* He had folded his six-foot-four self into the front seat of the grey car, and immediately moved the seat back to accommodate those thin legs in skinny black leather pants. The big black boots with the uncharacteristic bright orange laces barely fit under the dashboard. He had turned to her, held out a tattooed hand with long fingers and said "Crik meets Poppy," and that had been all he'd said for the first ten minutes. *Maybe his nose ring is giving him trouble,* she thought. It had looked a little inflamed. *Gross!*

Finally, she could stand it no longer. "So, *Crik*, is that your real name?" she asked turning in time to see him scowl.

"Could be," was all he said.

Oh, so this is how he wants to play it. Very well. I'll shut up. Let him smolder! Poppy felt her patience running thin. At some point they'd have to talk strategy. After all, they had a job to do, one that paid good money. And he looked like he could use it as much as she.

When Janek and Sarah pulled into the parking lot of Culver's Antiquarian Locks and Keys, Poppy pulled the car over to the curb a block away.

"So, they are getting copies of that key made that they found in the walls of the Castle!" and turning to Crik, she filled him in on the details of how Sarah had tricked their colleague Colin by giving him something other than the new found key, after Colin attacked her on the castle ramparts.

"Well, it was dark, Colin couldn't see what she passed to him, and at the same time, Janek was running towards him, to help Sarah."

"Amateur!" was all Crik said.

"Oh, so you would have done better, would you? We'll see Mr. Overconfident! Here, take my phone and call the Boss. Someone will have to get us a matching copy of that key one way or another!" she snapped.

A half-hour later, the two cars were on the road again. Janek and Sarah drove past the Elstree Open Space and continued on the M1 past the Hilfield Park Reservoir, bypassing a lot of residential housing mixed with light industry. Further, the view became greener and flatter, with large farms stretching for miles and smaller hedgerows protecting them from prevailing winds.

"'Potters Crouch,' what a lovely name!" Sarah was smiling broadly as she read the road sign.

"Would you like to stop for a cup of tea? There's a great little place called the Holly Bush down the road."

"Sure. Why not? We're in no rush are we?"

Janek turned onto the Bedmond Line Road and soon came to a small village with a few homes, all well-kept, and some with sculpted yew trees and lovely gardens. Sarah practically squealed with delight and Janek laughed. "Glad you are enjoying yourself!" he smiled at her fondly.

The Holly Bush was a white painted brick cottage with gables and black shutters. Inside, the atmosphere was cozy, with a brick fireplace, traditional black wood beams across a white ceiling, and benches covered in thick upholstery. They ordered tea and scones and settled back against the comfy cushions.

"This pub was built in the 1600s, so perhaps even Mary and Matthew stopped in on their way to Houghton House!" Janek smiled shyly at her.

Her eyes were wide. "It seems more modern, but the thatch roof betrays it, doesn't it?"

"Yes, it's been bricked over, once red and now painted white. But the beams are original."

As they ate, they spoke excitedly about their plans to visit the ruins of Houghton House.

Earlier, the driver of the grey car had been irate. "Oh for goodness sake, they are stopping for a tea!" Poppy braked and went off on the opposite side on Bedmond Line to wait by the culvert so their car would not be noticed. "Typical nerdy thing to do!"

"Hmm, bothered are we?" Crik's left eyebrow had shot up.

Poppy immediately turned on him.

"Look, Crik, or whatever your bloody name is, let's get one thing straight, how about? If we are going to work together we have to first be communicative and second, play nice! I'm not your enemy. But I could be, very quickly, if you keep up this stupid posturing thing you're doing!"

"Oh, big words," he started to say, but then caught Poppy's look and raised the right eyebrow, the one with three rings in it. He was quiet for a long time, considering her words. He seemed to come to some decision, because he began to speak, at first quietly and then with more animation.

"OK. You asked if Crik is my real name. No. It's my gang name. Got it given me when I was ten, as part of a gang where I grew up, in the back end of Blackfriars. Learned a lot there, specifically how to rob places, or follow people without being seen, pickpocketing, the like. A regular artful dodger. That's why the Boss hired me 'cause I'm expert at becoming invisible."

Now it was Poppy's turn to raise an eyebrow. "All six-foot-four of you?"

"Don't question 'til you see me in action. I'm a cat burglar with a mean streak, if you know what I mean. Not afraid to use me knife, if I hafta. Only way I survived the streets. I've said enough, now what about you, Miss Redhead?"

She gave him a stern look again.

"My name is Poppy. It's a nickname for Penelope. I'm from Manchester and this is a part-time occupation, I have to make quick cash when I need it. I'm older than I look, and I have had more experience than you might think, so take that as a warning: don't mess with me. This is my first assignment with the present 'Boss' but I've had worse. I've been trailing these two for almost three weeks now. I met Sarah personally; that was planned. That's why you're hereShe would recognize me if I was seen."

"So, these are a coupla nerds who are trying to find out if Shakespeare was really who they all say he was? What a far-out assignment! Couldn't believe it when the boss explained it over the phone. What some people get up to. Boggles the mind! Should be a piece of cake though with these two!"

"That's what the last guy said, and he's behind bars as we speak. So don't get overconfident. These two are real smart, kinda like the Boss and a lot like Colin, the last guy. In fact, he worked with Janek, and got outsmarted. She's one tough cookie too. Consider yourself warned."

His eyebrow went up again but this time he said nothing. Silence descended over the two, and Crik closed his eyes. Poppy watched the road for signs of a green Mini. Forty minutes later, it finally emerged above them on the M1 and she took off so fast that Crik awoke and shouted "Yow! Warning next time OK?"

Poppy smiled. "Gotta keep you on your toes!" was all she said.

A half-hour later, as Janek and Sarah arrived in Ampthill, Poppy followed at a safe distance, watching as they turned into "The White Stag" a large red brick building, with three storeys and rows of windows.

"So we won't be staying there. How about the hotel across the street, and about half a block down? By the way, we have to request a street view of this lovely Dunstable Street, so we can spy on them. And separate rooms!" She said the last with emphasis.

"Don't flatter yerself!" said Crik, a big smile plastered across his face.

They waited until Janek's car was safely out of view, before pulling into their hotel's parking lot.

Sarah and Janek deposited their suitcases on the stands by the door of their room. It was a pretty place, with a wide queen-sized bed with bright fuzzy cushions tossed across, a big window facing the front of the building, brick walls and dark beamed ceilings. Small and cozy.

"So, do you want to explore Ampthill a bit before going to Houghton House?" Janek asked.

"It's early, only eleven o'clock. Why not?" Sarah agreed. "Maybe visit the house after lunch, while it's still daylight?"

They donned jackets and runners and left their room.

Across the street, Crik was setting up his binocular stand facing The White Stag. "Bloody hell. They're leaving already!" He phoned Poppy and told her to grab her coat and meet him at the front door. *Not even time for a pint!* he thought.

"There's a neat piece of history I wanted to show you, Sarah. I'm sure you know all this from your own research and studies. When Henry VIII was in the process of separating from his first wife, Catherine of Aragon, he placed her under castle arrest here in Ampthill, but often visited her. I suppose he was trying to reason with her. History tells us he really had loved Catherine. But Anne Boleyn, being a student of theology like himself, somehow drew him, not to mention that Catherine was aging and unable to give him a son, which he had been obsessing about for some time. In the 1700s, a prominent citizen of Ampthill, Lord Ossory, erected a large cross in honour of Catherine."

They walked for about twenty minutes, following signs for Ampthill Park. The park was a beautiful space, stretching for miles off into the distance, with walking trails, a play area for children, a visitor centre, coffee shop, and rows of grassy land looking out over a large pond in the far west. To the south was a green area with rows and rows of small white crosses, each with a poppy in its centre. Catherine's Cross stood out from all else on a slight incline. They strode towards it. It was a very tall thin cross, carved from grey stone, placed upon a square base, and rising solemnly above the landscape. The three points of the cross were ornately carved, and Catherine's family crest lay before the cross bars. In front of the monument stood a plaque with the words:

"In days of old here Ampthill's Towers were seen
The mournful refuge of an injured Queen
Here flowed her pure but unavailing tears
Here blinded zeal sustain'd her sinking years
Yet freedom hence her radiant banner wav'd
And love aveng'd a realm by priests enslav'd
From Catherine's wrongs a nation's bliss was spread
And Luther's light from Henry's lawless bed."

Both Janek and Sarah were quiet for a few moments and then Sarah spoke.

"I've always been fascinated by the love story of Henry and Catherine. It seems she continued to love him throughout her entire trial and tried so desperately to encourage the return of his love. A very prayerful and religious woman, who died declaring her love for and forgiveness of a man who hurt her so much. Sometimes I even wonder if Henry did not, in his later years, regret that he had let her go. He was a complex character and I suspect he grew deranged over his lifetime of bad decisions."

Poppy and Crik watched from a safe distance. "I think we can safely return to the hotel. They're out for a walk, that's all," Poppy decided and the two walked away from the large cross. Sarah and Janek circled the open central area of the park and then made their way back to the White Stag. On the way they passed a series of interesting thatched rooved cottages, which looked like a thick, dark brown blanket had been gently moulded over the gabled tops of the whitewashed homes. They looked like the houses hobbits would live in, but above ground, and Sarah was again delighted.

After lunch and a short nap, the two again got in their car and headed for Houghton House, a little over a mile outside the village. Poppy and Crik were close on their trail but made sure to park a quarter-mile from the road leading into the grounds, and walked up the pebbled path on foot. Crik had used the internet to map out the land. He realised he could watch them from a copse of trees about two hundred yards from the property without being seen, but advised Poppy to stay back in the woods beside the footpath. He set himself up in a tree and pulled out binoculars and long-range camera and waited.

The House as it had appeared to Sarah on the internet was nothing like the real thing. As they walked up the rough path towards the ruins, Houghton House loomed far larger and more severely from the hilltop it towered over. The brick was an orange-brown weathered colour, exposed as the building was to all the elements. It was the huge size of the gawking empty windows that impressed her most. Janek had told her as they walked towards them, that the windows had been bowed at one time. The glass was long gone and whole sections of the home had crumbled, especially the corner towers. The wind wailed as it invaded the spacious open rooms, eerie in its pitch. There were several visitors entering and leaving through the various doors. Sarah felt her heart sink at the sight of the house.

"It's kind of a foreboding place," she whispered to Janek. He nodded.

Above the entranceway, carved into the sandstone, was a chained bear on one side and a lion on the other and in between them, were the letters M and H formed by carved spears. Janek explained that the bear was family crest of the Dudleys— Mary's maternal family— and the lion represented the Sidney coat of arms. They walked beneath these symbols of Mary's life, through the entrance, behind a young family, into an interior lit by the sun, which also threw deep shadows into corners and under the high thick stone window ledges. A large fireplace graced the left wall and a sign indicated this was the Great Hall. They moved towards the fireplace and, waiting until everyone else had left the room, got down on their knees and looked up into the chimney. All they could see was black darkness, until Sarah shone her flashlight upward. Janek ran his hand around inside the brick chimney but found nothing.

They moved towards an improvised modern day staircase which took them up another half level to what was advertised as the Great Chamber where Mary and Matthew would have entertained more privately. Moving to the back, they were now in what had once been family bedrooms, and they could see the dark recesses of former closet spaces. Sarah ventured tentatively into one of them, but it was full of cigarette butts and some debris in the corner, and nothing else. Another sign indicated the expansive windows in these rooms had once looked out onto cultivated gardens, and further afield, grassy wildflower plains with woods in the distance, where grand hunting expeditions would have been held. To the east, Janek pointed out the terrace with its Grecian columns. They left the house to stand beside the massive posts and felt dwarfed by them. "We can see here the influence of Philip's *Arcadia*," Janek said quietly. "What an incredible view!" They looked down into a wooded valley stretching for miles towards the horizon.

The sunrises must have been magnificent.

"This sign says that Paul Bunyan visited Houghton House and placed it in his novel, calling it the *House Beautiful*, Sarah read. "But to me it feels very sad, even a little creepy." She had hoped to feel Mary's presence here, but it had eluded her. Everything was either wide open or thrown into dark shadow by massive walls. It was depressing.

Janek picked up on her change of mood and suggested they sit in the sun on the broad side steps for a little while. He looked at Sarah and she smiled wistfully. "It feels sad here," was all she could say. He put his arm around her and hugged her close to him. "I feel it too, the lifelessness of a place once full of high spirited entertainment. It's a forlorn house now."

They decided to leave, and took a few last pictures of the house from a distance. Crik jumped down from his perch and walked quickly back along the trail to where Poppy stood, and the two headed for their car. "They didn't stay very long!" Crik stated. "I thought it was a cool spot."

"*You* would," was all Poppy could muster.

"Now what could you mean by that?" he queried, a teasing smile on his face.

"Just that I could see you there with your mates late at night whooping it up and drinking 'til the sun came up."

"Me? Little old me? You've got me figured wrong, missy. I'm a regular night bookworm."

Poppy regarded him with a smirk. "Who are you trying to kid?"

"I'll show you my books when we get back, smarty pants!"

CHAPTER EIGHT

"My ashes, as the phoenix, may bring forth
A bird that will revenge upon you all:
And in that hope I throw mine eyes to heaven,
Scorning whate'er you can afflict me with."

Henry VI, Part 3 - Act I, Scene 4

Many days after her sister-in-law, had returned home, Mary remained in her room, unable to rise, even to be with her children. Henry tried desperately to speak with her, but her eyes remained hollow and her words were few. She could not eat very much, drank little, and rapidly weakened. The doctor was called, but he merely shook his head and declared she had to come out of this grief in her own time. He told Henry to let this run its course and to summon him if Mary absolutely refused to eat or drink.

Alone in the dark, sitting by the window in the daylight, with or without her husband, it was as if she was blinded. Her thoughts would not connect to her body and she felt herself floating in a space a few feet above. Day became night, became day again and there was no change.

Her heart and mind clung to one thought: *He has been taken too soon.* Her poor brother Philip, always the one to bring her joy, was forever gone. She wondered how she would go on without him, and this thought always brought a heavy flow of tears. There had been too much death. Her soul felt frozen, her body the same, and even her thoughts seemed suspended in space. Everything had come to a silent standstill.

A fortnight later, she woke with a start, her throat sore and gasping for water. Henry brought a cup and she drank quickly, being parched. Great gulps were followed by hiccoughs and then loud gulping uncontrollable sobs. She cried for over an hour without stopping, and her head ached until she thought it would burst. Henry held her and stroked her back, her hair, her face. She could not look in his eyes, so troubled was her soul.

After the tears came deep sighs, as if she was now gulping for the air about her. Her eyes grew wild and she jumped at the slightest sound. Trembling with cold and fever, she finally succumbed to a fitful sleep, crying out from her dreams and waking the household. This time, a new doctor was summoned, a Thomas Moffett, who practised the controversial ideas of Paracelsus. Moffett spent a long time with Mary, and eventually managed to have some form of communication with her. This he accomplished by first asking her only to nod or shake her head in answer to his short pointed questions, delivered in a soft, kind voice. He later discussed his treatment with Henry:

"Your wife began to speak, after I introduced a kind of subterfuge of sorts, a benign trickery. Knowing of her interest in the study of chemicals, and her laboratory, which you helped her establish, I spoke about my training in the theories of Paracelsus, and his fascination with the natural world and botany. She listened for a long while to his theories and then began to speak about his later ideas about the mind, the imagination being a cause of many illnesses and also Paracelsus's deep understanding and kindness towards those with sickness of the brain. She became adamant that hers was such a sickness. I agreed. She was barely recovering from a deep grief over the three earlier losses of child and parents, when Philip was taken from her too. She had looked up to him with more than sisterly admiration. Theirs was a relationship of like mindedness and with his death, she feels a big part of her has died, never to be born again."

"She spoke all this to you?" Henry was incredulous.

"No. She spoke of Paracelsus and Philip. Your wife has a brilliant, and if I may say, questioning mind. As well as a very tender heart. The combination of these two in concurrence with four deaths, has overcome her. I recommend a long period of rest, combined with much fresh air, walking long distances every day— once her strength returns, of course— and much intellectual stimulation. She needs to rebalance the element of salt in her diet, to recover from the physical weakness she now experiences."

Henry allowed a pent-up sigh to escape. It had been a long time since he had felt any hope. Another man might have been jealous that a relative stranger had been able to reach his wife, but Henry was moved only by his great love for Mary. He asked Dr. Moffett to remain at Wilton for another fortnight, and Thomas agreed.

Over the next few days, Mary, with the help of Henry, the doctor, and several servants, finally left the safety of her room, to venture out into the gardens of Wilton. Though weak and thin, she seemed to welcome the fresh air. Gradually, she began again to spend short periods with her children, and this seemed to give her some joy. Frances visited and the two spent an hour together discussing Philip's funeral. Afterwards, Mary endured a setback.

For another week, she refused to leave her room, and became ill again with fever, chills, disturbing dreams, and delirium. This time, Dr. Moffett administered a new drug called laudanum which had been a favourite of his mentor, Paracelsus. The medication seemed at first to have an adverse effect on Mary as she sunk deeper into depression and melancholia. The doctor extended his stay at Wilton House.

One evening, after persuading her to walk in the lovely gardens, Dr. Moffett saw a change in Mary. She was very talkative that evening and also angry. She was upset at not being included in Philip's funeral, and told the doctor about its grand organization by the Queen and of Her Majesty's decision to exclude all women except his widow and her ladies-in-waiting. This infuriated Mary and she could speak of nothing else. Moffett began to explain that this was the way state funerals were generally conducted and

Mary immediately cut off his words with her statement: "If we are deemed necessary to give birth to our men, we must be worthy also of burying them!" She felt complete rage inside and wanted to talk about her fear of not being able to contain it.

"I will not see Elizabeth, nor will I have any communication with her! I believe her to be partly responsible for Philip's death. He was always seeking ways to please her, as do all her courtiers. They parade about Court, waiting for her to bestow a favour here, her wish there, a little pittance of a salary to do some work that she requires. She has impoverished my family! Philip was forever torn, trying to make his way under her haughty glance. When she finally gave him his 'assignment' in Amsterdam, he was so excited. Little did he know he was going to his death!"

She began to weep angry tears of frustration. The doctor led her back into the house, gave her a large dose of whiskey, and put her to bed.

He later wrote in his notes:

I fear Mary Herbert is in a deep melancholy, due to years of over responsibility, and efforts to cope with the deaths of those very close to her, all within a short time of one year. Her anger concerns me. If it is not reconciled in some way, she will sink further into this mire of black feelings. The family's long history of service at Court and their subsequent penury are facts few know about, as they have proudly hidden this from society. The Queen's action in taking Philip's funeral out of their control has injured Mary's sensibilities perhaps too much. Who is to say? I am not a judge of such matters. I can only observe that a split has occurred in her soul, a great wrenching, which, if it is not repaired, I fear will undo her. I recommend she continue to rest at Wilton and not engage in society, especially as she is unable at the moment to censor her thoughts and her words. It could be dangerous to her reputation and to that of her family. I prescribe sedating herbs to insure she rests at night, lots of time in the outdoors and constant companionship to guard against further relapse.

Henry frowned as he read the letter given him by Moffett. While he agreed in principle, he realized how difficult it would be to follow these instructions. He was not his wife's master, though other men felt that was their role within their own households. Henry had only ever indulged Mary with whatever she felt she wanted. Knowing her so well, and also grieving deeply himself over the loss of their child, his father and mother-in-law and his bosom companion, Philip, made him sympathetic to her feelings of anger and melancholia. He was making a supreme effort to be strong for the children and the family, but he now feared greatly losing the love of his life to depression and eventual madness. Despite his wife's absence from society, he was still obliged to serve Elizabeth and to do this, meant entering into the social world of Court. Otherwise, their family would fall out of favour with the Queen and they could lose all they had gained throughout the years. The Queen favoured Henry Herbert and his family was more well to do than Mary's had been. He needed to keep his world stable, but how?

On Frances's last visit, she had left a huge trunk, containing all of Philip's written works, which he had asked be passed on to his sister. At first, Frances had been disappointed that these writings were not left to their daughter. But on his deathbed, her husband had requested they be given to Mary and then, after she had perused them, destroyed. He had rambled on in his final delirium about vanity and how much it had taken him away from himself and his true work. He felt it was the cause of his misfortunes and he believed Mary would honour his will and do nothing with his "trifles", as he called all his stories, prose and poetry. Frances had wanted to read them herself but he had begged her not to, saying it would only lead her to falsely believe that he had loved another more than her, which was no longer true. He had come to see, through his great suffering, how important Frances and little Elizabeth were to him and how his earlier relationship had led him astray from the truth. This poignant request then, meant more to Frances than he could ever know, and she honoured it immediately after Philip's grand state funeral.

At first, Henry felt it was best to keep the trunk away from Mary, as she was so ill. But it now occurred to him that the trove of letters, poems, and stories of his best friend, might be a Godsend. He believed and hoped with all his heart that they had arrived in timely fashion, to help Mary connect again with Philip, as she had for many years before, through the exchange of correspondence and each other's writings. Mary had never been happier than when poring over her brother's words. And hadn't Dr. Moffett also ordered intellectual stimulation as an antidote to depression?

He brought the large container to their room that evening and found his wife pacing the floor, an angry expression on her face. When he gave her the box, he thought she would faint, so surprised was she and so touched. It was as if her brother was there again, passing her his notes for correction as he had done so often in the past.

Mary sat and read the first letter on the pile, and burst into tears.

"He finally realized how much Frances and Elizabeth meant to him! How late he came to this! But come to it he did, Henry, exactly as we all hoped he would! He must have then died peacefully knowing he had made things right in his marriage and with God. That is such a great relief to my heart!"

So, he had been right about the value of Philip's gift to Mary! Over the next few days, the family noticed an engaged expression on her face, as she spent hours poring over the contents of the trunk. She would be seen in her library, editing his words as she always had in the past, sometimes with a smile on her face. She had been pulled out of her suffocating inner focus into a renewed energy. That week, she made a decision, one which was to change the course of her illness and her future: she would work towards having Philip's works published and made known. It seemed to be her new mission in life. She refused to consider destroying this lifeline he had thrown her. And Henry could see no harm at that moment in again indulging her.

Mary decided to first organize this great mass of Philip's writings by date.

Her brother had been fastidious in dating his work. Many of his notes from schools he had attended were already divided by date and subject, as were his diaries. Mary could not at first understand why Frances had not kept the diaries and resolved to ask her the next time they met. Glancing through the earlier ones, she caught the name *Penelope* lovingly written across page after page. Perhaps that was what had caused Frances's reticence.

Sifting through Philip's history caused much pain in Mary and she realised she would have to take it in stages. Her heart was overwrought, but her innate curiosity was stronger. Not for her to shrink from any intellectual task, no matter how uncomfortable. After a few days, the organizing was complete. Every surface of her library was covered with Philip's treasured words. She decided to start the very next morning with his first school notebooks, written in a slanted, childish hand that made her heart ache to look at. *I must be strong for him,* she resolved.

One evening at dinner, her husband and the household servants sensed a subtle change in Mary. Her chin was up and she looked in each person's eyes as she spoke. The meal went much better than it had for some time. The house seemed to breathe a collective sigh. Henry was careful in his attentiveness to Mary, not wanting to break the spell around the evening, with its soft candlelight and hushed sounds.

Philip's school notes proved to be very amusing and made her laugh out loud at times. In one record, he described the day he first met with Fulke Greville, who became a lifelong friend. Philip had collected samples for a botany lesson and, on the way home, had slipped on a mossy rock while crossing a creek but had managed to hold high his treasured petals and leaves. Fulke had been right behind him and in his effort to help Philip get up both had fallen back into the brook, but again managed to salvage their morning's work. Sliding into class, each had left a puddle beneath their chairs. The adventure had forged their friendship.

From early on, Philip had been concerned about others, even above and beyond himself. When Fulke developed a fever days after their botany adventure, Philip had spent his relief hours visiting him, reading to Fulke and playing dice. He had saved the remains of his meals and passed these on to his friend. In his nine-year-old hand he had written, "I am rich, for I have a friend." Mary's eyes filled with tears. Often her brother had seemed lonely, bearing his burdens himself, not wanting to put trouble on another's shoulders. Melancholia had often gripped him. What a dear and holy heart he had possessed! Not for the first time did her own heart swell with gratitude at being his sister.

She had taken to keeping a journal of quotes which struck her as she read through her brother's notes. She decided to keep this record always near her, as if he, Philip, were actually accompanying her through the remainder of her days. Words were becoming life for her now and those words, she was discovering, were very powerful. Over the months this first journal grew fuller and a new one was begun. Mary kept these small leather-bound books hidden with the other box of Philip's works, in a safe place in her library, known only to herself and Henry.

Months passed in a scurry of reading, reminiscing, writing and copying into her journals, the nuggets of Philip's wisdom. At the moment, Mary was researching about her brother's trip to the continent after he had completed his formal education. What adventures he had experienced and Mary was fascinated by the people he had met! Of course, she had heard much of this before, in Philip's retelling of his journeys and in his letters home, but the stories came to life through his diaries. Her brother was such an entertaining writer! But he was also graphic. His descriptions of the St. Bartholomew's Day Massacre were so horrific that she had to take a break from her reading for two days.

By now it was spring and she played in her gardens with her children. The gardener and the cook smiled as they watched from a distance because they could hear laughter, a sound which had been quite foreign in Wilton House over the winter months. "Lady Mary is coming back to herself!" exclaimed the cook, wiping a tear from her eye. "And not a moment too soon!" reiterated the gardener. William was now seven, Anne, four and the baby, Philip, almost three. Mary held Philip in her arms as the other two picked early primroses for posies. The sun was shining brightly and Mary's cheeks were rose coloured, her long red hair blowing in the wind. She looked radiant that day.

Apart from Frances, and her immediate family, though, Mary was unable to muster the strength for company or for the parties of the past. Henry was quite satisfied with her progress, feeling that little by little his wife was becoming stronger. *We shall celebrate the small victories,* he told himself, *for they are great to our Mary.*

One afternoon as she and Frances took tea in the library, Mary read to Frances the description Philip had written of his time at the home of the Walsingham family in Paris that infamous St. Bartholomew's Day. "I will read only the bearable parts, but Philip speaks of you, Frances, as a five-year-old girl, on that day of the Massacre:

All about us were the sounds of a terrible struggle, with screams that made every hair stand on end, the smell of smoke, the sound of gunfire. We could see from Sir Francis's small anterior balcony to a corner of the street and what we saw was too horrific for words. Many of us felt we should try to stop the fighting but knew in our hearts that we would be exceedingly outnumbered

As I raced past a large window I heard a tiny mewling sound like that of a little kitten. Pulling back the heavy curtain, I discovered little Frances Walsingham, hiding there and softly crying as she covered her two ears. I bent low and touched her shoulder. She was trembling. Opening her eyes, she reached for my collar and clung on tightly as I picked her up in my arms and cradled her tiny golden head in my shoulder. She heaved a great sigh and began to sob and hiccough at the same time, taking loud gulps of air. She was shaking and I tried to comfort her by speaking softly and taking her far away from the noises at the window.

After some minutes she became calmer and fell asleep out of sheer exhaustion and terror, her head again on my shoulder. This beautiful little innocent should never have witnessed such a thing and at that moment I felt God had put me in her path to help her find peace. She had the look of a small angel and I will never forget the peace she inadvertently brought to my soul that day. *I would have this strange day end in second childlikeness and the oblivion of sleep, just as it has for sweet little Frances. But it was not to be, for the men of the household sat up all night guarding the doors and windows against attack.*

Frances's eyes had brimmed with tears. She remembered clearly the tall slender young man who had rescued her that day and her immediate trust of him. How her heart now ached to have Philip back and she let out an anguished sob. Mary was crying too. The two women huddled together by the fire remembering this gentle man and how he had touched their lives. As the fire burned itself out in the grate Mary wrote in her ledger:

"Here was a man of such virtue that we shall not look upon his like again."

By autumn, Mary began to dread the approaching anniversary of Philip's death. She spoke to Henry one evening of her dread. "How can I mark this day, but not again succumb to the old melancholy that will come with it?" Henry came to kneel beside her chair. "We will live through it together." "Shall we attend service in Salisbury?" Mary asked. "Whatever you wish my dear, whatever will bring you peace," her husband said.

"I have reached the part of his journals where he is translating the Psalms into a more beautiful form of the English language. He had only completed Psalm 42 when he died. You remember Henry, how he began reworking these Psalms here at Wilton House, while visiting us two years ago? I have an idea—what if I were to read his newly worded entries to you on that day, here in the library where he struggled to bring more understanding to the words? What could be more fitting? We will have a little service of our own then, right here, in his honour."

On October 17, 1587, Henry and Mary hid themselves away in their library for a while. In the end, both were exhausted, having cried and laughed over their memories. Then Henry had suggested that Mary complete Philip's work, finishing the translation of the Psalms he had begun. "It is a task I am not sure I am worthy of or able to complete," she replied. "Perhaps he will help you, just as he did many times before," her husband stated as he left the room.

When she did not come to bed that night, he decided to let her be. In the morning he found her fast asleep over her notes, newly worded Psalms 44 and 45 beside her. He smiled, then helped her up to their room and drew the curtains against the rising sun. "I have begun Henry!" she whispered and closed her eyes.

Over the next weeks, Mary persevered with her translation of the Psalms and made much progress, as her motivation increased. She felt closer to Philip through this effort, because she was doing it all for him, completing what he had started. She often talked to him, out loud, asking him for a word here, a sentiment there. The more she created, the more confident she became and the more enjoyable the task as well. It was a revelation to her.

During the first year after Philip's death, the Wilton Circle which Mary and Philip had begun at her home, continued to meet every two months. Mary hoped the initial meetings without Philip would not be as difficult as she had expected, because her brother had often been forced to miss meetings due to his posting in the Netherlands. Unfortunately, they were heartbreaking, as each member felt they had to talk about their grief. Many tears were shed and many poems written in commemoration of her noble brother, and for the first two months, Mary was completely exhausted and sometimes even ill after all the guests had departed. The group, all men, except for Mary herself, was comprised of Fulke Greville, the best friend of Philip, a courtier, Member of the House of Commons, playwright, and writer of prose; Edmund Spenser, author of *The Faerie Queen*; Sir John Davies, who was later to became the Attorney General for Ireland; Samuel Daniel, the famous poet and author of history who taught Mary's son, William; Michael Drayton, a recognized writer of historical and religious works; and Ben Johnson, a playwright, actor, and poet.

Fulke insisted on staying at Wilton after each meeting, to console Mary and her family. He and Mary would walk for long hours in the woods on the Wilton estate, sharing memories, discussing Philip's writings and planning for future meetings of the Circle. On one of these walks, Mary shared with him her growing ambition:

"The more I read of Philip's notes, the more I want to— indeed *need* to— put words to his life experience! I feel I can no longer remain silent. It is as if his words live in me and I in them. They have given my life new meaning. I intend to proclaim him to the world, in my own way, in my own time, and I will not be stopped. He simply *must* live on!

It has taken me almost a year to quell the anger I have felt against the world for his death. The Queen I hold most to blame, because she refused to give him meaningful work, kept bypassing him in favour of others at Court. He was withering there! That is why he pressed so hard to be sent into battle! She squelched his creativity until he became so frustrated that he lashed out at the other courtiers, thus meriting her punishment. While he was banished from Court, he did his most creative work. Had she put his genius to work, or even trusted it, he would be alive today.

More so, I was furious with Elizabeth for refusing the women in Philip's life attendance at his funeral. I do not think I will ever forgive her for that slight!

No! I am now determined to speak through my writing, whether it be to my Queen or to society in general. Philip's death is such a tremendous loss to our nation and to the Protestant faith that I believe God Himself will show me a way to continue my brother's work, his passions, his causes. The rewriting of the Psalms, in the best English dialect our country has seen, is only a beginning. I intend to use his memoirs and notes to produce prose and plays, just as he and I did before, but which now will convey my brother's message and his spirit."

"But how will you..." Fulke began.

"Do *not* tell me I cannot do this, because I am a woman! I will find a way, and when I do, there will be no stopping me! I will become a force to be reckoned with should Elizabeth or any other person try to put me in my place. Continuing my brother's passion in the world is my new vocation. Through me, Philip will live again. Through my words, his voice will be heard again! I have spent too much time on my own loss. The mourning must end. It is time to act!" She stopped and shook her walking stick in the air.

Fulke stood staring at her in shocked admiration. She had never appeared so determined. He remembered how Philip would often say of his sister, whom he loved so much, 'though she be but little, she is fierce.' Philip and Mary had even placed these words in a play they had been working on together before his death, titled *A Midsummer Night's Dream*, left unfinished. Fulke now recited the verse:

"Oh, when she's angry, she is keen and shrewd!

She was a vixen when she went to school.

And though she be but little, she is fierce."

Mary misjudged Fulke's expression. "Do not judge me, Fulke! I have suffered much, as have you. Of all Philip's friends, you alone know how deeply I loved and admired my brother. His will be my life mission now. His greatest desire was to improve the English language and to use it to communicate his deepest values. How can I not honour this longing of his?" Her cheeks blazed.

Fulke embraced Mary. For a long time the two simply held each other. When he finally let her go, Fulke looked with new wonder at the young woman before him.

"Philip always believed that your writing would surpass ours. He said that because of your heart of gold, your superior intellect, and the unorthodox way you have of phrasing sentences, that your words would one day have more impact than any writer he had ever seen. We all admire you, Mary. You are a woman, yes, and that only increases the power of your words. I will do everything I can to support you in your quest to share Philip's life and virtue with the world, so that he does, indeed, live on."

These were heady, but prophetic words, which rung in Mary's ears long after Fulke had taken his leave.

Her dedication to her brother at the beginning of their joint translation of the Psalms included this phrase:

By the Sister of that
Incomparable Sidney

The dedication began thus:

To the Angell spirit of the most excellent
Sir Phillip Sidney
To thee pure sprite, to thee alone's addres't
this coupled worke, by double int'rest thine:
First rais'de by thy blest hand, and what is mine
inspird by thee, thy secrett power imprest.

So dar'd my Muse with thine it selfe combine,
as mortall stuffe with that which is divine,

Thy lightning beames give lustre to the rest...

To thy great worth; exceeding Nature's store,

86

wonder of men, sole borne perfection's kinde,
Phoenix thou wert, so rare thy fairest minde ...

Howe workes my hart, my sences striken dumbe?
that would thee more, then ever hart could showe,
and all too short who knewe thee best doth knowe

There lives no witt that may thy praise become.
Truth I invoke (who scorne else where to move
or here in ought my blood should partialize)
Truth, sacred Truth, Thee sole to solemnize

Those precious rights well knowne best mindes approve:
and who but doth, hath wisdome's open eies,
not owly blinde the fairest light still flies...

Yet so much done, as Art could not amende;
So thy rare workes to which no witt can adde,
in all men's eies, which are not blindely madde,

Beyonde compare above all praise, extende.
Immortall Monuments of thy faire fame,
though not compleat, nor in the reach of thought,
howe on that passing peece time would have wrought

Had Heav'n so spar'd the life of life to frame
the rest? But ah! such losse hath this world ought
can equall it? or which like greevance brought?

Yet there will live thy ever praised name.

To which theise dearest offrings of my hart
dissolv'd to Inke, while perm's impressions move
the bleeding veines of never dying love:

I render here: these wounding lynes of smart
sadd Characters indeed of simple love
not Art nor skill which abler wits doe prove,
Of my full soule receive the meanest part.

Receive theise Hymnes, theise obsequies receive;
if any marke of thy sweet sprite appeare,
well are they borne, no title else shall beare.

I can no more: Deare Soule I take my leave;
Sorrowe still strives, would mount thy highest sphere
presuming so just cause might meet thee there,
Oh happie chaunge! could I so take my leave.

By the Sister of that Incomparable Sidney

The translations were complete. Mary sighed deeply, contentedly. For a long, painful time, she had not experienced such a connection to her brother or God as she did in that moment. She felt a renewal of purpose and resolved in her heart once again, to spend her life insuring her brother was not forgotten.

Yet there will live thy ever praised name.
To which theise dearest offrings of my hart
dissolv'd to Inke, while perm's impressions move
the bleeding veines of never dying love…

88

CHAPTER NINE

As Sarah and Janek returned to the White Stag Hotel, rain was falling. It was late afternoon and they decided to have an early supper and plan their next day's trip north. After the meal, they returned to their room and propped themselves up on pillows on the bed, each with a laptop on their knees.

"We should go north on the Ampthill Road to the A421to Chawston, where we can then veer northeast onto the A428 to Cambridge. I want you to see Cambridge, Sarah— it's such a famous city! Then on to the Quy Road, which will take us into Burwell, where we can explore the ruins of Matthew Lister's Burwell House. The supposed secret passage connected to a church, and, as far as I can see, the only existing church in Burwell is St. Mary's, so that must be the one. The whole trip is only about sixty miles, maybe one hour's drive. What do you think, Sarah?" Janek asked.

"Sounds like fun! I have a few questions, one being, how will we get into the passageway to explore it if it has been closed off for decades? And where will we stay?"

"I think we should stay somewhere near Cambridge, because there is more choice for hotels. We can go back and forth from there. It may take us days to figure out a way to explore the passage. We'll have to befriend the local curate of St. Mary's and also take time to explore the ruins of Matthew Lister's Burwell house.

They chose a historical hotel in Newmarket, only a few miles southeast of Burwell, called Rutlands Hotel. The price was right and it looked beautiful, with an onsite restaurant and wine bar, a sheltered cobblestone courtyard, and ancient stable.

Getting to the secret passage presented a problem. Nowhere in the online references to St. Mary's Church was the passageway mentioned. Janek and Sarah knew there was another access to it which had been described to them by Gladys Wrothsey, a member of the Wiltshire Historic Society, whom they had met before going to Carisbrooke Castle weeks earlier. She had visited Burwell several times and had spoken to an old timer who claimed there was a hole in the ground hidden by a large rock, near ruins of an older house, thought to have belonged to Matthew and his family, just behind the church. These ruins were on top of old Norman burial grounds, long covered over with grassy mounded earth. If all else failed, they could look for this hidden entrance, but both Janek and Sarah had some trepidation about its safety and were concerned about violating a burial site. They decided to email Rev. Janice Noonan at the church to make preliminary introductions and leave their cell phone numbers.

At six in the morning, Crik was at the window, observing the hotel across the way. He and Poppy were dressed and had eaten breakfast, not knowing when Janek and Sarah would decide to leave.

"You know, this well and truly sucks," Crik muttered. "Is there no way we can get a listening device on these two so we have a better idea of their plans?"

"When they decide on a hotel, yes, but we won't risk it too soon. Once they stop closer to Burwell, we'll get into their room, or I should say *you* will, and set up a hidden microphone."

About ten o'clock, and after three cups of coffee each, they scrambled to their car to follow Janek and Sarah out of town. The day was cloudy, with a light drizzle. The car was moving at a slow pace, so Poppy was forced to stay far behind in the morning traffic, keeping them barely in sight. She realized the route they were following, the A421, would soon become the A428, meandering through small villages and lots of open countryside or farmer's fields on its way to Cambridge. Once they arrived there, she would follow more closely. Cambridge, a university city, would be very busy on a Friday. Students would be migrating out of the city for weekends in the countryside, or trips to London. But the next forty minutes to the great city would be easy driving.

"So, Crik, what are these books you were on about showing me?' she asked glancing at him.

He was silent for a few minutes, chewing on his bottom lip. He looked nervous. *Probably can't even read*, she thought, regretting she had asked him such a question.

"If you can't wait to find out and must know, I'm interested in archaeology," he said keeping his eyes lowered.

"Really? Ever been on a dig?"

"Nope."

"Are you in college or uni?"

"Nope."

"Man of few words aren't you? Come on, spill it! Why so secretive?"

"First, tell me about you, then maybe..."

"Fair enough. I'm from Manchester and live with Mum and Dad at the moment, 'cause I have a school-age daughter. As soon as this job is over, I'll have enough money to move out and get myself a proper job. I've decided I don't want this crazy life anymore. In fact, I intend to start saving for college."

"What do you want to study?" he asked, genuinely interested.

"Nursing or Paramedicine," she replied.

"Cool. You strike me as the type who could take that kind of work. You gotta be tough for those fields. And a daughter, eh? That's cool. Yeah, I can relate to that."

"Oh yeah, how? You got a kid too?" she asked, surprised.

"Not one of my own, no. See I've got this little brother. He lives with me. He's ten now. I make him go to school every day, see that he gets on the bus, eats okay, that kinda thing."

"What happened to your mum and da?" She asked.

"Died. In a fire, when I was fourteen. My brother Jack, was only a baby. Mom passed him to me and we ran out the door, but she ran back in to wake my dad who was drunk asleep on the sofa. Then the ceiling collapsed..." He became silent.

Poppy saw that he was biting his lip really hard. She felt a pang of sadness and wanted to say something but couldn't think what. Finally, she put her hand on his arm and asked what happened after that.

"We were both put in foster care, luckily in the same home. It wasn't so bad at first. We were in Notting Hill at that point, kinda hoity-toity, nothing like where we were from. I missed my street gang, but that was part of the reason they got us so far away. I had been in the gang for a while, there were lots of drugs and drinking and the worker thought I'd go clean if I had the chance to be away from those guys. But I hated the preppy school I was in and kept skipping classes, wandering the streets, and trying to get in touch with my mates. That wasn't hard, we all had cells, and finally when we met up, they wanted me to steal stuff from my foster parents to pawn."

"At first I stalled, thinking me and Jack would get kicked out if I got caught and then where would we be? Eventually my mates put on the pressure, threatening a break-in now that they knew the upscale place I lived in. So I started small, stealing this and that and cashing it in, over time. Thought I was pretty smart."

"It seems the parents knew all along and were just waiting to catch me, which they did a month later. That was a bad day. The worker moved us out to another house outside of central London and confiscated my phone. I was fifteen by then, with a giant chip on the shoulder, you know how it is. I was in a different school in the country, one where they sent kids having trouble with things. A private boot camp deal. I only saw my kid brother on weekends. I hated it!"

The car was now quiet. Poppy didn't say anything. The atmosphere was that tense. She hadn't bargained on this guy dumping his whole history on her. A few sentences would have been fine. But something in her shifted a bit, realizing how hard Crik's life had been. Though she was curious as to how he had ended up with custody of his brother, she felt hesitant to pry. Crik didn't say another word, and after ten minutes, signs for Cambridge began to appear and she had to keep her wits about her so as not to lose sight of the green car.

Once they were in the centre of Cambridge, Poppy figured Sarah and Janek were going to pull over and go for a tour. *Those two can't resist the lure of the libraries*, she thought, a smirk on her face.

"What's so funny?" Crik asked.

"Just watch. He's going to pull over any minute now and have to get out and show her around all these lofty places of learning. Mark my words!"

Two minutes later, the green car, flashed its signal and pulled into a free parking spot across from King's College. Poppy put her hand in the air, and Crik and she high-fived and laughed in unison. "You got them pegged!" he said. She pulled over a block away and looked at him. "Wanna see the sights too?" He actually looked excited.

They followed at quite a distance, and as the two entered the chapel of King's College, Poppy suddenly held back.

"I can't risk following in case I am recognized. You go ahead in and make sure you're not noticed, and I'll return to the car. Text me when you're coming out?"

Crik was not prepared for the beauty of the chapel. He stood still, looking up at the high fan shaped arched ceiling, surrounded on either side by the most magnificent stained glass windows he had ever seen. At that moment the sun came from behind a cloud, flooding the entire narrow space with multicoloured light. It bounced off polished wooden chairs set up in neat rows and sent rainbows undulating across stone tile floors. *Holy shit, this is*

93

amazing! he thought.

He could see Sarah, holding Janek's hand, amongst a large group of teenaged school kids in the centre aisle that led to the altar. They were so engrossed in what the teacher was saying, that he knew he'd be safe to wander behind them without being detected. He turned his back to them and examined the carved creatures and heraldry on the side wall at the back, and read some of the signs describing the history of the building. Then, feeling a little overwhelmed, he sat in a chair near the exit and let the dusty coloured rays of sun wash over him. It was the most peaceful he had felt in a long time. From his vantage point, the two lovebirds were highly visible and as soon as they turned to leave he was out the door and standing beside a large plane tree unnoticed by anyone. They came so close to him on their way back to the car, that he could hear Sarah as she said, "We have to come back tomorrow! Let's get some lunch and head to our hotel in Newmarket."

When they were out of range, he slipped across the street and got into the car. "You getting sick of driving?" he asked Poppy. She said she was fine and then hit his arm. "Be careful, you! They almost saw you back there!"

"Nah, I was behind the tree. But I heard her say they've booked a hotel in a place called Newmarket." Poppy whipped out her phone and passed it to him. "Research how many hotels are there," she said as she pulled out after the green car. "Good work!" she added, smiling. He smiled back and told her they were now going somewhere for lunch. Then he couldn't stop talking about how amazing the chapel was. Poppy finally exclaimed, "OK, Mr. Mouth, can it! They're stopping again!"

As Sarah and Janek entered a coffee shop, Crik offered to get them sandwiches to eat in the car, and walked in the opposite direction while Poppy sat back watching the restaurant from a block down the street. She was famished and restless. She wanted more action. This job was getting tedious, but she had to admit Crik was beginning to be entertaining. He had been like a kid in a candy store when he returned from the chapel.

A half-hour later, they were back on the road, following the A14 through the north of the city, and heading for the B1102, towards Burwell. She supposed they would go there first, and then head south into Newmarket. These two were so predictable! This time she stayed well back as there was far less traffic.

In the green car, Sarah turned to Janek and asked him about his family. He had a broad smile as he replied.

"I come from a great family, Sarah. My grandparents left France when Dad was young, and moved to Salisbury, out in the countryside, to farm. There, when he was twenty-one, my dad met my mom, Sylvia, at a barn dance. I have four siblings: two brothers and two sisters. I am the middle child. My oldest sister, Agata, or 'Aggie,' teaches grade school in Dublin. She married an Irishman, Sandy Malloy. Then there is my older brother, David, who is married and lives in Cirencester, in the Cotswolds, on the river Churn. He farms sheep. They have five children. His wife, Sadie, is great! I am godfather to their firstborn, Charlie, who is now seven. What a cool kid he is. You'll meet them all one day, Sarah. Then there's me, and after me comes Katie who is two years younger. She is finishing her studies in geology at University of St. Andrews, Scotland. She lives with her partner Sally who is also a geologist. Next year she hopes to continue her Master's in Earth Sciences. And last but not least is Magdalena, who is fifteen, and going to high school in Bishop Burton, a small town in Yorkshire. Dad was offered a job there teaching in the agricultural department ten years ago, so he bought a farm and we lived in that region, farming sheep and harvesting the wool. Mom and Magda run a wool shop on the farm. Mom also offers drama courses at the theatre in Beverley as she has a degree in Theatre Production."

"That's where you get your love of dramatics! What a wonderful family you have, Janek. You are so lucky!" Sarah exclaimed.

"Yes, I realize that. At one time, I wanted to be a sheep farmer, too, then a vet, and then a drama coach, and when I went to University of Sheffield, in

South Yorkshire, it was originally for Theatre Studies. I worked part-time in one of the libraries on campus. In the middle of my second year, I decided to switch to Library Studies, with a few Polish courses thrown in. So I eventually graduated with a Degree in Information Studies and a double minor in Theatre and Polish Language. I went on to do my Master's of Library Science, moving to London after I graduated last year, and getting the job I now have at the British Library. Pretty roundabout journey, wasn't it?" He laughed.

"Interesting, though! Did you like Sheffield?" Sarah asked.

"I loved it there! I was able to live at home and commute to Bishop Burton, in an old beater of a truck, every day. It was only an hour's drive. And Sheffield is right beside the Peak District, so you are never far from the outdoors if you want to cycle, rock climb, or picnic. It's been voted one of the most beautiful cities in the UK. In my Master's year I moved to a small bedsitter in Sheffield, so I wouldn't have to commute. Made more friends that year and continued to pay my way through the library job. I had a placement at the British Library in the Archives and they hired me straightaway after I graduated."

"Did you always want to live in London?" Sarah was curious.

"Not at all! Hated the busy pace at first because I wasn't used to it. But London has grown on me. With the research interest I have, I feel it's the best place to be right now. But enough about me! What about you, Sarah?" He touched her shoulder.

"Well, I consider myself very fortunate too. My family is great! Dad is a museum curator and guide who spent a lot of his life researching the Billings family of Ottawa. He works at Billings Estate and every day our dog Benji goes to work with him, which is a few blocks from our home on Pleasant Park Road. Dad is blind. Has been from age three when his eyes were removed due to cancer. That didn't stop him from doing anything, including being a guide at the estate. Mom is a writer of children's fiction and has published two books. I have two siblings, both older than me. Sam is thirty, he is married to Sal, and they have three kids: Jason is two, Amy is four, and Naomi is five. I am godmother to Amy. I love them so much! My sister Jennifer is a children's librarian and has three children, all redheads: Carolina is six, Martin is four, and baby Robert is two months old. They are so sweet and I am an aunt six times over! My parents and I can't get enough of them!"

"You must miss them when you are here, then?"

"I really do. But I have been so busy and preoccupied lately that I haven't had much time to think about anything but this research... and you, of course!" She blushed.

Janek smiled. He was worried for a minute and was silent. How would he and Sarah manage if she felt she could not stay in England? Would he be able to move to Canada? He looked over at her. Her face was pensive. He thought *I would follow her to the ends of the world and back!* She was thinking, *Wherever he is I want to be!* But neither spoke their thoughts.

"What do your siblings do? Janek asked instead.

Sam works in high tech, and so does Sal. Jennifer is at home now on maternity leave and her husband Harry works as a biologist for the University of Guelph, in western Ontario. It's far from Ottawa, about a six-hour drive. But they visit often and I always take a week in the summer to stay with them. I love Guelph. It's a farming town, about the size of Cambridge. In fact, we have a Cambridge in Ontario— just fifteen minutes from Guelph! It's a beautiful part of the province, where roses and fruit are grown. Lots of farms and a School of Veterinary Medicine at the University."

"Will you be disappointed to not be able to see them this summer, with your six-month extension here? That will take you to the end of December."

"I hadn't even considered it, to be truthful, Janek. I am so happy with you, and the joint research adventure we're on together. Pinch me, is this real?"

Janek gave a relieved sigh. How could he even think of being without

Sarah?

A minute later, the green Mini turned off onto B1103 and travelled southeast into Newmarket, where they had booked their hotel. In the car following them, Poppy turned to Crik, saw he was asleep, and poked his arm, saying, "Wake up! They're soon going to be at their hotel!" Crik stirred and roused himself, looking around him. "Keep a keen eye out for a hotel very near the one they pull into," Poppy ordered as he gave her a sidelong glance. "Who made you the boss?" Crik grumbled.

The Mini turned onto High Street and then into the brick gated entranceway to the Rutland Arms Hotel, which seemed to Poppy to be centred on an inner courtyard. *Nice place!* she thought. Crik pointed to a hotel a half block away, called the White Fawn, and they parked in the rear lot.

"I'm going to run back and watch them check in so I can find out their room number. Then later I'll sneak back and bug their room when they're out," Crik announced, looking excited.

"Just be sure you aren't noticed!" Poppy warned him. "By anyone, including the front desk staff." *He stands out like a bloody sore thumb, with all his piercings and black clothes, not to mention the fluorescent orange shoe laces!* she thought to herself.

Five minutes later, he was back, before she had even completed their registration at the desk. "That was easy! Room 207, I overheard!" he whispered.

Sarah loved their room at Rutlands. It was tucked away in the back right upper wing of the hotel and looked out over the courtyard. The ceiling sloped downward towards the antique sleigh bed, leaving a small alcove with two chairs and a desk by the window. It was cosy and calm with cream coloured walls, dark old wood beams and a soft green quilted coverlet on the bed.

Back at the White Fawn, Crik was posted at his window, observing the entrance to Janek and Sarah's hotel. He didn't have to wait too long before he saw them walking hand in hand down the High Street. Scooting across the street, he entered their hotel lobby behind a family of five with a youngster who was screaming at the top of his lungs. Knowing this would distract the desk clerk, he slipped up the central staircase as if he belonged there. Having surreptitiously studied the emergency fire exit plan on the wall by the stairs the first time he'd entered Rutlands, he easily made his way to the second floor. The hallway was empty, with Room 207 being at the end of the long hall next to an exit. He dashed to their door, withdrew a lockpick, and in no time was inside the room. Moving quickly, he placed two bugs out of sight. Whistling as he let himself out, he used the fire exit and was in the courtyard in record time.

Back in her room, Poppy anxiously awaited his arrival. If he got himself into trouble, she reasoned, she would simply leave him to deal with it, just as she had done on the Isle of Wight when her former colleague had got himself arrested. There was a rap at her door, and Crik called out "Room Service." When she opened the door he was standing there with a frosty beer in each hand and a bag of crisps dangling from his teeth.

She smiled. He really was a corker! Dancing into the room, Crik sunk into the soft sofa, patted the spot beside him, placed the two beers and the crisps on the coffee table and said "Come and sit, Milady! The job is accomplished!"

After dinner, Janek and Sarah made a phone call to the rector, Rev. Janice Noonan, of St. Mary's Church in Burwell. They had planned to be truthful and say they were researching Matthew Lister's life but had decided not to mention the Shakespeare authorship debate, thinking it would only complicate things. Sarah made the call. The rector was very personable and even somewhat interested in the research angle. She came from the area but claimed she did not recognize the family name Lister. Nevertheless, Sarah made an appointment to meet Janice the following afternoon.

"That was very disappointing," Sarah said sadly to Janek. He hugged her and said "Tomorrow's another day. While you are speaking with Reverend Janice, I'll look for the ruins of Matthew's old house, near the church."

Back in his room, Crik monitored everything. He smiled and picked up his laptop. In no time, he, too, found the reference Janek had used years before, which discussed the other entrance to the tunnel which existed among the ruins. He discussed strategy with Poppy. Sarah and Janek would leave at one to drive to Burwell, where Janek would explore the ruins and Sarah would, at two o'clock, meet with "the Rev" in the church. He and Poppy planned to arrive in Burwell earlier, about nine in the morning, and explore the ruins themselves first. If they could find the hole in the ground which led to the tunnel, that would be a bonus. Poppy would have to wear a disguise, in case the other couple arrived early or happened to see her. "Now we're finally getting some action!" Crik said, giving Poppy a high five.

Meanwhile, Janek had been reading Mary Sidney Herbert's translation of the Psalms.

"Sarah, listen to this! I never noticed it before! This is the poem of dedication to her brother, that Mary Sidney wrote as a preface to the Psalms, which were included in their publication. It is entitled *"To the Angel Spirit of the Most Excellent Sir Philip Sidney."* She signs her poem with *"...By the sister of that—"* he raised his voice *"— incomparable Sidney!"* Sarah, where have we heard that very phrase before?"

"In the dedication of the First Folio to the *"incomparable paire of brethren!"*

"Let me research further to see how common that phrase was in Mary's day!" Janek was excited. Sarah loved his intensity and the happiness she felt at that moment was almost overwhelming. This quest was truly exciting! Her mind buzzed with energy as she picked up her computer and began the same research. It never hurt to have pairs of eyes on a problem.

"The etymology points to Late Middle English, say 1450-1499, and comes from the Latin *incomparabilis* and fifteenth-century French *incomparable.*"

After a half-hour without finding further information on the use of the word "incomparable" in the sixteenth and early seventeenth centuries, they decided to call it a night. They would search out better books on the subject when they returned to London.

The next morning, at eight-thirty, Crik and Poppy arrived at St. Mary's Church. It faced onto the High Street, which was busy with traffic at this time of the day. No one paid them any attention. Poppy sported a blond wig and sunglasses and a wide brimmed hat. Strolling casually up the stone walkway, they passed several graves, some tipping sideways and others decorated with fresh flowers or well-tended plants. Crik tried the front door of the church but it was locked. "Just as well," he said and the two made their way past the large rectangular tower, alongside a paved pathway to the back of the building.

There was a wildflower field behind the church, surrounded by a small stand of trees. Behind that large space, they could hear the sounds of traffic on busy roads. "Well, let's find those ruins!" Poppy declared.

The field itself was about nine hundred square feet, the size of a very large football field. They stood in the middle and turned in a circle. There wasn't a ruin in sight. "Are you sure we have the right church?" Crik asked.

"It's the only church in Burwell!" she snapped back, clearly annoyed.

"OK. Don't get your knickers in a knot now, Little Miss Redhead!" he exclaimed. "Ruins are just that, ruins. That means they break down over time. So start looking for crumbled rocks. That may be all that remains of them now."

Realizing he was right, she headed for the first rock she saw.

After half an hour they sat down on the rough grass and looked at each other. "They're havin' us on! There are no ruins here!" Crik kicked at the earth with his big Doc Marten boot.

Poppy had to agree, worried that Janek and Sarah had discovered they were being followed and were leading them on a wild goose chase. They decided to return to the hotel and listen in on the pair.

An hour later, they were no further ahead. Janek and Sarah had not given them the slip as they had expected, and Sarah was still intent on meeting

Reverend Janice that afternoon. So, at two o'clock, Crik and Poppy were back in their car, parked a block-and-a-half from St. Mary's Church, observing as Sarah entered the church and Janek went to investigate the same field they had earlier stomped around. Crik left the car and ventured to the wooded area surrounding the field, secretly watching Janek as he, like they had earlier, circled the field in vain. Janek joined Sarah inside and they emerged together an hour later. Crik had been fidgeting in the car, wondering what they were doing in the church. "Probably exploring that secret passage, while we're sitting here twiddling our thumbs!" he said.

Now Poppy and Crik were again following the green car back to the hotel. Listening in to the couple's conversation later, they were surprised at what they heard.

"I can't understand it, Janek," Sarah said. "Reverend Janice was completely in the dark about a secret passage leading from her church to supposed ruins behind it. She claimed there have never been ruins there, nor has anyone ever mentioned a tunnel from the chancel to the backyard region of the church property. She knew of no Lister family listed in the church records. I think she thought I was crazy or pulling a practical joke. In fact, the chancel doesn't have a door that is barred or even locked. There's simply an archway that leads from one room to the next! But I am glad she let us look at the church records. Weird, isn't it that these records have never been photographed for storage in Kew or some other repository?"

"It was the same frustration for me too, Sarah! There are no ruins behind this church. There's just a wildflower field and barely a rock in sight. It couldn't have disintegrated that much in the time since Gladys Wrothsey last visited Burwell." Janek was shaking his head. "But you'd be surprised how many old church records across England are decomposing, all that valuable information often kept in binders, exposed to the air. That would be a great research project, to go around the country collecting information from the early days to today. And thank God we found those papers, which are an anomaly in and of themselves. I don't think they belonged in St. Mary's Church records at all and I wonder how they even got there?

In their room across the street, Poppy and Crik looked at each other. Crik mouthed *What papers?* and Poppy slapped his arm. "You don't have to *whisper!* They can't hear us!" she said scowling.

"Let's get on the internet and try to find out more about those letters," Janek was saying. "Can you read the first one to me?"

"OK. It is dated November 24, 1636 from a Dorothy Lister, Towchester, Northamptonshire, to her sister Amelia Pigott, housekeeper at the rectory of St. Mary's Church, Burwell. It says:

"I will come to visit you at the rectory, if you can spare a room, a fortnight from now, by carriage. Martin, my dear husband, will accompany me. He will then go on, up to Burwell, a journey of two days, to investigate, for his brother, Matthew, some lands and properties there. Matthew wishes soon to retire from his medical duties to the royal Court in London and is pursuing the purchase of a manor in Calceby. Martin will retrieve me when this business is completed. Please write as soon as you are able to confirm this happy visit. Now, I must ask, how are you and the rector managing this damp and dreary spring?"

Poppy and Crik were listening. They were as confused by the letters as Sarah and Janek were, but were happy when the couple resumed their internet search for more details concerning Matthew Lister. All was quiet for about a minute and then Sarah exclaimed, "Are there two Burwells?"

Janek looked at her and then typed a few words into the computer. "Of course! You genius! There's a Burwell in Lincolnshire as well! It's about two-and-a-half hours' drive from here, almost two hundred kilometres northeast."

They burst out laughing at the same time that Poppy and Crik shrieked in their hotel room a minute down the road.

After another half hour of research, Janek and Sarah discovered that indeed a Matthew Lister had purchased a property, the manor of Burwell and Calceby, in Lincolnshire, and that manor was now gone, but that there were ruins of an older church, St. Andrew's, behind another church, St. Michael's, itself closed since the late 1980's, and no longer in use. "That's our Burwell!" exclaimed Janek. "Let's leave right after breakfast, tomorrow morning, for Lincolnshire and visit the real Burwell and Calceby. We'll explore the standing church and the ruins of St. Andrew's!"

CHAPTER TEN

"O proud death, What feast is toward in thine eternal cell,
That thou so many princes at a shot
So bloodily hast struck?"
Hamlet - Act V, Scene 2

For over two years, Mary had struggled to finish her brother's works, while at the same time reading everything he had ever written, researched, or studied. In some way, she became her brother, trying to see the world through his eyes, attempted to live through his thoughts and delved much deeper into the mystery that had been Philip than anyone before, even his wife. She was determined his memory would never die and to this goal she committed herself. After a while, she began to feel as though she were bringing him back to life.

To those around her, Mary seemed imbued with a new purpose and a vigour she had not previously felt. She had always been an energetic, involved woman. Now she was a woman on a mission. Any chance that presented itself, she brought her brother into conversations. Her loved ones would listen politely, all the while thinking they were helping her with her grief. Little did they realize how very deep was her determination to actually live through her brother.

As a woman, there were few creative outlets in which to express her thoughts, dreams, and hopes, without being perceived as a threat to male writers. She was highly skilled at needlework and continued to produce as much if not more than her share of artistic creations, but they now had a purpose. She illustrated her brother's *Astrophel and Stella* in sections, just as she finished his original book with her own words. Philip's passion for Classics was well known. Most of her designs now involved Classical themes and through these efforts she educated herself even more than in the past, in all things of Antiquity. He had loved history. She now voraciously read every history book she could get her hands on. The former kings of England occupied her thoughts.

Her Queen began to make much more sense when she was placed beside former rulers who had gained the throne through devious means. Her view of Elizabeth changed dramatically with this understanding. Philip had been very frustrated with the Queen. Mary, too, was both frustrated and increasingly angry at Elizabeth for constantly thwarting the hopes of the Sidney and Dudley families. She now believed her parents' lives were ruined by Elizabeth's selfishness. Philip would have married his first love, if not for the Queen's interference. And he would not be gone now, had Elizabeth given him work suiting his station and true talents. Philip had never had the temperament of a warrior.

But here was the rub: how to tame this anger, this constant resentment, the desire for revenge against a royal system and control that had caused her family so much grief? How to escape the possibility of a charge of treason? She knew she was treading on dangerous ground, knew how unsafe it would be should her true thoughts and feelings be detected. For two-and-a-half years she kept herself out of Court life, away from politics, and far from London. But as the months became years, she grew stronger in herself. After these isolated years, she was more determined than ever before to represent her brother by taking up his true talent as writer and thinker and offer Court and the people of Britain new works based upon his ideas. She knew he had tenuously navigated the troubled world of politics and intrigue. She would have to be just as careful, or her family would suffer.

Late one afternoon, alone on a walk through the woods surrounding Wilton House, she stopped to sit on a large rock in the sunshine. She was so weary that day and had a headache. She began to cry out to her brother to show her the way. No one answered. Mary stayed where she was for an hour. The sun came and went behind the clouds; it looked like rain was imminent. Wrapping her shawl around her shoulders, Mary closed her eyes and thought for the hundredth time of death. Would it not end all her present strife? Could it not be the very thing that would bring her brother, her parents, her little daughter back to her? Her aching heart was so broken. She then began to pray for death, speaking out loud to the heavens. The silence was deafening.

"Is there no way out?" she whispered.

What came to her overwrought mind were the simple words from the Book of Genesis: *And God saw everything that He had made, and behold, it was very good.*

She looked about her, opening her eyes. Evening was coming and she could hear the blackcap warblers and nightingales singing their goodnights in the trees behind her. The sun was setting and pale orange and mauve bands of light were thrown across the western sky. Life was going on as it had from the first day. Her heart stirred despite itself, with the sheer beauty of it all. Life itself was good. *I, in myself, am created good, by Someone much bigger than me. The small part of the world I and my family inhabit, is very good. At the roots.* Her heart strengthened. She let out a long breath and took in a bigger breath, watching and waiting as the sun set gently behind the trees and the haunting last notes of the mistle thrush filled the void.

Rising, she made her way home by the familiar path. She walked slowly. Her anger was spent for the moment. Perhaps it would rise up again. She would be more ready for it, more accepting of it. She hoped never again to deny what she had to give. And she had much to give. She would not apologize for who she was, for what she felt strongly about or for her talents. They came from God. And that was good. The will of God, the will to live, was stronger than any other worldly power.

And so it was that two months later, on Ascension Day, Mary orchestrated a triumphant return to London. Henry was surprised by the fervour with which she planned her entrance to the city and to Court. Nevertheless, he went along with all the plans. The Queen had organized several celebrations to honour Jesus's ascension into Heaven, forty days after Easter each year. For the first time in two years, the Herberts would again be part of it.

Mary left Wilton House in a carriage, decorated with the Sidney and Herbert arms, with several other carriages behind hers, pulled by horses dressed with ribbons. All the chariots held girls or women. Behind them, were forty men on horseback. And behind and alongside this group, were the servants, dressed flamboyantly. They paraded into London and were hailed by hundreds of people celebrating in the streets. Henry had moved to the front, and sat on horseback with other relatives at the head of the procession. He looked back to see Mary and the ladies, his daughter and nieces, waving to the crowds lining the cobbled streets. His wife's face was serene. *She has mastered herself,* he thought with a great deal of pride, mixed with a hint of trepidation, for he was not yet sure what this new Mary would do or say.

When they arrived at the palace, he helped his wife step down from her carriage. The Queen watched them from a distance, seated on her white horse and resplendent in her finery. Her expression was one of surprise. She was clearly taken aback by Mary's presence. As Henry and his wife bowed before Elisabeth, she said haughtily:

"I see you have changed greatly in your absence, Lady Herbert!"

To which Mary, with a curtsy, replied, "By the grace of God."

The Queen said nothing more, merely nodded and waved them on, past the line of bowing ladies and small girls, her royal head held high.

Mary turned to Henry, smiling. She too lifted her head. "That went well," was her only comment.

After Christmas that year, Mary decided to finish a translation her brother Philip Sidney had begun: Phillippe Du Plessis Mornay's work, *A Discourse of Life and Death*— in the original French, *Excellent discours de la vie et de la mort*. She had left this work until she felt stronger, and now was the time. As she sat at her library desk at Wilton House, Mary reminisced about her brother's close friend. She had met him when she was seventeen, when Philip had brought Phillippe and his wife of one year, Charlotte, to visit Wilton House. Mary had been married two years herself at that point, and had felt she had much in common with Charlotte, though they were a decade apart in age. Both women were politically astute and committed Protestants, like Philip and Du Plessis Mornay. Mary and Henry had been overawed by the famous Phillippe, but he soon put them at their ease. The visit lasted a week and Mary never forgot it.

Du Plessis Mornay had been on a year-long mission to England, sent there by the Huguenot Henry III of Navarre, to elicit support for his ambitions to become the next ruler of France, as well as to support the Protestant cause in France. Right away, Mary had sensed the deep respect Phillippe had for her brother. She had felt privileged to observe these two leaders in the Protestant movement discuss theology and politics. She had begun to understand more deeply, her brother's passion to spread Protestantism throughout Europe. He had accomplished this through travels to the continent and his writings. His was a creative mind and a deeply spiritual one. The values he had embodied came from a grounded Protestant faith. In truth her brother had become less a political theorist than a theologian with a creative mind.

She met Phillippe and Charlotte several times over her lifetime. When Philip died, she received the most consoling letter from Charlotte, who spoke of a special service held in Navarre. She had taken pains to write out every word of her husband's eulogy to Philip. It was only years later that Mary realized that Charlotte herself had composed most of the text. Her skills at writing had by then become legendary. After Charlotte herself passed away in 1606, her husband collected together her works, under the title *Memoires de Messier Phillippe de Mornay*. After his death, these were published in 1623. Years earlier, Charlotte had sent Mary her other recognized work, an observation of the St. Bartholomew's Day Massacre, which she had personally witnessed. It was a horrifying tract, and it helped Mary see the event through eyes other than those of her brother Philip, also a witness.

It took her a long time to translate the *Discourse*, even though she was an expert in the French language. The words needed careful thought and Phillippe's reflections were all the more poignant now after the deaths Mary had experienced over that shocking year in her life. In the end, the words became a balm for her soul, as she hoped her English translation of his words would for others. She was thrilled to finally sign her own name as translator. She realized how rare it was for a woman to do this, but with little hesitation, she did so anyway, knowing, in her heart, she had earned the right. That was all Mary needed. She remembered her long walk in the woods and her determination never again to denigrate her talents.

By 1593, Mary had finished another literary work: a story her brother had called *Arcadia* and which he had dedicated to her. When she was first married, he had sent her his finished drafts of what he called his trifles, a story for her alone. Each time he finished a chapter, he would send it to her from wherever he was at the time. In short, it was a work in progress. But when he died, he was in the middle of a sentence in Book V. Little did he know then, that his trifles would bring grief to both Mary and Fulke Greville, his dearest friend.

At the same time as Mary was rewriting and finishing the *Arcadia*, Fulke used a handwritten copy of the original, obtained from Philip's widow, to add his own ending, finishing the story abruptly where it had been abandoned. He then commissioned its printing by William Ponsonby, with the title *The Countess of Pembroke's Arcadia*. He included a touching letter from Philip to his much-loved sister. This action, perhaps initiated in kindness, ended in disagreement with Mary.

Mary strongly disagreed with Fulke's interpretation of the work. In anger, she added an ending she thought more appropriate and had *her* final version printed, also by Ponsonby. Both versions therefore existed side-by-side and were distributed in London, against the original wishes of Philip. Both Fulke and Mary were exceedingly proud of Philip and did not think his major work was a trifle. They each felt justified in publishing their own versions.

Though in the past, rumours that Mary and Fulke were lovers had swirled about London, all evidence now was to the contrary. Not only were Mary and Fulke at odds over the editions of Philip's *Arcadia*. Both sides of Mary's family had argued with Greville for many years, due to Fulke's usurping of Robert Sidney's position in Wales. Robert was Mary's younger brother. He had gained the title Viscount Lisle upon inheriting Penshurst Place, a Sidney family home in England. While in his last years in Wales their father, Henry, had tried to replace Fulke Greville, then a member of his Court of the Six Marches in Wales, with his son Robert, but to no avail. The Queen would not listen. When Henry died in 1576, Fulke retained the political office in Wales. Fulke had always been a favourite of the Queen, whereas none of the Sidneys were. In 1577 Fulke resigned from this position to return to London.

As early as 1590, Fulke also became embroiled in a fight with Mary's husband, over monies Henry thought should have gone to the Crown, but instead went to Fulke's personal coffers. All of this conflict added to the rift between Fulke and Mary, which led to the two publishing different versions of the *Arcadia*. They tried speaking to each other concerning their differing revisions but relations remained strained. In the end, by 1623, Philip's

Arcadia had been further revised by yet another author, Sir William Alexander, who, in trying to link the last two books of the *Arcadia*, actually created a bridged version, which eventually became the most popular of the three versions. Other authors followed suit. The disputes between Mary, her family, and Fulke became buried in history. Philip would have been saddened by the conflict between his best friend and his sister. He had often tried to defend his friend's position with his family, but the Sidneys and Herberts, over time, grew to distrust Fulke.

CHAPTER ELEVEN

Crik and Poppy were ecstatic. Not only had they overheard everything about Janek and Sarah's plans for the next day, but they had decided to beat them to Lincolnshire in the morning. Crik listened to the couple's further conversation and when they left their room to go to dinner, he turned to Poppy.

"I'm going to whip over there while the lovebirds are eating and remove the wiretaps from their room. Easy as pie. Want to come, see how it's done?"

"Not on your life. I can't risk Sarah seeing and recognizing me. You go, and I'll figure out our route to Burwell."

Twenty minutes later, Crik was back. Poppy heard him whistling in his room. Then he knocked at her door, holding up a bottle of red wine.

"Thought we could use a little drink tonight to celebrate. Dinner's on me!"

Poppy looked at him for a second then quipped: "There'll be no funny business!"

"Ooooh…the lady pronounces!" he taunted.

She smiled despite herself. "Give me a minute while I call my daughter."

"Your room or mine?" his eyes twinkled and she slapped his hand.

Her telephone conversation made her all the more determined to get this job over with as soon as possible. Samantha, cried into the phone. "I miss you, Mummy! I love Granda and Granny but I really, *really* want you to come home. When will you?"

"Soon, honey. Soon. Mummy is just busy with her job, but after this I'm going to change jobs and work in Manchester and never have to leave you again. OK? Now, how's school going?" she asked.

Back in his room, Crik had placed a call to his young brother. There was no answer. "Blast it! He should be home eating or at his homework!" he said as he pounded the desk. His message was short and not too sweet. "Jack, I'm gonna kick your ass from London to Scotland if you don't call me back before seven tonight. You are grounded, boy, until I get home. Except for school!"

Poppy was standing outside his door and overheard the last few words. She waited a moment, then knocked. He came to the door and flung it open, a scowl on his face. Seeing her, he quickly adjusted his expression and stood aside, sweeping his hand in a welcoming gesture. "Milady, my humble quarters."

He had ordered fish and chips and borrowed two wine glasses from the bar downstairs. The wine was chilling in an ice bucket and he even had a small bouquet of daisies on the table.

Poppy smiled. "Did you nick those from a little old lady's garden?"

"No! Never. I may be a thief, but even *I* wouldn't stoop that low!" and he reddened.

Poppy eyed him thoughtfully. He was growing on her, she had to admit, and she felt she had really hurt his feelings. "They are beautiful! My favourite in fact. How'd you know?"

"Oh, I have a way with the ladies, I truly do!" he said, obviously pleased.

At the crack of dawn, Poppy and Crik were entering Burwell, having made excellent time on the empty highway. It was almost six, and they stopped near the church a half-hour before sunrise. This would allow them at least four hours to investigate the two churches before Janek and Sarah arrived. The early light would help them to see, and at that early hour they would not draw as much suspicion to themselves as if they were exploring the site at midday. Nevertheless, Poppy wore her blonde wig. You couldn't be too cautious.

They got out of the car, grabbing cameras, knapsacks, and an extendable shovel, hidden in Crik's heavy canvas shoulder bag, along with flashlights, screwdrivers, lockpicks, and other various tools of the trade. Pretending to be tourists, they strolled down the road. The church was a block away, and in the early morning light, they approached it cautiously. They needn't have worried; the village seemed to still be asleep.

St. Michael's Church was not huge, but rose out of the dawn-lit bracken like a venerable old lady, dressed in light grey and white. The steeple was three storeys high and square, with a small arched wooden doorway, equipped with a huge padlock. Above this door was a larger triple-arched window, then a modern looking black and white clock telling the correct time, and above this another smaller arched window in the top floor of the tower. Parts of the upper floor were made of red bricks, perhaps a later addition. These were crumbling far less than the grey ones, which appeared to be greenish sandstone, here and there replaced by a whiter stone. This church had definitely seen better days. Poppy hit Crik's arm, pointing upwards with her other hand. "Relative of yours?" she asked, eyeing the ancient gargoyle whose poked out eyes stared in perpetual surprise and whose huge mouth, as per custom, held a water drainage pipe. Crik laughed nervously.

A handwritten sign covered with plexiglass, indicated that the church was now maintained by the Redundant Churches Fund of England and that each day it would be opened to visitors by a local volunteer of the Churches Conservation Trust between the hours of 8 a.m. and 6 p.m.

"That gives us about two hours to find that tunnel at the old ruins behind the church. St Andrew's, the ruins were called?" Poppy asked Crik. He nodded.

"Unless you want me to pick the padlock and get us inside this one?" Crik asked her.

"No, we could be seen! Let's look first at the ruins behind this building because according to our overheard research, it was there the old lady found the entrance hidden in the ground," Poppy decided.

They looked around. The nearby graves were in poor shape, tilting like old soldiers, and worn by time and weather. The grass was overgrown and the place was derelict.

They made their way through high, dry thatch past the side of the building, only to find an extension on the back end. Beyond that was hilly ground containing more old gravestones in the same forlorn condition as the ones in the front. Here and there were more modern stones, decorated with wreaths and kept up with small well-tended primrose or English daisy patches. A twisting natural path led the way to the top of the knoll. At the peak, they stopped.

"There's no bloody ruins of any church here!" Crik yelled.

"Shut up eejit, you'll wake the village!" Poppy whispered.

"The bloody disappearing ruins— again! I'm gettin' fed up!" Crik was livid.

"Sit down! Have a ciggy," and Poppy passed him one. They both lit up, sitting together on the slope. "OK. They talked about the ruins being near Burwell and Calceby. I'm looking it up now on my phone." There was a pause.

"There we go. No problem. It's eight miles further down the road. By car. I guess 'behind' for them in the sixteen hundreds meant way out back through the woods, across five farms and off the beaten track to Grandma's house."

Crik laughed with relief and looked at her sideways. "Love your sense of humour, darling. OK. So let's get back in the car and beetle it down that beaten track, aka Highway A16!"

Within six minutes, they were in Calceby. While Crik drove, Poppy read him the various descriptions of the ruins of St. Andrew's Church that she was able to find.

"In fact, the entire village of Calceby is pretty well deserted, so Matthew Lister's house no longer stands. But the ruins are just over that hill, behind the copse of trees on your left."

Crik parked on the side of a small worn path out of view of the highway. The two jumped from the car. It was already 6:15 a.m. and still grey, but within a minute the sun could be seen rising on the horizon. This time, climbing the hill by the trees, they saw before them the ruins of St. Andrew's Church.

"*Hallelujah!*" cheered Crik, slapping Poppy hard on the back. She turned and scowled at him. "Sorry, sorry. Don't know me own strength!"

Poppy forgave him, so happy at finally reaching their destination after what seemed like endless detours. She raced Crik to the ruins and sat down on the ground, breathless, in front of them.

The stones sat as they had for centuries: silent, grey, and bulky, looming over them. The two were quiet before the stones. The ruins were chalk, drawn from the area centuries ago. All that remained now of this ancient building were three fourteen-foot walls, with an open archway at one end, which joined two opposing walls. The third wall stood alone about thirty feet from the other two, and seemed to be eroding faster. The chalk was covered with green spring moss and there was a curious arched metal structure protruding from the earth at the centre of the joined walls. No roof existed. In the crisp morning air, the sounds of birds could be heard nearby, and a cool wind whistled about them. Otherwise, Poppy and Crik were alone with the ruins.

For several minutes, they looked up at its worn strength, neither feeling like disturbing the peace surrounding them. Finally, Crik whispered, "Pretty awesome place. The quiet makes you feel kinda small, doesn't it?"

The sun rose over the distant eastern fields and fingers of light and scuttling clouds moved towards them. Poppy roused herself and said, "Time to get at it!"

For five minutes, the two circled the structure, looking for any sign of an opening in the ground, the walls, or the earth. They found nothing. The ruins sat on a high incline. Crik began to scale the incline on his hands and knees, feeling the scrubby grass for signs of loose earth, holes, indentations or the like. He worked quickly, like a rabbit digging its burrow. At one point he leapt up and held up a small bone. "Looks like someone's finger! I think we're getting close! Remember Janek mentioned this site was near a Norman graveyard?"

Poppy shivered. They shouldn't be disturbing old graves. As she stood worrying, Crik called out again.

"I've found something here!"

Rushing to his side she saw he was digging in the earth with his bare hands, parting the long dead scrubby thatch to reveal an indent in the hill. It was about two feet wide and had a huge flat piece of sandstone above it. Crouching below the stone, and looking at it from ground level, she could see a large hole in the ground. It looked like an animal's burrow to her. Crik grabbed the expandable shovel from his knapsack and carefully began to dig below the large slab. Poppy held her breath and looked around. There was no one for miles and the trees in front of the hill hid them from view of the road. Not a car had passed since they arrived and the nearest farmhouse was miles off in the distance.

Ten minutes later, Crik had cleared a four foot opening which seemed to point downward, into the ground below. He put his boots into the large hole and there was only space below.

"I'm going to ease myself down. You watch out for me and yell if anyone comes along!"

Poppy looked horrified. "You can't be serious! What if it's an animal hole and you get attacked? Or worse still, a grave?"

"It can't be an animal hole, 'cause I had to dig it, right? Use your noggin, my pretty one," and he pointed to his head. Then he was gone, down the rabbit hole.

Poppy gasped despite herself. "I'm too small to pull you out! What if the ground caves in?"

He popped his head up from inside the hole and touched her cheek. "I'm standin' on the stairs here, my love! See? No issue! Now I'm going to head down these stairs if you'll be so kind as to pass me my torch and my coat please. It's as cold as the grave! And throw something over the hole, my knapsack maybe, in case someone comes along?"

She reluctantly did as he had asked. He called out at the stair bottom, his voice quite faint. "Blimey, this really *is* a tunnel! I'm about seven feet under now, and it's a clear path ahead, with rounded stone walls heading north, towards the road where we came from. Wait for me. I shall return!"

Poppy began to walk around the hill, heading north, simulating his journey. Of course she would not hear anything with Crik being so far below her. She began to pace.

Crik, by now, was well into the tunnel. What an adventure! He imagined himself telling Jack all about it when he returned to London. He swung the torch to the right, left and above him, looking for something, anything. The walls were thick and made of stone, with the occasional sound of water droplets. The tunnel itself was reinforced in places with heavy timbers and it proceeded straight ahead. It would have been pitch black, had it not been for his light. The structure, he could tell, was entirely man-made. Every ten yards or so, he felt a small bit of air on his head. At first he had jumped in his boots at the touch of the slight breeze. Throwing the beam of his torch upwards, he saw there was a space between the bricks, from which a large piece of metal piping extended, just an inch above the surface. *Air vents!* he thought with relief.

After about five minutes, the tunnel came to an abrupt end. He was startled to see a small archway opening to the right of the end wall. Following its lead, he found himself in a tiny room about nine feet by nine feet, which looked a little like a stone cellar. There were several small recesses in the walls which he explored one by one, but found nothing. At one end of the room, in the far wall, was what looked like a thick metal ring. He pulled on it, but nothing happened. He pulled again, and again nothing. It was then he noticed that the wall below the ring, had a wide space carved out of it, right at ground level. A space about four inches high and six feet wide. He got down on his knees and shone his torch through the space, putting his ear to the damp earthen floor and looking through the opening.

Meanwhile, on the surface, Poppy was frantic. *Where is the chancer?* She returned to the hole Crik had disappeared into. All she could do was sit and wait. And bite her nails.

Below the ground Crik could see only a few feet in front of his eyes. The space below the ring led to another space, with what looked like very wide wooden crossbeams on angles. He reached through and touched one of them. He was right. Wood beams. Covered now with moss or lichen. Slightly damp on the surface, but solid. And beyond the maze of them, about two feet away, were steps leading upward. He could see three of them, made of stone, rising one above the other, in the light of his torch. He felt the movement of air on his face, ever so slightly, and recoiled back. This was a doorway. Getting to his feet, he moved his hands over the edges of the stone walls and soon discovered a very minute indentation in a line about six feet tall from floor to ceiling. This was then a large stone entrance, or exit, but his way out was blocked by huge heavy beams of wood on the other side, leaning their weight against the door.

It was then he noticed how very cold he was becoming and how little air there was in the tunnel. Deciding to turn back, he counted his steps until he again reached the first stairway. Approximately six hundred steps. Now feeling weak, Crik mounted the stairs and poked his head through the opening, taking great gulps of the fresh air outside. He completely startled

Poppy. At the sight of him she shrieked with happiness. There were tears in her eyes. "You little eejit! You... you had me scared!" and she fell into his arms, hugging him tightly.

Now Crik was scared too. He had never seen this gentler side of Poppy. He was momentarily frozen with fear. He wasn't sure he felt comfortable with this side of her.

"Sorry, I guess..." he said tentatively, but by then she had straightened up, dusting herself off and removing herself from his stiff embrace.

You are a sight! Look at you! Covered with the dust of ages, which you've gotten all over my new outfit! Move away. You smell like dirt!"

Ah, that's better, he thought with a sigh.

Sarah and Janek had decided to leave earlier than they had planned. They had woken at the crack of dawn and were so excited about the upcoming adventure that they had a quick breakfast and were packed and on the road at 6:45 a.m. They were ten miles from Burwell when Janek's phone rang. It was only 8:40 a.m. He pulled over into a lane and by this time the phone had stopped ringing. Curious, his eyebrows raised at Sarah, he dialed the unrecognized number.

"Simon Culver, Culver's Antiquarian Locks and Keys," the voice at the other end stated.

"Hi, Mr. Culver. It's Janek....Janek Wieczorek. You just called my cell?"

"Yes! Hello, Janek! Let me take the phone in my office. We will have more privacy there. Ah, that's better. I'm afraid I have some rather bad news for you. You see my shop was broken into three days ago, the evening after you picked up your copy of the medieval key!"

"No! I am so sorry, Mr. Culver!"

"Yes, no need for you to be sorry, sir. No. Not at all. But I must tell you the only thing missing in the store is the mold I made for the copy of your key! So strange! We arrived the next morning to find my desk in complete disarray, and drawers pulled out or emptied everywhere. You see, I had stored one copy of the key, as I mentioned to you, in my hidden safe, so they were unable to get to it. But unfortunately, I had left the mold under some papers on my desk. I usually take the special molds and place them in the safe as well, but I had a curious phone call to my office right after the new keys were made, and I'm afraid I didn't have time to put the mold in a safe space. I have two safes for storing valuables or unusual items but the second one for molds is larger and is off the premises. So I had hidden the mold under some obscure papers, Lord knows I have a ton of them on my desk! I was diverted by that strange phone call and was busy with its request the rest of the day. I had to leave hurriedly after work to go to a meeting regarding the earlier call. Curiously, the other party never turned up! Oh, I am rambling. I apologize!"

"I am so sorry to hear this!" Janek was distraught. "No. You are not rambling. Please, go on."

"Yes, well. There's more to it. I know you asked me to keep everything confidential regarding your found key, and I know I should have called you first, but all I had was your home number and there was no answer there. So I simply ended up calling the police before reaching you to tell you I would have to do so!"

"Perfectly understandable, Mr. Culver! I'm happy you did call the police. Of course you had to!" Janek felt sorry for the man who was obviously upset. "Then what happened?"

"Well, straight away the police came over. They fingerprinted my desk, but I daresay I had touched things to see what was missing. So silly of me! But don't these thieves wear gloves now, what with all the coverage of crimes? Anyway, the police did a thorough job here. I had to mention your name because yours was the only related article stolen. They should have called you by now as well. Have they?"

"No, but Sarah and I are away in the northeast of England," Janek answered.

"Right. Of course. I should explain how I got your cell number and why I did. Let me back up a bit. Last evening I thought a lot about the whole affair and I reasoned you may be in some danger. After all, it was only your mold that was targeted. I began to wonder if that strange call I received was a way of getting me out of the shop, of ensuring I would not be there during the break-in. It was all so strange! The call was from a man who claimed to be an old client, from the 1990s, who had left with me a mold for a special key that he had found when selling his house twenty odd years ago. He said he needed the key returned as soon as possible, as he was only in London for the day. He was unable to come to the shop, but would meet me after closing hours at the coffee shop on the ground floor of the British Museum.

I confessed to him that I had no recollection of his name, and a quick online search revealed nothing, but he insisted I would remember him when we met. Acted kind of like an old acquaintance on the phone, all jolly good and so forth. I agreed quite reluctantly. Then I spent the rest of that afternoon researching his name. Molds older than twenty years are kept in an archives unit we rent on the other side of London. Myself and the secretary there searched high and low and by closing time I had found nothing. I tried to call the gentleman back and explain but he would not pick up. So I had no choice then but to get over to the museum as soon as I could. He never appeared!"

"That sounds very fishy, Mr. Culver!" Janek agreed.

"So, to make a long story short: this morning I traced your home phone number to your apartment and I visited there on my way to work. The landlady, who lives downstairs, was very reluctant to give me your cell number. But she finally gave in when I explained I had a special key made for something you owned and couldn't put it in the mail. I showed her your sales receipt for the purchase of the key and mold, and she realised she knew of our business, a family member had spoken highly of us, so here I am, calling you on your phone."

" Sir, I think you may be in danger, or at the least being watched by some pretty shady characters! I also called the police to report the no-show of the person who called me and told them I thought that person had tried deliberately to get me out of the shop. They listened but thought it was all a little far-fetched."

"Mr. Culver, I very much appreciate all you've done. I have no problem with you having my cell number, and when we return I would like to invite you to our apartment for dinner and explain more to you about why I believe every word you have said about us being watched. This has happened before. If you are interested, that is?" Janek asked.

"Please, call me Simon. I feel we are more than business colleagues. Yes, I am ever so interested, Janek, and I would love to hear the story of all you and your Sarah have been through. I am now much relieved that I have called the police again this morning, for your safety alone. I did not want to spoil your trip, and I daresay I have, but please forgive me?"

"Simon, you have nothing to apologise for. We are becoming quite used to this scenario lately. Not that we like it or even understand it, but we have been followed before. I am just sorry your shop became involved in this mess!"

"No, no, none of this is your doing! We will talk again soon. I look forward to it! Let me give you my police contact 's number, shall I?" Soon Mr. Culver rang off.

"Oh my, something has happened!" Sarah said, putting her arm on Janek's shoulder. "I'm afraid so!" he said and then explained the call to her.

"I'm so glad Mr. Culver wants to hear our story," Sarah said. "I think we should call the police, don't you?"

Janek agreed. "I didn't feel this time that we were being followed, but we must have been. Whoever is behind this bizarre ordeal is just not willing to let go! I confess I don't understand it at all!" Janek looked both angry and discouraged. Sarah leaned over and gave him a kiss.

"We're in this together and I have every belief we will defeat this guy or group, whoever they are. We can't let them intimidate us any longer!"

Janek smiled at her in his lopsided way. "What did I ever do without you?" he asked, kissing her again.

Janek dialed the number and was put on hold for a long time. Finally, the officer in charge of the investigation came to the phone. He seemed belligerent towards Janek, complaining that he had been trying to get a hold of him for two days. Janek explained that he and Sarah were away. Detective Paul Smithey asked when they would be returning to London. Janek was unsure, so the officer decided to speak now on the phone.

"Look. You've come up in our database. Something about Shakespeare and your research being stolen, a computer theft of a device owned by a Miss Sarah Churchill— your girlfriend, I suppose— an attack on her at Carisbrooke Castle, a car accident outside of Salisbury after your car was tampered with, now *this*! The theft of a mold for a key that you found that you think will lead you to something or other! Sir, it reads like a fantasy, I must say!"

"You can see it any way you like, sir, but it is all the truth!" Janek's face was red and his eyes blazed. He was very angry, Sarah could see that.

"What are you and this Sarah playing at? I warn you, the police have no time for craziness like this."

"Neither do we! If you are not willing to take this seriously and help us, not to mention the innocent Mr. Culver, then we don't have time for this call either!" He was about to ring off, when the detective spoke out loudly.

"Look, Mr. Wieczorek! You have to admit the story sounds fishy. I was partly testing you to see how scared off you'd become. I *am* taking seriously the reports of other officers— outside of my jurisdiction, I might add— but to fully understand this unique situation, I'll need to ask you and Ms. Churchill to come in to the precinct and speak with me when you return. Will you do that? In the meantime, we have absolutely no leads as to why someone would break into Culver's and steal something so obscure, but I will let you know if anything comes up."

Janek sighed. He knew what that meant. Nothing further would be done until they returned to London, but he and Sarah agreed they would call the detective on their return. Then Janek thought of something else. He gave them detective Louis's number saying they had hired the private detective to help them while in Carisbrooke and Salisbury. He ended with the statement, "*Louis* certainly took our story seriously!"

For a long time, both were silent. Janek felt very discouraged and also, again, quite responsible for harm done to Culver's because he had visited the store. He began again to worry and wonder if he was putting Sarah and others, in unnecessary danger.

She could see it in his body language, so she hurriedly said, "Don't you go thinking you'll drop all this to keep from hurting me or anyone else. Janek, listen! You have a perfect right to your research, your ideas and your life! If you give in, they win! Whoever "they" are! And I for one won't let them win. In any case, this is more fun than I've ever had in my life. Please don't consider excluding me from the adventure?"

For a long moment, he stared straight ahead. Then he turned to her and said, forcefully, "You are so right Sarah! I won't bring this up again. We are in this together and we are going to win in the end!"

He turned the car out of the lane, and sped off towards Burwell. In the car, he and Sarah continually checked behind them, to see if they were being followed. There were no other cars on the road, it was that early. Burwell wasn't the most sought-after tourist spot in the UK. Nevertheless, they agreed to carefully watch the goings on around them from now on. They knew they must have been followed this time and that their pursuer or pursuers were upping the ante. Breaking into Culver's was a new twist on the bizarre behaviour their followers had already exhibited. Not only were they out to harm Janek and Sarah, they now seemed not to care that they involved innocent people. What could possibly be their goal in all this? "Is it just that they want to be first to discover who was the real Shakespeare?" Janek voiced his inner turmoil. *Or is there something, some vendetta this person has against me?*

"Janek, I think it's bigger than you, or me, or anyone else. I think that if a discovery of this magnitude is made, the discoverer will become famous. Overnight. Shakespeare is *that* big. Whole industries all over the world, are based on Shakespeare. People's livelihoods are at stake. Especially scholars. It's like a proverbial can of worms. It will turn the world on its head, I think," Sarah was a little taken aback herself by her own words. "You start out on this trek because you are so curious, you love the words of the Bard so much, your life is so *influenced* by the writings, the world has been touched by these words! Who can't help wondering what the person was like who wrote these wonderful words, who changed the entire English language, who was so psychologically astute that the words *still* speak to us after centuries! But as we get curious about the writer, holes begin to appear in the theory that it was the man 'Shaksper', or that only one person had the type of genius it would take to write this way. The question has been begged far earlier than you or I begged it."

"Exactly. It's curiosity, basic human questioning, that's at stake here. If we cannot safely question something, we all know what that does to the human spirit, and to the world we live in! History has more than given us examples of what stifling personal freedom can do."

They had reached the Church of St. Michael. It was beautiful, representing far more than an old, tired building long past use. Even the fact that it had been declared redundant had a special meaning as they walked towards the ancient door. It was for them the culmination of their mutual decision to continue their quest despite the possible cost. It meant the world to them.

CHAPTER TWELVE

"Who is't can read a woman?"
Cymbeline - Act V, Scene 5

Mary put down her pen and laid her head upon the pages scattered around the wooden desk. The fire had all but burned out in the grate. She shivered. Sitting up, she gathered the papers before her and read the verses one last time before retiring to her chamber:

Ay me, to whom shall I my case complaine,
That may compassion my impatient griefe!
Or where shall I unfold my inward paine,
That my enriven heart may find reliefe!
Shall I unto the heavenly powres it show?
Or unto earthly men that dwell below?

To heavens? ah they alas the authors were,
And workers of my unremedied wo:
For they foresee what to us happens here,
And they foresaw, yet suffred this be so.
From them comes good, from them comes also il
That which they made, who can them warne to spill.
To men? ah, they alas like wretched bee,
And subject to the heavens ordinance:
Bound to abide what ever they decree,
Their best redresse, is their best sufferance.
How then can they like wretched comfort mee,

The which no lesse, need comforted to bee?
Then to my selfe will I my sorrow mourne,
Sith none alive like sorrowfull remaines:
And to my selfe my plaints shall back retourne,
To pay their usury with doubled paines.
The woods, the hills, the rivers shall resound
The mournfull accent of my sorrowes ground.

Woods, hills and rivers, now are desolate,
Sith he is gone the which them all did grace:
And all the fields do waile their widow state,
Sith death their fairest flowre did late deface.
The fairest flowre in field that ever grew,
Was Astrophel: that was, we all may rew.

What cruell hand of cursed foe unknowne,
Hath cropt the stalke which bore so faire a flowre?
Untimely cropt, before it well were growne,
And cleane defaced in untimely howre.
Great losse to all that ever him did see,
Great losse to all, but greatest losse to mee.

Breake now your gyrlonds, O ye shepheards lasses,
Sith the faire flowre, which them adornd, is gon:
The flowre, which them adornd, is gone to ashes,
Never againe let lasse put gyrlond on:
In stead of gyrlond, weare sad Cypres nowe,
And bitter Elder, broken from the bowe.

Ne ever sing the love-layes which he made,
Who ever made such layes of love as hee?
Ne ever read the riddles, which he sayd
Unto your selves, to make you mery glee.
Your mery glee is now laid all abed,

Your mery maker now alasse is dead.

Death, the devourer of all worlds delight,

Hath robbed you and reft from me my joy:

Both you and me, and all the world he quight

Hath robd of joyance, and left sad annoy.

Astrophel: A Pastorall Elegie Upon the Death of the Most Noble and Valorous Knight, Sir Philip Sidney, Spenser, Edmund, Collector; subtitled "The Doleful Lady of Clorinda" sung by Mary Sidney

Reading the poem again, she felt her heart had not been fully in her words. Her friend and fellow Wilton Circle member, Edmund Spenser, had begun compiling a book of tributes to Philip and had asked each of the group to contribute a piece of writing.

Mary asked herself why, at this time, she was unable to portray her true feelings about the loss of Philip. An insight came quickly: she had been able to finish his works, to write about death and to grieve her brother spiritually, but her spent emotions were just that— spent. It was time to stop mourning. Mary now only wanted to see her brother's dreams become realities in her lifetime.

She was determined to complete everything they had started together: the bits of verse, the plays, the sonnets, the prose. She would attempt to imbue them with the spirit of her brother. She would try to enlarge and improve the English language and champion his Protestant cause. This was her new goal, one that she wished to fiercely pursue to the end of her days. Mounting the stairs to her chamber she felt a renewed zest for life.

The very next morning found her at work on Philip's papers, at her library desk, her brother's school notebooks scattered about.

Philip had been keenly interested in history. There were long passages about Henry V, Henry VI, Henry VII and Henry VIII. Each King was very different in personality from the others. One was weaker than the rest.

Henry VI stood out as a studious man, more interested in his books and religion than in war, happy to promote peace when to all around him, war seemed inevitable. He was oblivious to the anger of the lords and dukes who had fought for his cause in France. And now these warriors were forced to watch as Henry forfeited lands they had gained for England. In accepting the conditions of the French King Charles II upon his marriage to the King's niece, the power-hungry Margaret of Anjou, Henry VI negated all their heroic efforts.

Philip had puzzled long and hard over the studious but, he suspected, mentally-unstable, Henry VI, as shown by the scribbles in the margins of his notes. There were phrases like: *I am glad he saw book learning as essential to his rule*, followed closely by *What was in his mind with this marriage bargain, so poorly conceived?* and then, ultimately, *Is peace at any price wise? I must think on this more...*

The story of Henry VI perhaps made Mary feel closer to Philip than the other histories he had researched. In this king, she saw a shadow of her brother's lifelong struggles, his religiosity and intellectual curiosity warring with a deeply political nature.

Mary decided to immerse herself in everything written and available to her, beyond her brother's notes, which dealt with Henry VI and his reign. She consulted a text which had been her brother's and which she and Philip had often read together as students in Penshurst, the original Sidney family home. Written by Edward Hall, it was called *The Union of the Two Noble and Illustre Famelies of Lancastre and Yorke*, and was published in 1548. She noted scribbles Philip had made on every page of the text and remembered their many discussions of the history recorded in this book.

Mary was well into Henry VI's life by noon. The story fascinated her and brought her back in time. Her imagination was certainly up to the task of picturing every word, and when she put the book down to pause for refreshment, she realized it had helped her forget her aching sadness. Not once throughout the reading had she had the time or inclination to think of her heartache, for the story captivated her.

When she returned to her library, Mary took down from the mantel the great tome she had recently received from her brother's estate, *The Firste Volume of the Chronicles of England, Scotland and Ireland Faithfully Gathered and Set Forth by Raphaell Holinshed*, published in 1577. She had her own copy of this book, also given to her by Philip, but she wanted to note and think about Philip's handwritten observations found on its many pages. Philip had known Holinshed personally, but was even friendlier with Edmund Campion, whom Holinshed had employed to help with the compilation.

Mary shook her head as she thought about Campion. His life had been a whirlwind of fame, fortune and, ultimately, misfortune. Along the way her brother had become involved, almost to his detriment, in the man's struggles. Originally a Protestant deacon, Campion had been employed in 1570, by her father, who was posted to Ireland as the Queen's Deputy. Henry Sidney had commissioned Edmund to create a history of Ireland. Philip had been sixteen and Mary nine, when they met the young man, as he had often visited the Sidney children in their home. Campion had been particularly fond of Philip, and of his uncle, Robert Dudley. Many an evening the three men sat long into the night discussing the politics and religion of their day. But over time, Campion became more convinced of the truth of the Catholic Church, and this led to a troubled conscience and a need to leave Britain to study Catholic theology. Being highly intelligent, he had eventually been drawn to the Jesuit Order, into which he was ordained in 1578 in Prague.

Originally, Edmund had made a great impression upon Mary's uncle, and through him, Queen Elizabeth herself. Later, when he returned to London in 1580, Campion's Catholicism and missionary activities had become suspect. Mary remembered fearing for Philip during that fatal year, because he and Campion had become such good friends that Philip openly spoke of Edmund's ideas. Campion had even believed Philip may one day convert to

Catholicism. That had not happened, but Mary now wondered how close her brother had come to questioning his Protestant faith. Philip had been torn. His questing mind had often led him into troubled waters.

She thought back to the early months of 1580, when Philip had spent himself trying to convince Queen and country to go to war against Spain, to further the Protestant cause. His efforts had been unsuccessful. Here was evidence of how very conflicted Philip had become. At the same time as he was befriending and entertaining the ideas of the newly converted Catholic Campion, Philip was also pushing for war against Catholic Spain, for his own religious reasons.

Later that year, Campion, was being interrogated by the Queen's ministers, including her uncle, about his purpose in England. When asked if he would be loyal to the Queen, Edmund had replied in the affirmative, which had bought him time in the country. But there were royal spies everywhere, and Campion's days were surely numbered. He was turned in many times for further interrogation, and finally the charge of treason stuck. He was put to death in early 1581, in a most brutal and torturous way.

Where had Philip been then, and what had been his thoughts? Most of 1580 he had lived at Wilton House, writing alongside Mary, meeting with Robert Dudley, banished from Court by a Queen who was unwilling to tolerate his outspoken disappointment with some of her policies and his angry outbursts against her favourite courtiers. He had returned to Court in 1581.

Mary spent much of that week searching through Philip's notes trying to find a hint of his true relationship with Campion, and even with his own faith. Surely, he had not wavered under the watchful eye of their uncle and herself?

When the questions became too heavy, Mary retreated to her study of Henry VI's England, safer territory for her troubled mind. She realized how close she herself had come to questioning God and her Protestant faith, through the last two years, surrounded as she was on all sides by death. *Better not to enter that fray. I am on my way back out of the woods, and must stay the course,* she thought. She opened Holinshed's great book once again and immersed herself in her country as it had been in 1422, upon the death of Henry V. His death left his nine-month-old son the inheritor of the throne of England. Months later, that same son became King of France when his grandfather, King Charles VI of France, before his imminent death, negotiated the Treaty of Troyes, which proclaimed his English son-in-law his rightful heir. This effectively had ruled out Charles VI's own son, the Dauphin Charles of Valois, which, throughout the Hundred Years' War, led to a tumultuous relationship between the two nations.

As she researched, Mary began to notice how often the women in the historical stories, though not front and centre, inevitably influenced the course of royal history around them. In her younger days, her tutors had only mentioned the men of English history, their valour, their conflicts. Women were rarely spoken of. But here, in the story of Henry VI, were valiant and troubled women. Joan of Arc; Margaret of Anjou, Henry's wife; Eleanor Cobham, the second wife of Henry's uncle, Humphrey Lancaster, the Duke of Gloucester, in short, all figured largely in the events of their respective lives. She realized that Henry VI, a vacillating, peace-loving man would have been overpowered much earlier by his lords and dukes, were it not for Margaret's strength and unwillingness to be defeated. Eleanor, accused of resorting to witchcraft, wanted more than even her husband, to obtain the throne and be Queen. In fact, these two women had become enemies while Henry VI ruled. Joan of Arc was a formidable legend unto herself, the world never having seen another like her!

The more she thought about these strong, but often-unhappily-misguided, women, the more Mary felt she had to write about them and to make their stories and passions known. Henry VI's and England's history would have been entirely different without them.

Mary was very excited by this sudden realization. Rarely did women read about other women, unless that woman was the Queen of England herself, and— God only knew!— *she* was a mighty force to be reckoned with!

So Mary set about organizing her plays into three parts. *Henry VI, Part 2* would revolve around the adult Henry coming of age, while his lords and generals preyed upon his weak nature, behind his back. The feisty Margaret and the scheming Eleanor would feature highly. In *Henry VI, Part 3* she would show how Margaret rose in power, surpassing the King and defending his throne against the House of York, so that her son would one day become King. Finally, after the other two stories were written, she would draft her version of *Henry VI, Part 1*, the story of Joan of Arc. As much as it would be a history of the men of Joan's time, she would make it more the story of the woman herself, the saintly, powerful mystic. She had decided to wrestle with Joan's character last, because hers was a fascinating story, and she wanted it to be a reward for her hard work of portraying the adult King Henry VI in all his studious dysfunction.

Mary introduced *Henry VI, Part 2* with the King and his lords meeting Margaret of Anjou, soon to be Queen. In this scene, Margaret's uncle, King Charles VII of France, had sent a proclamation of his conditions of marriage, which was to be read before the actual marriage ceremony could occur. Mary had decided that Margaret would appear fearless, confident, and cunningly manipulative. She would make sure her audience got the message right away that the king, Henry VI, was mesmerized from the beginning by her beauty. Margaret would know she had power over him and would plan to use this against him to get her way. She planned to infer, further into the play, that Margaret and the Duke of Suffolk, William de la Pole, had become lovers while he was conducting her from France to wed Henry. Mary knew there was no historical evidence of this, but surmised from what she knew of Court life in her own country, that powerful women such as Elizabeth, always insured one or more of her courtiers were lovers, in order to protect herself from the others, to upset the balance of power among them, and to find out the nature of rumours circulating about her. In that way, the Queen was able to maintain her power. Mary assumed it would be no different in Margaret's day, perhaps especially as she was a foreign Queen:

Queen Margaret
Great King of England and my gracious lord,
The mutual conference that my mind hath had,
By day, by night, waking and in my dreams,
In courtly company or at my beads,
With you, mine alder-liefest sovereign,
Makes me the bolder to salute my king
With ruder terms, such as my wit affords
And over-joy of heart doth minister.
King Henry VI, Part II, Act I, Scene I, Lines 24-31

As the play took hold of her imagination, Mary could picture Margaret: tall and confident, upset with the weaknesses her husband exhibited, and attempting to rule his lords and leaders through Suffolk, at that time favoured by Henry. In the end, her quest for power was to prove greater than her love of Suffolk. Though she pretended, she had never really loved this England which was her new country. She wanted to rule it all, and even went to the battleground to ensure the lords would respect her power over them as a replacement of their King.

Mary wondered at her ruthlessness, and in her mind, compared Margaret to Elizabeth in their thirst and need for ultimate power over everyone around them. She had learned from her mother, Lady Mary Sidney, Elizabeth's chief lady-in-waiting, that Elizabeth's need was based on very real fear. From her youngest years at the hand of a ruthless father, King Henry VIII, and until her death, Elizabeth trusted no man— so no man would become her husband "King."

She searched her history books for more information about Margaret of Anjou and was not disappointed. During his reign, Henry VI had suffered the effects of mental illness, in fact, had been pronounced insane and thus unfit to rule on several occasions. Margaret moved in to take over the reins, just as her mother before her had done. From 1435 to 1438, while her husband— Margaret's father, René of Anjou— was in prison, his wife Isabella, the Duchess of Lorraine, ruled so well in his place that she was able to safeguard his territories in France and in the Kingdom of Naples. Isabella was known to be formidable. Ahead of her time, she made sure her daughter had the same education as her brothers. Margaret was highly intelligent, highly-educated and hungry for power.

Her father's mother, Yolande of Aragon, was described as a masculine ruler, who did not shy away from violence, and who provided the money so that Joan of Arc could defeat the English. The Grandmother's sympathies were never with the English.

From these two redoubtable women, in combination with her fierce temper and hunger for power, Margaret was well-prepared to be both Queen Consort and regent when Henry was incapacitated. Not only did his mental illness affect his ability to rule; he was also captured by Yorkist factions and imprisoned from 1455 to 1461, during the War of the Roses. All this time, Margaret strove to support the Lancastrians. She participated in the Second Battle of St. Albans, and actually rescued her husband. Henry's captors had kept him safe, despite imprisonment, and Henry had said they would suffer no punishment. But Margaret, asking her young son's advice and completely ignoring Henry's promise, put them on trial and had them killed. She had put others to death in the past and had ordered the assassination of the Duke of York, but unsuccessfully. The eventual victory of the Yorkist faction, through the effort of the Duke of York's son, ended with him being crowned King Edward IV. Henry VI went into exile for a year and was then imprisoned in the Tower of London. Margaret, her young son, and those aiding her, escaped to France.

There, the former Queen plotted with the new French King Louis XI, and Richard Neville, Earl of Warwick, to restore Henry VI. This was accomplished in 1470, but it lasted only a few months. By 1471, Edward IV was again victorious, Richard Neville was killed and Margaret and her son— Edward of Lancaster, Prince of Wales— returned to fight together in the Battle of Tewkesbury, that May. Edward was killed, leaving his mother, Margaret, broken-hearted. Henry VI was sent to the Tower of London where he was found dead within a fortnight, possibly murdered. Margaret was imprisoned and later put under house arrest. In 1475, King Louis XI paid for her to be returned to France where she lived under his support, until she died in 1482. The death of her son and all the violence she had initiated, had finally broken her.

In Margaret, Mary saw her own Queen mirrored. To say so directly, either in public or in a written story was far too dangerous. But in a play, that would be the thing! Through her play she could highlight the lust for power that she saw not only in Margaret, but in Elizabeth, and in the intrigues of Court. Philip had spoken to her often of the machinations from, and behind, the throne, and often had he warned her not to speak of this knowledge. Mary Sidney herself had been an unwilling witness to the struggles, the underlying fears, the spying and the violence when she lived at Court as a young woman before her fortunate marriage to Henry Herbert. She knew how to hide her opinion in the words of a play, seemingly divorced from the English court, by their appearance in the mouth of a French Queen.

As for Lady Eleanor, Mary would portray her as manipulative and devious as well:

ELEANOR
What seest thou there? King Henry's diadem,

Enchased with all the honours of the world?
If so, gaze on, and grovel on thy face,
Until thy head be circled with the same.
Put forth thy hand, reach at the glorious gold.
What, is't too short? I'll lengthen it with mine:
And, having both together heaved it up,
We'll both together lift our heads to heaven,
And never more abase our sight so low
As to vouchsafe one glance unto the ground.

GLOUCESTER
O Nell, sweet Nell, if thou dost love thy lord,
Banish the canker of ambitious thoughts.

Henry VI, Part II, Act I, Scene II, Lines 5-17

Mary very quickly set the scenes so her readers would see the ambition in both women, how they attempted to control their men with charm and coaxing, to get their own way. Both wanted power and were already very powerful in their own worlds. That is why they were to become enemies.

For weeks, Mary scribbled away, long into the night. Henry knew from experience not to interrupt her flow of thoughts when she was thus consumed. Finally one night she ran to their chambers and threw two manuscripts down in front of him. "They are done, Henry! You must get them to your troupe of actors as soon as you can!"

Henry looked at his wife. Her cheeks were flushed from having run all the way from her library. He thought she was never more beautiful than when she completed a play.

"I am your humble servant, my dear. But may I have a day to peruse them myself?"

CHAPTER THIRTEEN

The sun was now brilliant in the sky and it shone down on Crik and Poppy as they sat by the ruins of St. Andrew's Church, a few miles outside of Burwell. They had been discussing what to do next. Poppy wanted a chance to explore the tunnel herself and Crik had finally, reluctantly, agreed. "What do I do if Janek and Sarah turn up while you're down there?" he asked her.

"Sit on the entrance to the tunnel! And don't move!"

Minutes later, he was helping her down into the hole, making sure her feet landed safely on the stone stairway. "I'm not used to being taken care of like this. Would you stop it?"

"Can't help being my gallant self."

Poppy looked around, and shone the torch in all directions. She was really afraid to be down here herself. What if an animal appeared, or the tunnel collapsed, or Janek did show up? She didn't like the sound of that dripping water, coming from a dark spot above her head, fearing it had been eating away at the ceiling over the centuries. *It's only groundwater! Don't cave in today!* she thought and clutched her coat closer to herself. She had decided to examine the walls very carefully. After all, where else would that Matthew guy have hidden something? She wanted to understand exactly why he had felt he *had* to hide Mary's letters, papers, and plays anyway. What was with that? It seemed kind of pointless to her to go to all that trouble of writing and researching for all those years only to have your work hidden from people! There had to be a good reason and she was determined to find it. Before Janek and Sarah. Wouldn't the Boss be pleased then?

The walls were mostly stone, reinforced with thick pillars every couple yards. She knew a thorough search would take hours, which they didn't have, but so far nothing looked out of place, there were no obvious chinks in the walls and there certainly weren't any signs saying "Here it is, over here! The papers, yoo-hoo!" She supposed Matthew, being clever— after all, he *was* a doctor— would have hidden them pretty well. Their hidey-hole would not be obvious. *What would I do?* she asked herself. A thought came to her: *I would put them in the wall or in one of the beams, but make it look natural.* Say, lines in the beams would really be seams in a small doorway. She felt the surfaces of each and every wooden piece as far as she could reach, until she came to the dead end. When she entered the small room at the far right of the tunnel, she was sure she would find something there. Poppy let her hands roam over all the short walls, in the dark, relying on the touch of her fingers, but nothing surfaced. Like Crik, she shone the light of the torch into each and every recessed hole, which were all at eye level, but to no avail. *That would be too obvious*, she thought in retrospect.

She wondered if there was a secret compartment in the stone stairs at either end. The only one she'd be able to examine would be the entrance at St. James's ruins, because the door here was completely blocked by what felt like the weight of ten large timbers. *We can look for the entrance at this end, once I get out of here*, she thought, noticing as Crik had at this point, that the air was stale and she was weakening. She headed back, running her hands along the walls in the dim light of the torch, feeling for holes or knobs or anything unusual.

A thorough examination of the stairs revealed nothing more, but maybe Crik could look further. For one minute, panic rose in her as she climbed back up the staircase. What if he wouldn't let her out? She almost screamed his name, such was her sudden claustrophobia at the thought. But when she raised her head to take in the fresh air, even before her eyes readjusted to the bright sunlight outside, Crik was at her side, gently taking her arm to help her out, sitting beside her on the grass, patting her back while she breathed deeply of the country air. Never had she appreciated the British countryside more. He was alright, this Crik. Not as bad a bloke, as she had first feared.

"Ain't you the brave one? I'm proud of you!" he said, giving her shoulder a tap. "I take it nothing was found, but we have some time left. If they have stuck to their schedule, they'll just be leaving Burwell now."

"*If* is a big word," she said. Let's look for the entrance at the other end, where the door is so blocked up, shall we?" Poppy was now on her feet.

"There's no keeping a good woman down," Crik replied, hauling himself up.

The great old wooden door to St. Michael's opened with surprising ease. Janek and Sarah entered the dimly lit space at the entrance, known as the Tower. A sign said that the arched window, casting light onto the stone floor below them, was erected in the mid-fourteenth century. Janek looked up into the roof of the rectangular tower, and pointed upwards. Carved into three corners of the inner ceiling were three praying figures, made of wood, all life-size. The top figure was placed upside down while the other two looked down on them from a lofty height. To Sarah, it felt comforting, like guardian angels watching over their shoulders.

To get inside the church, they gently pushed on one of four Gothic doors, which were about the height of a tall man, each one bearing glass windows set in carved wooden frames, and some with miniature stone carvings on top of each door. The empty spaces above the doors held screens, creating an airy entranceway.

The interior of the church was well lit with sun streaming through three large square windows, curiously not aligned, and seemingly randomly placed. The building was about sixteen feet across, its nave consisting of double rows of dark wooden pews on either side of a narrow central aisle. The floors were very roughly hewn with two or three different colours of hexagonal stones, showing a great deal of wear. Some were a deep russet colour. You had to continually look down to avoid tripping on their uneven edges. Standing in an awkward, off centre spot on the stone floor was an ancient baptismal font, carved but not ornate, with Latin words written around the base. The symbols on the font looked like four-leaf clovers or rounded crosses, matching the carvings on the screen doors behind them.

Entering the chancel, they couldn't take their eyes off a carved pulpit which looked to be centuries old. The inner chancel was sparsely decorated with one small altar at the back. It was beautiful, simple and carved with stylistic flames and crests. The altar railings were also striking, made of stone carved in grape clusters. On the far right wall, below the interior chancel, was another wooden carved table and behind it, a roughly hewn stone basin with a sign indicating it was an original piscine, the stone sink for washing of hands and chalices during the service. Keeping vigil over everything was a single panelled stained glass window depicting St. Michael. The oranges, reds, and blues of the Archangel's clothing were vibrant as the sun stole through them, casting bands of coloured light about the altar. Janek was fascinated by the age of everything and by the church's stark but moving minimalism.

Sarah had wandered back to the pulpit and something about twelve feet off the floor, on the white wall to the left of the chancel arch, caught her eye. She walked over and then excitedly motioned to Janek.

They stood looking up at an exposed very old painting of a woman, wearing a crown, with a halo about her head. The colours in the painting were faded but there were the remains of rusty brown and grey paint lines. The woman's mouth was almost obliterated. To the right of the drawing was a crown, and under that, an image which looked like an upright anchor, or the letter M.

"The *M* is in the Lombardic script, from the seventh century. It has a crown above it!" Janek exclaimed.

They heard a noise coming from the back of the chancel and both turned. A middle-aged woman was standing with a vase of flowers in her hand. She smiled at them and came over to greet them.

"Hello. Pleased to meet you. My name is Lillian Hawkins. I volunteer with the Churches Conservation Trust." She held out her free hand, and Sarah and Janek each shook it, introducing themselves.

"I see you've discovered our treasure! Isn't she beautiful? This painting was discovered underneath the last layer of stucco, when it was removed a century-and-a-half ago. Rather high up, and nothing else like it was found. Made us all wonder a little. There are several theories as to who she might be. As this was once a Catholic church and originally a Benedictine priory under John de Hay in the 1100s, many think she represents Mary, Queen of Heaven. Janek, I heard you mention the Lombardic *M*, so you are a historian, I suspect?"

"Not by training," he answered modestly. Lillian smiled and continued.

"Another possible candidate is Marguerite de Navarre, who was born in 1492 and died in the mid-1500s. She had dealings with Calvinist reformers, including Queen Ann Boleyn, and was a tolerant Catholic married to King Henry I of Navarre, kind to the poor, and a woman ahead of her time. There was another Marguerite, called Queen Margaret of Navarre, born in the *twelfth* century, who gave her full support to Thomas Becket against Henry II. Becket was assassinated by Henry's supporters. The fourth candidate is Queen Maud, who was Henry I's daughter, also known as the Empress Matilda, whose accession to the throne was thwarted by Stephen of Blois, her cousin. However, eventually Matilda's son became King Henry II. She also tried to work things out between her son and Thomas Becket. There were several women coming to Thomas's aid, weren't there? And finally, the last candidate is Queen Maud of Scotland, the religious wife of Henry I. So there you have it: a lot of Henrys and a lot of Margarets! Personally, I opt for Mary, Queen of Heaven."

Sarah and Janek stood speechless. This woman was a font of historical information! Smiling, Janek shook her hand again, "You are so knowledgeable! Maybe we can ask you some questions?" He turned to Sarah and raised an eyebrow to ask if that was alright with her. She nodded.

"Do you know anything about the Lister family? Specifically Matthew Lister, a doctor, who moved to this area from London in the mid-1600s?"

"Yes, as a matter of fact, I do. Please, just let me put water in these flowers and we'll sit and chat?" she asked and then hurried away through a door in the chancel.

Sarah smiled at Janek and squeezed his arm. The two sat down in the first pew and discussed what they could comfortably share with Lillian. She seemed thoroughly trustworthy to both of them, but recent experience had taught them to be wary.

Returning with a tray of tea and biscuits, Lillian sat down from them, in the same pew. It was to be a wonderfully pleasant exchange, complete with tea!

"Yes, now Matthew, the doctor. I have read some of his family's reports, letters, historical records, and such. They are housed at the Lincolnshire Archives on St. Rumbold Street in Lincoln, not too far from here. The Listers are distant relatives of my own, but probably also of half the population of Burwell." She chuckled. "Yes, he married a local girl and settled here. Before that, he was a big wig in London, treating the royals. But when he returned home, he remained somewhat anonymous. In fact, he once lived about eight miles down the highway; his home, the Manor house, is long gone. It was right near the old ruins of St. Andrew's Church."

"The St. Andrew's ruins purported to have a secret passage leading to Matthew's manor?" Janek asked.

For a moment Lillian looked shocked.

"So, you've heard of that passage! Yes, that's it exactly. The passage truly exists, but it has been boarded-up for over a century, almost two, now. It is not at all safe to venture into. But by the historical accounts I have read, and photos I have seen, it consists of a small room and a six hundred-foot passageway, linked by stairwells at each end. Matthew built it to have a safe place to hide, if he was ever attacked during the Civil War, back in the later 1600s."

"So there is no longer a possibility of a tour of the passage?"

"I'm afraid not, no," she said. "Why are you so interested in Matthew, if I might ask?""

"Well," Sarah began, "he was intimately involved in London with a woman whom Janek and I are interested in: Janek for a book, and me for my thesis."

"Mary Sidney Herbert?" Lillian asked, her brown eyes twinkling beneath a fringe of salt and pepper hair.

"That's right," replied Sarah, stealing an arched look at Janek.

"Yes, the lovely and talented Mary. He had quite a whirlwind romance with her, and some even believe they may have married, though clandestinely. I did come across a brief note Matthew had left in his will— a peculiar note, really. To a woman relative of Mary's in the north, asking that a rather large box be delivered to her, a box of Mary's things that were not detailed and were not to be opened by anyone but this woman. For the life of me I cannot remember her name! Now, why is that?"

"It dovetailed with other letters I had read," she continued, "correspondences of Matthew's second wife, the Burwell wife that is, who was younger and outlived her husband. She had written to a cousin on several occasions, expressing sadness that her husband's heart always seemed to be elsewhere, and several times had mentioned the name of Mary Sidney Herbert. She was quite upset by it all. Impossible to accuse him of unfaithfulness, because Mary had died long before his second marriage. At one point, she complained that he would never talk to her about Mary. That was what started her obsession. The fact was he was unforthcoming. There is nothing worse for a curious mind, is there?"

Both Janek and Sarah were holding their breaths. This was too good to be true! A box, unopened, to which they possibly had the key? They simply *had* to follow this lead.

"So, Lillian, do you know what happened to that box?" Janek asked, his eyes on Sarah's excited face.

"Well, I remember something about it. The solicitor was charged with its delivery and he sent a series of correspondences to the intended recipient, who was to make a trip to Burwell to retrieve the box. Now what was her name? Well, you can find out by visiting the Lincoln Archives, can't you?"

"Did the solicitor leave any confirmation that he had dispatched the box?" Sarah asked quietly, trying to conceal her excitement.

"There was some problem with that, something about the wife being involved and wanting to be allowed to view the contents. It was a little 'messy' as they say. It's all there in the archives for you to read though."

"You have been more helpful than you know!" Sarah exclaimed.

"Well, I am very pleased to have been able to shed some light on your questions. I do remember that the box was removed from its original hiding place, which was, curiously, that tunnel you earlier mentioned. Matthew brought it to the solicitor a month before he passed away. I suppose as a doctor, he must have known his death coming on."

"I'd be interested in finding out what you have discovered when you complete your research, if you would let me know?" Lillian asked. "I have an insatiable curiosity about the history of our little part of Lincolnshire."

Janek and Sarah exchanged email addresses with her. Then Janek spoke tentatively.

"Lillian, this may sound crazy to you, but we both agreed we would like to take you into our confidence. This information— the information about

Matthew, Mary, and the box of her belongings, is also being sought by a third party, and their reasons for wanting it have been dubious, to say the least. They have even followed us about on our research stints, and once or twice have caused us injury!"

"No!" she exclaimed. "Why would this information be that important to them?"

"We do not know for sure, but, crazy as it sounds, we are telling the truth. We do not want to involve you in any danger, but, should anyone come asking questions about us or our work, would you let us know? And would you be prepared to say you did not speak to us? You don't have to lie, you can just say we were here, or people vaguely answering to our descriptions were here for a few minutes and then left? Without revealing that you spoke to us?"

"Certainly! Unless asked otherwise, I will not point them to Lincolnshire Archives. Unfortunately, I cannot lie if they ask me about Matthew Lister, but I will not elaborate. This is rather shocking and nothing like this has ever happened here, in all the years we have opened the church for visitors. We do get some pretty interesting questions, but this one has topped them all! I am so glad I was here when you two visited. Do you intend to publish your findings someday so I can read about this mysterious research of yours?" she asked hopefully.

"You seem to be a kindred spirit to us, I feel that," Sarah said. "We'd be happy to let you know if we publish anything. Thank you so much for your understanding."

"One more thing. I hope you have called the police?" Lillian asked.

"We have, but they have not taken us very seriously," Janek replied, shaking his head. "I hope you will not share anything we have said with anyone, because I wouldn't want you to come to any harm!"

"Certainly not. I am a librarian and I understand the need for confidentiality!" she declared.

"Then we *are* kindred spirits, as I work at the British Library and Sarah works at the Ottawa Public Library part-time, when she is not completing her Master's studies at the University of Ottawa," Janek informed her.

They parted with hugs. Back in the car, they let out a grand whoop and hugged each other, laughing until tears streamed from their eyes. They knew this was an outstanding lead in their search for Mary's papers and decided to leave for Lincoln then and there, realizing there was no longer a need to search for the hidden passage at St. Andrew's ruins. It would have been great to see the site but it was too risky to visit in case they came upon their "watchers" there. Another time. Right now, it was important to get to Lincoln without being followed and they were determined to do just that.

As Janek and Sarah were happily leaving Burwell behind, Poppy and Crik were searching for an opening at the spot where a manor house might have been, six hundred paces from the entrance they had found behind St. Andrew's Church ruins. After thirty minutes, they were ready to give up.

"If there ever was an entrance, and we know there had to have been, it's been carefully and deliberately covered over. I wouldn't be surprised if they used cement!" Crik looked up from his digging. He had left various holes, the earth overturned, in search of an opening.

"Someone seeing this overturned earth will wonder what kind of animal dug around here!" He was hot, sweaty and getting cranky. They had risen that day at four to get a head start on Sarah and Janek.

"Come on, then. Let's get back to that other church down the road. Janek and Sarah must be there by now, it's ten *bloody* o'clock in the morning! I'm surprised they didn't come here first. We should have been watching the time. This mystery thing is getting seductive, don't you think?" Poppy asked.

"Seductive?" his eyebrow, the one with the piercing, shot up and a smile appeared for the first time in an hour.

"You know what I mean! Now that we are both safely above ground, I can relax! You have to admit it's kind of fun exploring secret tunnels and searching for past treasures. The stuff of books!" Poppy's eyes had a dreamy look. "You know, before life threw me a curveball, and before wanting to be a paramedic, I always thought I'd make a good copper—a detective, I mean. Loved those Nancy Drew books, I did!"

Crik watched her pensively. She had that kind of determined toughness it would take to be a copper, a sort of "Don't mess with me" attitude.

"I could actually see that!" he said, and Poppy felt a small glow in the pit of her stomach.

They packed up, tried to smooth the earth over the holes Crik had dug at the ruins to make it look like no one had ever disturbed the ground. "Wouldn't do to have some little kid falling down a hole!" Crik cautioned.

"Well that was exciting!" Poppy sighed happily as they drove away. "Even though we didn't find anything, it's whetted my appetite for adventure."

Crik looked sideways at her. He had to admit an attraction was growing for this tough little redhead. She was a few years older than him, but she acted much younger. Yet she was very responsible, kind of like he had become since taking on Jack. *But she'd never go for the likes of me*, he thought a little sadly. And then she turned and smiled radiantly at him and for one moment he felt like he was young again and carefree and life was one big adventure. *Maybe I will have a chance if I don't piss her off too much*, he thought, imagining how he could impress her.

It was almost ten thirty when they pulled up to the church. The street was deserted but the church door had been left open. Janek's car was nowhere in sight. Poppy sent Crik on ahead. He walked inside and, seeing no one, returned to the car for Poppy. Entering this church, just as before, Crik felt this kind of quiet awe coming over him. Again, he just sat down and looked around him, taking it all in, resting in the silence.

Poppy walked up the aisle and looked about her. She felt the simplicity of the place and it soothed her in some way. She wondered where Sarah and Janek were. They hadn't passed them on the road, on their way to the ruins. She had thought their car would be parked outside the church by now. Maybe they had stopped somewhere in town for lunch. Speaking of lunch, her stomach was growling. She had her wig on, and it was becoming itchy in the heat of the church. She walked to the back of the chancel and looked for an exit, just in case Janek and Sarah should enter the church and she'd have to leave quickly. A lovely vase of fresh flowers decorated the altar at the far back wall. It reminded her of her dream of having a small country home with a garden. *I'm getting sentimental in my older years,* she thought but at that moment, leaning over and smelling the lilacs, bluebells and daffodils in all their glory, she really didn't care about anything else. She was enjoying living in the moment, something that was so unfamiliar that it sometimes could frighten her.

Finding a door at the side of the chancel, Poppy walked through to a small, bare room, once used by priests or ministers as a dressing room for putting on vestments. There was no one there. A back door leading to a garden would serve as a quick exit route.

Just as she was about to turn back into the church, a middle-aged woman came down the garden path towards the door. Poppy rushed back into the chancel and down the aisle to where Crik was sitting. She whispered that someone was here and just then Lillian came around the corner of the pulpit, walking towards them, a big smile on her face. "Can I help you in any way? I just popped back to my car to get my lunch, sorry I missed you entering the church. My name is Lillian and I volunteer here," she thrust out her hand to them.

"Hello," Poppy said brightly.

"If you need me for anything, I'm about. Otherwise, enjoy looking,"

Lillian said. She thought it best not to engage because then there would be no need to lie. The tall dark young man looked quiet, but also a little threatening with all those piercings. *Best to stay by the back door, should I have to make a quick exit.* She moved back to the chancel and busied herself with dusting. The thought occurred to her that these may not be the people who were following Janek and Sarah after all.

Poppy and Crik just sat for a few minutes in the old church, side by side. She thought about asking the Lillian lady if she had seen her "mates", as she would refer to Janek and Sarah. But at the moment, she wasn't that way inclined. A sleepiness had come over her. Looking at Crik, she saw he felt pretty much the same. His eyes were closed and he was breathing evenly, as though meditating. She decided she should probably rouse herself with a walk about the church.

Like Sarah, Poppy stopped in her tracks at the sight of the painting on the wall above the chancel arch. She called to Lillian to ask her if she could take a picture of it.

"Certainly!" Lillian answered, without elaborating.

Poppy retrieved her camera from their knapsack, and this time Crik also accompanied her to the front of the church. Taking a long range closeup of the image, because it was so high up on the wall, Poppy showed it to Crik, who seemed fascinated by it. He walked closer to Lillian to ask her about it.

"That is our little treasure," she replied. "It was discovered during renovations a century-and-a-half ago, and was left exposed by the workmen, who realized it was something from history that needed preserving. We think she is an image of Mary, Queen of Heaven. Are you interested in historical research?" she asked Crik.

"I am becoming more interested by the day," he answered. "Especially in archaeology. Hope to study it one day."

Then with a pleasant smile, he turned back to Poppy. "Well, dear, is there anything else you wanted to see?" he asked a big grin on his face.

Somewhat taken aback, she raised an eyebrow. "Well, we'll be going I guess. Looks like we are the only visitors you've had today, aren't we? Do you have a guest book, Lillian?"

Lillian made a non-committal noise in answer to Poppy's first question and then told her there was a book on the little desk at the entranceway.

Poppy and Crik walked down the aisle, he taking her arm like a devoted husband. Once through the screen she whispered "What was that about?" and he laughed.

"Just playing along," he said.

The book lay to their left. Crik beat her to it. As they left, she noticed he had written *Mr. And Mrs. Drew*. With a big heart beside it and the word *romantic*.

"You really are something else!" Poppy slapped his elbow as they exited, but she had a big smile on her face.

After they had gone, Lillian decided to close up the church for an hour. There really had been a lot of excitement today. She wanted to sit and think about it all. She wasn't sure if that couple was in fact a couple, nor if they were the ones Sarah and Janek were worried about, but she was glad she had not given anything away. She felt suspicious of the two and always trusted her instincts. Going quickly to the front door, Lillian turned to lock it. The couple was slowly pulling away from the curb, and as she watched and waved, she memorized their license plate number. *I really must email Janek. Maybe it's nothing, but those two might not be Mr. and Mrs. Drew after all*, she thought.

CHAPTER FOURTEEN

My courage try by combat, if thou darest,
And thou shalt find that I exceed my sex.
Resolve on this, thou shalt be fortunate,
If thou receive me for thy warlike mate.
Henry VI, Part 1 - Act I, Scene 2

Henry Herbert finished the last of the lines of Mary's *Henry VI, Part 3*. He scarcely knew what to say to his wife Mary, who by now was asleep beside him. Her written words had both surprised and delighted him, but more than anything else, he felt awe, deep and abiding, for this woman he called his own. What had she ever seen in him, to have committed her life so many years before? How she had grown and changed over those years. The suffering, great as it had been for both of them, and their children and relatives, had almost lost him his dear Mary, but she had somehow found her way through it, back to him and their family. Had she been a less-sensitive woman, he thought, she would have succumbed to her melancholy. But her awareness of everyone and everything going on around her had finally pulled her back into life, and with what a flourish! Thank God he had the means to give her a library, and a troupe of players to furnish an incentive to write. Then again, had there been no actors, Mary would have dragged the whole household into her plays, as she had in earlier days, to his mortification. Henry was no actor.

Lately, his health was failing, and periodic episodes of gastric pain plagued him. He had decided not to tell Mary. She would worry herself over it and set to work developing concoctions in her laboratory, also established by him to keep her intellect and interests challenged. She had developed many remedies and he had tried them all. They had worked for the most part, but not on his present condition.

I must ensure my will and testament is intact, he thought morosely. All the talk of death and battle in the *Henry VI* plays he had read, had shaken him out of his normal complacency. He knew his wife would be up to the task of running their several estates, when he would pass away, but he hoped he had a while yet.

What a melancholy spirit I have tonight. It won't do! I pray God I have many years ahead of me. My age being so much greater than Mary's is just that. Age. We are all aging, but she, my dearest wife, carries hers with such a grace and determination to pursue every chance she can to make sure her brother is not forgotten. It keeps her young, somewhat trapped as she is in the days gone by, in his every passion, his words, his ideas. She lives so much for him, but manages to live for us too. An extraordinary woman I have here! And he leaned over and kissed her cheek and tucked the quilt over her shoulder.

The next morning, Henry had no sooner left for London, with her two plays, than Mary was again at her library desk, quill in hand, Philip's history books, along with her own, spread out before her.

"It is time to confront Joan la Pucelle, heroine of France!" she said aloud, with a wave of her pen.

Long and hard had she thought about this Joan. Her life was an enigma. Mary, who had studied Latin and Greek, knew the word's origins: as *aenigma* for riddle and the Greek *ainigma* meaning an obscure or dark expression. Joan had troubled Mary's conscience.

Mary knew that, with Joan being an enemy of England, she should hate the peasant girl who became a warrior in armour, claiming for France the lands which Henry IV and V had conquered. But as Mary read through *The Union of the Two Noble and Illustre Families of Lancastre and Yorke*, popularly known as *Hall's Chronicle*, of which she had Philip's Fourth Edition, and

Holinshed's Chronicles of 1577, she could only admit to admiring the very young peasant's courage and faith. Hearing voices which she said were from God and Mary, Queen of Heaven, Jeanne d'Arc, eventually won the trust of the Dauphin of France, Charles VII, his men, and her country. She won back lands for France in the famous Siege of Orléans, relying on her trust in God, His mother, Mary, and the voices she heard. She had claimed to be a maiden, and wanted to be known as Jeanne la Pucelle, the Maid of Orléans.

Among Philip's favourite books, Mary had found another treatise marked with extensive observations. It was called *A Brief Discourse of Rebellion and Rebels*, by one George North. Upon opening the unpublished document, she saw it had been dedicated to "Roger, Second Baron North." She smiled as she remembered the man, a trusted friend of her uncle Robert Dudley. He had been one of the few invited to the clandestine marriage of Robert with Lettice Knollys, so many years before. And, turning over the pages, she noticed the book had been stamped as originally owned by her uncle. Philip must have borrowed the treatise. She made a note to ask Lettice, Robert's wife, if she would like it back for her library. Mary spent the rest of the day and most of the next, reading this rare work, which was a treat, as she realized that because it had not been widely published, few in Britain would have seen the book.

As Mary began to write her play about King Henry VI, she had not only the three major sources to help her: George North, Hall, and Holinshe. She was further aided by the annotations her brother had written in the margins of these copies. Philip had visited and studied in France, where he was influenced by both Protestant and Catholic theologians. He had written a specific notation about the earliest biography of Jehanne d'Arc— as she signed her own name— which was written by Guillaume Cousinot, the son of a father of the same name; both had served under the French Kings Charles VII and Louis XI. Both wrote accounts of Jehanne d'Arc which were known to scholars, churchmen, leaders and citizens of France, when Philip visited that country.

Mary could see how conflicted Philip had been over vying accounts of the Catholic Joan and the English historians who had slandered her name. He had read the English versions of the history but had heard tales from French scholars of her heroism, during her trial at Rouen, in the face of interrogation by English nobles, Bishop Peter Cauchon and the other bishops. Philip had left a long description in the margins of *Hall's Chronicle* attesting that, according to French witnesses and chroniclers, Joan had always maintained she was doing the will of God in all her actions. She had also protested her virginity against attacks to the contrary. Only one French chronicler had said she reneged once and admitted sins to Bishop Cauchon, but later returned to her insistence that she had always followed God's will, sent to her through the voices she heard.

Mary knew that Philip had been taught from an early age by his father to seek and speak only truth. She knew her brother had practiced these virtues from an early age, much to his detriment at Court. So she saw in his scribbled notes his effort to be faithful to the truth, to give both sides of this argument their due.

Mary, in the end, was as conflicted as her brother had been about Jehanne la Pucelle. But she had an even greater mental struggle than he. In Joan, she saw similarities to Elizabeth, her Queen, the woman she had grown to distrust and perhaps even hate, over the death of Philip. Joan, like the Queen, proclaimed virginity, in order to serve her nation. Elizabeth had also taken up arms and fought alongside British soldiers. She was quoted as having said, at the Battle of Tilbury, where British soldiers led by Elizabeth, herself in armour, waged war against the Spanish Armada:

I have the body of a weak, feeble woman; but I have the heart and stomach of a king, and of a king of England too... I myself will take up arms, I myself will be your general, judge, and rewarder of every one of your virtues in the field.

Elizabeth, like Joan, had armed herself to go to battle. Joan suffered wounds, and Joan rewarded those who fought beside her. She was known to have promised wives of soldiers they would return from battle. She had singularly been responsible for Charles VII finally being crowned King, due to her relentless urgings and her successes in battle. But Elizabeth, in Mary's mind, rarely rewarded anyone but herself. The Sidney family had impoverished themselves in her service, and when Mary's father begged for troupes, he received none. In this, Mary could not help but admire the selflessness and humility of La Pucelle as it contrasted drastically with the self-centeredness of Elizabeth and her overriding arrogance.

Perhaps the strangest coincidence Mary found between the two, involved the presence of a Duke of Alençon in both their lives. In 1578 and 1579, Elizabeth had been courted by the Duke of Alençon, named Hercule Francois, who hoped to wed her. He was Catholic, she Protestant. There were rumours of great sexual attraction between him and the Queen when he visited Court. Mary was under no illusions of the Queen's virginity, being the niece of the Queen's lover, Robert Dudley. By a curious twist of fate, Jehanne d'Arc battled alongside another Duke of Alençon, who is said to have admired her and refused to criticize her as did other French knights. However there was no evidence of their having been intimate except for British accounts of her trial, where, to save herself, the English chroniclers declared she said she was pregnant by him, denied it later, and named other men as fathers. In the end, Joan never was pregnant, as history proved. Her English captors were said to have waited nine months before they executed her, just to be sure. She was burned at the stake.

But herein lay the danger: if Mary's writings displayed an admiration of Joan, the words would be seen as treasonous. How to remain true to what she now saw, as had her brother, the real heroic nature of the young Joan, while also holding to the English view of the warrior woman as a plague to England and a usurper of Kings? How not to anger the Queen, who would one day surely read her words, albeit anonymously?

She decided to give Jehanne la Pucelle her due. In her lines, the audience would judge for itself her truth or deception, her innocence or duplicity. Just a she herself had done and her brother before her, in hearing both sides of the story. Though the French and English versions differed greatly in their portrayal of Joan, the truth lay somewhere in between. That was the way of truth, in Mary's experience. There was always more to the story, beneath the surface, in the hearts of the players. No one was one-dimensional.

She would put forth the English view in the mouths of the English characters of her play. She would let Joan speak for herself. Charles VII would be seen in his true colours, as one who never really trusted Joan, though she had his Kingship and his honour foremost in her mind always, second only to her greater wish to serve God. Charles could have ransomed her but refused and she went to her death. She had done nothing to deserve that treatment.

Here, Mary saw a parallel between the unfortunate Joan, and her brother Philip. Both were used as pawns by rulers of their day. Elizabeth could have given her brother gainful employment worthy of his true talents, but instead he had gone to his death in service to her ambitions in the Netherlands. The Queen had not liked his advice about the Duke of Alençon when he had strongly advised her, in writing, not to marry the French Catholic. He had been shunned by the Queen afterwards, even though it was thought by Mary and the Sidney family that she was only dangling the Duke as a threat to her lover Robert, with no real interest in pursuit of the marriage. In some ways, both Joan and Philip were naive about the political arenas they inhabited and perhaps trusted too much in the fallible rulers, the knights and courtiers who fought for them.

"Joan la Pucelle

DEATH STALKS THE HOUSE OF HERBERT

Dauphin, I am by birth a shepherd's daughter,
My wit untrain'd in any kind of art.
Heaven and our Lady gracious hath it pleased
To shine on my contemptible estate

and

Why, no, I say, distrustful recreants!
Fight till the last gasp; I will be your guard.

and

Behold, this is the happy wedding torch
That joineth Rouen unto her countrymen,
But burning fatal to the Talbotites!

and

Besides, all French and France exclaims on thee,
Doubting thy birth and lawful progeny.
Who joint'st thou with but with a lordly nation
That will not trust thee but for profit's sake?
When Talbot hath set footing once in France
And fashion'd thee that instrument of ill,
Who then but English Henry will be lord
And thou be thrust out like a fugitive?
Call we to mind, and mark but this for proof,
Was not the Duke of Orleans thy foe?
And was he not in England prisoner?
But when they heard he was thine enemy,
They set him free without his ransom paid,
In spite of Burgundy and all his friends.
See, then, thou fight'st against thy countrymen
And joint'st with them will be thy slaughtermen.
Come, come, return; return, thou wandering lord:
Charles and the rest will take thee in their arms.

161

First, let me tell you whom you have condemn'd:

Not me begotten of a shepherd swain,

But issued from the progeny of kings;

Virtuous and holy; chosen from above,

By inspiration of celestial grace,

To work exceeding miracles on earth.

I never had to do with wicked spirits:

But you, that are polluted with your lusts,

Stain'd with the guiltless blood of innocents,

Corrupt and tainted with a thousand vices,

Because you want the grace that others have,

You judge it straight a thing impossible

To compass wonders but by help of devils.

No, misconceived! Joan of Arc hath been

A virgin from her tender infancy,

Chaste and immaculate in very thought;

Whose maiden blood, thus rigorously effused,

Will cry for vengeance at the gates of heaven."

When she read these words again, Mary was happy with them. The words of the English captors were different. Mary carefully crafted the final scenes. She knew her audiences would want to feel the British had been victorious in doing away with Joan, because that was what they had been taught by their history: that Joan was nothing but an enemy who had resorted to witchcraft and eventually was eventually put to death, after being declared a heretic.

YORK

Ay, ay: away with her to execution!

WARWICK

And hark ye, sirs; because she is a maid,
Spare for no faggots, let there be enow:
Place barrels of pitch upon the fatal stake,
That so her torture may be shortened.

JOAN LA PUCELLE
Will nothing turn your unrelenting hearts?
Then, Joan, discover thine infirmity,
That warranteth by law to be thy privilege.
I am with child, ye bloody homicides:
Murder not then the fruit within my womb,
Although ye hale me to a violent death.

YORK
Now heaven forfend! the holy maid with child!

WARWICK
The greatest miracle that e'er ye wrought:
Is all your strict preciseness come to this?

YORK
She and the Dauphin have been juggling:
I did imagine what would be her refuge.

WARWICK
Well, go to; we'll have no bastards live;
Especially since Charles must father it.

JOAN LA PUCELLE
You are deceived; my child is none of his:

163

It was Alençon that enjoy'd my love.

YORK

Alençon! that notorious Machiavel!
It dies, an if it had a thousand lives.

JOAN LA PUCELLE

O, give me leave, I have deluded you:
'Twas neither Charles nor yet the duke I named,
But Reignier, king of Naples, that prevail'd.

WARWICK

A married man! that's most intolerable."

Even in this, and despite herself, Mary's humanity came through. Joan was a helpless teenager, a young woman sure of her faith and now terrified that she had been betrayed by those she fought for and with. No one was coming to her rescue. She was about to die. And die she did in an excruciating manner, abandoned by all.

Mary sat staring ahead, tears in her eyes. To her mind came a picture of Philip, dying in the Netherlands, away from his country, disillusioned with his vanity of a life, his young wife whom he had only just begun to love by his side. Pain overcame Mary. There were no victors in his war. There were no victors either in the story of *Henry VI, Part 1.* Mary made sure of that. She picked up her quill again and wrote an ending which flew in the face of the heroics which came before it. A weak Henry VI was persuaded by the description of a beautiful Margaret from France who was to become his Queen, herself deceptively cunning, in a manipulative move by Lord Suffolk whose plan was to usurp his throne:

SUFFOLK

Margaret shall now be Queen, and rule the king;
But I will rule both her, the king and realm.

All this as a poor maid burned in France and English lords negotiated a wavering "peace" with Charles VII of France. Nothing was really as it seemed. No one was a winner, and as history proved, not even the deluded Suffolk, who was to die on his way to exile, murdered by his countrymen, condemned by a mock trial.

At last Mary put down her quill pen. It truly was all vanity.

CHAPTER FIFTEEN

It was getting close to noon, and Sarah suggested that they buy a picnic lunch and eat it on the grounds of the Lincoln Archives, while searching its catalogue online on their phones. Janek agreed, knowing that Wi-Fi would be accessible outside the library.

Life with Sarah is so easy, he thought, a happy smile on his face. The future looked so bright. He looked over at her. She was contentedly gazing about at the people coming and going on their lunch break. Sarah was beautiful, with her golden-red curls and a dash of freckles across her nose. Janek was sure he had never been happier.

He thought back to his years with Sybil. When she had first pursued him, he had not believed his good fortune. Sybil was beautiful, vivacious and mysterious. She was an extreme extrovert and he a true introvert. She moved in fast circles, while his career revolved around books, research, and the steady, but highly engaging life of a librarian. He was intellectually-inclined and she was drawn to people, social life, and glamour. They had lived in two different worlds, trying to meet in the middle. Initially, dating had been exciting: going to galas, driving her here and there, her father's sports car always at the ready, meeting the celebrities and well-known people her charity work revolved around. But he had soon tired of it all. Sybil had at first tried to cover for his awkwardness in conversation by answering for him or talking over him. They had argued often and she had never seemed happy with him. When he had asked her why she was still seeing him, she remained vague and non-committal about where their relationship was going. His family had found her standoffish and had been uncomfortable around her, just like she had been with them.

By the beginning of their third year together, Janek and Sybil barely had any alone time together. She had become distant, travelling more with her work, and refusing to discuss their relationship. More than once, he had asked if she wanted to take a break and she had agreed, only to come back within a week— as if she were driven by something he could not understand. When he had questioned her further, she had asked him to trust her, appealing to his kindness. And she would often cry, extremely frustrated that he didn't understand her. He attempted to listen more; he tried to change but the whole thing was unsustainable.

Glancing again at Sarah, he knew immediately that they were right for each other. Theirs was a mutual, peaceful relationship of shared passions. He realized he had stayed with Sybil because he had felt sorry for her. He had mistaken those feelings for love. He now knew that real love meant he and Sarah could be themselves, fully and freely. And he was happy for the first time in three long years. He hoped Sarah was as happy as she seemed, because he wanted the best for her.

By one-thirty, they were at the front desk, eager to start their search. The Head Archivist was summoned and helped them locate the Lister family papers. After a search, they were able to pinpoint the letters they wished to peruse, all related to Matthew's correspondence with his lawyer and friends as well as the letters his wife had sent to relatives.

They were provided a separate study room and gloves to use while handling the fragile papers. For an hour, they went through everything, familiarizing themselves with Matthew's writing, his terminology, and interests. Janek finally came upon the first communication to his solicitor, citing Mary's name.

"Sarah, here it is! Matthew's letter to his solicitor Harold Alington! He speaks of discharging a metal box, containing Mary Herbert's treasured correspondence, mostly with her brother, including her own writings, and those of the Wilton Circle, excerpts from plays, stories, and musings."

He looked at Sarah, who jumped up so she could read over his shoulder.

Matthew had left the box and its key in the safekeeping of his solicitor in 1655, almost two years before his death. At eighty-four, he had been an old man, especially by the standards of his day. There were specific instructions that the box was to be forwarded, upon Matthew's death: *to the illegitimate daughter of Mary's son William and his cousin, Mary Wroth.* William had fathered twins, a girl and a boy, but he had refused to acknowledge them. He had since married another woman, while Mary Wroth had been widowed.

Matthew had claimed the contents of the box included many secret writings from his first spouse, Mary Sidney Herbert, which, at the time of her death, she did not want revealed to anyone but him and those she chose. Several other works had been willed to him by her niece and goddaughter, the very same Lady Mary Wroth, in 1653, the year of her death at home at Loughton Hall. These he had received and also locked away in the safe box. In one poignant sentence, Matthew indicated the depth of his feelings for the long-dead Mary.

As Sarah sat down, Janek read aloud:

"I desire to honour the wish of the precious wife of my early years, Mary Sidney Herbert, who was and is dear to my heart still, that all the works she undertook, along with her dearly loved brother, Sir Philip, and all she wrote after his untimely death, be guarded with my life and not allowed out of the safekeeping of a family member that she deemed worthy of reading her innermost musings."

Sarah and Janek looked at each other across the table. The seriousness of Matthew's instructions hung between them and somehow each sensed that the weighty responsibility he had voiced, fell that moment gently but fully upon their shoulders.

When Sarah spoke, it was in a whisper, "Janek, there is such secrecy hidden beneath those words."

Janek nodded.

"As there is today, Sarah. We seem to have stumbled upon matters of historical intrigue and secrets well-kept, as you say. The cloaked nature of the works of Shakespeare still commands respect of whoever tries to uncover the truth of them. I think we must take this discovery as a serious warning from beyond the grave. For reasons still unknown to us, the Folio and the revelation of its true author, had a powerful effect on many of the historical characters of the day. And today, our own harried experience is teaching us just how compelling the authorship question has become. People on the same quest are trying to prevent us from following our private research to its conclusion. So, I feel we must maintain the stance Matthew adopted of carefully protecting whatever we may find, until such time as we feel we can reveal it safely."

They had come to the end of Matthew's letter. There were other bits of correspondence and papers to peruse.

The next was a death certificate for Matthew Lister and burial instructions. His last will was not included, but they knew this was housed in London at Kew. There were many letters of condolence written to his young second wife, Anne. And then a letter dated January 4, 1657, from her, to his solicitor asking for the box of contents from his previous marriage. Harold Alington, Esq., replied that this box was to be forwarded to a person named by Matthew in his instructions and to no other witness. There were more letters from Lady Anne to another solicitor at the same firm, asking for his help in releasing the box to her before forwarding it to its proper recipient. The letters became increasingly pleading and then this solicitor wrote back that, in fact his partner, Harold Alington, had died. By this time it was the end of 1657, close to Christmas. The information for all Harold's clients had passed to him, Martin Aberworthy. He suggested a meeting with Anne. This happened early in 1658 and according to his notes, the box had still not been dispatched to the specified Katherine Wroth, daughter of Mary

Wroth and William Herbert, who apparently had not answered any of the letters sent to her various residences. It was known that she had married twice, her first husband, a John Lovet, died early into their marriage. She was thought to be living at the time in Wales, near Tredegar Park, and remarried to a wealthy man by the name of James Parry.

Based on the non-delivery of the box, the persuasive Anne Lister was able to convince the new lawyer to allow her to read through its contents, claiming widow's rights over a husband's property. It was also noted in a letter to her sister, that she had married this lawyer the following year, perhaps an indication of how she managed to convince him to allow her access.

And that is where the trail ended. There was no mention again of the box, its key, or of Katherine Wroth coming to collect it.

All the letters in the box were read. Their research was stalled yet again. Sarah and Janek were quiet in their mutual discouragement.

"We will have to find out where Katherine lived out the rest of her life, and see if the box ever did reach her," Janek said, shaking his head. "I feel so frustrated at this moment!"

Sarah leaned across the table and held his hand.

"I do too, but we still have other leads, not least of which is Matthew's will. What do you say to finding a hotel, having some supper, and an early night?"

Janek rose from his chair and came across the room to embrace her.

"If I were on my own I'd be tempted to give up, but not now. Not with you beside me. We are getting closer to the discovery of Mary's papers and I hope we are the only ones on this quest at the moment. I think one piece of good news is that we've managed to lose our followers!" He smiled. "And that was no mean feat!"

Miles away, Crik and Poppy were realizing the same thing. Their quarry had indeed given them, as Crik declared, *"The slip, sir, the slip..."* as Shakespeare would say."

Poppy had to laugh. "Look at you, quoting the Bard!"

"Of course, milady, and it's from the wonderful play *Romeo and Juliet*: Second Act, Scene Four. Shall I identify the line number?"

"How would you know that? Have you got the play on you?"

"I'll have you know I played Mercutio in a school performance. And it's Line Forty-One by the way."

"Yes, Mercutio," she said in a sly tone. "You are so like him! Unpredictable, witty, even, with a tendency to be silly!"

"I will take all as compliments, Poppy— thank you kindly. Now what are we going to do?"

Poppy looked across the car at him. He suddenly seemed deflated. She liked him much better when he bantered with her.

"We don't get discouraged. We head back to London, because they have to land there some time. Above all, when talking to the Boss, we act like we know what we are doing at all times. We never let our guard down around him! This is your first assignment under his rule and you'd best know that he is a hard taskmaster. He would destroy you as quick as he'd use you, make no mistake about it."

"I gathered as much in my one and only meeting," Crik admitted. "Not one to be crossed, him."

"I am seriously impressed that you know some Shakespeare!" Poppy exclaimed, hoping to change the subject to something lighter.

"You just wait. I will continue to surprise, never fear."

She laughed and headed the vehicle back in the direction of London. There was a small smile on her face, which Crik did not miss. She was alright, was Poppy after all, he thought.

A day later, Sarah and Janek had returned to their apartment in London. Sarah was excited to visit Kew, where the National Archives was located, and to be able to see the actual, physical will of Sir Matthew Lister.

They headed out in the green car a little after ten that morning. Poppy and Crik were not far behind in their own new rental car, having kept surveillance on the apartment.

"They'll be watching for us," Poppy declared. "So, it's best to change cars every day."

Crik was almost asleep in the passenger seat, as he had spent a long time talking with his brother the night before over dinner. The boy was starting to trouble him, with new antics like skipping school and not handing in his assignments. *Chip off the old block*, he thought. He would have to get a handle on this situation quickly before it escalated.

"I guess your daughter doesn't give you too much grief yet?" he asked Poppy.

Sensing his worries, she answered that it helped to have her parents looking after Samantha. "You're on your own and that's a lot harder, given Jack's age. Have you got no support at all?"

"Not really, not someone that I could entrust him to. Definitely no family connections. There *is* a boy's club he is supposed to be attending every other night, where they do sports and activities, but he's even missing that. He used to like it there, but lately he seems to avoid the place like the plague."

"Have you found out why?" Poppy asked glancing over at him.

"I've tried, but I'm getting nowhere. It's really worrying me. Couldn't sleep last night."

"What about counselling for him? That really helped Samantha and she's a lot younger than your brother."

"That is one thing he's adamant about *not* doing. Says he'll run away if I try to force him."

Crik was despondent today. He looked like he'd been wrung out. Poppy sensed his fear and also his great love for the boy. "It's a good thing he has you."

This seemed to encourage Crik. He looked over at her and tentatively asked, "What would you think about meeting him? I cook a mean spaghetti sauce and we'd love you to come for supper. That is, if you would want to. No pressure, though."

"I'd like that very much," she returned, giving him an uncharacteristically shy smile.

On the way to Kew, in the southwestern Borough of Richmond upon Thames, Sarah and Janek chatted happily. Janek was explaining a theory he had read that Edmund Spenser, a member of Mary's Wilton Circle, may have secretly identified her as Shakespeare when he wrote and dedicated to her, his poem mourning the deaths of Philip Sidney and his uncle, Robert Dudley. The poem was titled *Ruines of Time* and was printed in 1591. There is a stanza which many believe was a reference to Mary Sidney Herbert's grief after the deaths of two of her favourite people:

There, on the other side, I did behold
A Woman sitting sorrowfully wailing,
Rending her yellow Locks, like wiry Gold,

About her Shoulders carelessly down trailing,
And Streams of Tears from her fair Eyes forth railing:
In her right Hand a broken Rod she held,
Which towards Haven she seem'd on high to weld.

"I think 'weld' is meant to be 'wield' which, in the England of Spencer's day was used to mean 'to brandish' as in 'wave around' like one would a sword. In other words, Mary 'shakes a spear' or a lance, broken as it is. Thus 'Shakes-speare!'"

"Interesting! Could it be a clue? It is an intriguing line, and by this time, many of the plays of Shakespeare had been released and acted by several troupes of players, so his work would have been known under the name Shakespeare."

"It gets better. Later on the poet asks her name and she replies":

"...shedding Tears awhile, I still did rest,
And after, did her Name of her request.
Name have I none (quoth she) nor any Being,
Bereft of both by Fates unjust decreeing.

"She was not able to be named as a writer, especially of plays, nor was a woman published in those days. This was unjust, as she was equally as prolific a writer as her brother by this time. Also, a recognized author by the attendees of the Wilton Circle. Yes! It makes sense! Spenser could be teasing out a revelation, without coming right out and saying it. Mary would suspect he knew, as the poem was dedicated to her!" Sarah conceded.

"Being part of the intimate Wilton Circle, Spenser would have known of the exchange of works between Mary and Philip, and though it was a well-kept secret, he probably wondered if her hand was behind the plays popular in his day. That is why he would have cloaked his words when he described

Mary," Janek suggested.

"There is another intriguing thing, Sarah. The title page of the original copy of Shakespeare's Sonnets, which was published by Thomas Thorpe and printed by George Eld in 1609, reads *Shake-Speares SONNETS Never Before Imprinted*! Again the reference to wielding a spear! And the Sonnets were released well before the First Folio of Shakespeare's works, which was in 1623, fourteen years after the Sonnets! Of course, eighteen of the thirty-six plays in the First Folio *had* been reproduced and printed in quarto, or eight-page, format early on, and had been distributed and sold in London before 1623. Curiously, there were few Folios per se printed in London, before Shakespeare's, but two of the most well-known were Philip's *Astrophel and Stella* and *The Countess of Pembroke's Arcadia*. Mention of the Sidneys and Herberts constantly surrounds the works of Shakespeare, even to the point, as you already know, of the Folio being dedicated to Mary's sons, William and Philip, the *incomparable paire of brethren...*" he broke off, a worried look on his face.

"I think I'm making you feel lectured to, Sarah!"

"Not at all, Janek! I am amazed at how many passages you can quote verbatim though!"

He smiled at her. "We can go to the British Library and view the original manuscript of *The Sonnets*. Would you like that?"

"Incredible! Yes!" she nodded her head vigorously.

They had reached the turnoff into Kew. Janek pulled into the parking lot.

"It's a long walk from here, but it's a pretty one. Shall we? It's such a beautiful day!" Janek held the door for her.

Sarah linked her arm in his. They strolled up a wide pathway and before them were two fountains spurting water which rose in fourteen-foot columns, high up into the air. Birds circled overhead as the sun shone over the water, causing bright stars to dance across it. Ahead were a series of linked buildings in a modern design, and as they entered the main door, the large foyer felt cool and airy.

"What a modern, open space!" Sarah exclaimed. She had been expecting something old and historical, but Kew was anything but. Janek explained the National Archives had come into existence in 2003, through the amalgamation of four organizations: Historical Manuscripts Commission, Public Records Office, Her Majesty's Stationery Office, and the Office of Public Sector Information. All four had eventually come under the one roof and were now known as the National Archives, Kew. The property stretched for blocks, comprising several buildings all constructed in a state of the art stacked style, each with many windows. The Thames River ran alongside the back portion of the complex.

Unbeknownst to Sarah and Janek, Crik had sidled up to the line for the information desk and, though a good distance behind them, he heard them explain their need to see the will of a seventeenth-century gentleman, Dr. Matthew Lister of Burwell. They had done their research ahead of time and had the reference citation ready. He was able to keep the pair in sight as they followed an archivist to a general research room. Within fifteen minutes, the archivist returned with a box containing many folded, browning papers. Crik overheard the explanation that the will of Sir Matthew Lister was in this box along with others from Burwell who had passed away in the last months of the year 1667.

When the archivist left them, they eagerly opened Matthew's will and laid it out on the table, using the weighted blocks provided to hold down the folding corners. They read silently. Then Sarah, taking out a pencil, said:

"I am going to make a note of the details: Matthew's wife Anne received the rent from his home in London. His nephew, Martin, received the house in Burwell, as well as the rents from Matthew's tenants in Calceby, Thorpe-Arnold, Muckton, and Anthorpe. Friarshead, the last of his holdings, went to his brother, with whom he had co-owned the property. That sort of left Anne homeless?"

"It sounds unkind, yes, and it was a common practice in the day, but Martin would have provided for her from the many properties he had been willed. Or she could go back to her family, who also lived in Burwell. There were no children from their marriage so the nephew would have assumed responsibility, if he had any integrity," Janek said.

"There's no mention of any box of documents," Sarah said with a sigh.

"No," Janek replied. "Matthew really must have wanted to ensure no one but his lawyer knew about that box!"

"How would his wife have found out about it?"

"Your guess is as good as mine. Wives usually know most about what a house contains."

"Well, can we make a copy of this will?" Sarah asked. Janek went to search for the archivist, who collected the box. A copy was obtained after a ten minute wait; it was paid for and they left the building.

Crik jogged to the parking lot once they were out of sight. He could hardly wait to tell Poppy what he had overheard.

"They found the will of Matthew Lister, and though I wasn't able to see it, I was able to overhear their discussion about it. They mentioned a box of documents, but it wasn't mentioned in that will. Somehow the guy's wife, Anne, had found out about a secret box he and his lawyer were guarding. Guess what, that Matthew guy only gave his wife a small part of his fortune. Some catch he was!"

"A box of documents! Very interesting! Did they give a hint as to where they are going next? Poppy asked.

"Not at all. But there they go now, so we should follow them. They looked really disappointed and kind of fed-up. I think they had put a lot of hope into finding something in that will. What motivates these two to traipse all over Kingdom Come for a box of papers? I don't get it."

Poppy glanced over at him, surprise on her face. "Didn't the Boss fill you in on why we are on this quest?"

"Yeah, he did. The discovery of who Shakespeare really was, of course. But what does it matter? Finding out who actually wrote those plays won't change them one bit. There's no money in it!" Crik declared, with a head shake.

"Is that what you think?" Poppy asked, incredulity in her voice. "There's no money in it? There'll be a ton of money Crik! The Boss is positioned to profit greatly in many ways from this discovery! He's been researching for years on this topic! He's in an academic world, boy, and a discovery like this would mean grants, research students, offers of employment at prestigious universities, publicity, conferences, papers, notoriety! He'd be a celebrity! Set for life! He is way too smart for his own good that guy! Why do you think he's investing his own savings, copious as they are, in us and others to get any info we can for him? Believe me, his whole life is invested in this. And he's not beyond using force to be the first to declare proof of the real Shakespeare!"

"The guy is a jerk— surely you can see that, Poppy! He has no life. He's cruel and acts sophisticated but he's obsessed. He's a meal ticket for me and my brother, that's all he means to me. Frankly, he pissed me off with his superior ways. Looked down on me royally. He's no better than you or I, in fact he's worse! He hasn't got a kind bone in that manicured and pampered body!" Crik was really angry.

Poppy looked at him sideways as she drove. She had never seen him so mad. The Boss had hit a nerve with him, that's for sure. He had done the same with her, put her down, made her feel insignificant somehow. But, as Crik admitted, the Boss was her meal ticket and her daughter's too. The sooner this job was over the better. She was more determined than ever to make this her last job of this kind. *I'll waitress if I have to*, she thought grimly.

CHAPTER SIXTEEN

Love's not Time's fool, though rosy lips and cheeks
Within his bending sickle's compass come;
Love alters not with his brief hours and weeks,
But bears it out even to the edge of doom.
Sonnet 116

Mary sat in her garden, reading the letter her brother Robert had sent her from London. The news was good and she was delighted to hear it. He was home in Baynard's Castle, on a visit from Vlissingen, also known to the English as Flushing, in the Netherlands, where he was Governor, under appointment by Her Majesty Queen Elizabeth. The letter was dated March 20, 1597 and she read it aloud:

My dearest sister Mary,

I hope this finds you in excellent health of mind and body and all your household as well. I am gladly home for a time from the continent. Barbara and I would like to visit you at Wilton House with our children at your convenience. We would only stay a short while. I am expected back in Flushing within a month's time. I have a request to make of you. Our daughter Mary, your goddaughter, loves to spend time with your family and has asked if she may stay at Wilton, yet again, to continue her education under your tutelage. I know we have imposed on your kindness many times over her ten years, but she seems quite insistent on this and for once does not beg to be taken with the entire family back to Flushing. Usually she clings to her Mother, my dear Barbara, but of late we notice she is much more self-sufficient and perhaps a little too 'worldly-wise' for our liking. I think she would benefit from the grace of your company and the intellectual and leisurely stimulations Wilton has so generously offered her in the past. Please reply soon my dear. I await your response.

Humbly,

Your brother, Robert.

Mary was overjoyed. She felt she needed the company of loved ones, and was thrilled that her extended family would be there for the celebration of William Herbert's eighteenth birthday. She had planned a huge ball in his honour, as he was to leave for the Queen's Court in May. She and Henry had worked hard to secure this, hoping he would follow in the footsteps of both his relatives, Robert Dudley and Philip Sidney, now deceased, as well as his esteemed father, now retired from Court.

She quickly dispatched an affirmative response and began to plan for the family's visit. Her thoughts travelled back in time, as she remembered the birth of her goddaughter, tiny Mary, named after her. How she had loved watching the child grow! She was perhaps closer to Mary than to any other nieces or nephews for that matter. Mary was a dark haired, dark-eyed beauty. She had excelled in learning and had been extremely precocious, a trait which endeared her to her father, who had nicknamed her his *Moll*, and doted on her. At the age of three, Mary had entertained the entire family at Wilton House with her dancing and her knowledge of letters, taught by a proud Aunt Mary. Over the years, the young girl had learned to play the lute, virginals and piano, had a golden voice, and had, through her dancing, attracted the attention and admiration even of the Queen when Her Royal Highness had visited Penshurst.

On April 8, with all the Sidneys and Herberts present, the great ball of the season was held in William's honour. He was a very handsome and confident man, fair of hair and strong in physique. Mary and Henry were extremely proud of him. He was intelligent, presented himself courteously, and had serious ambitions already. He loved to write and to dance. After a sumptuous repast, the musicians were assembled. William walked to the centre of the floor and held out his hand to his mother, Mary. She gracefully took his in hers and smiled up at him. They began to dance the galliard, a dance which was set at a moderate pace, with much foot-kicking and high-spirited movements. As they danced, William signalled the musicians to increase the pace, and Mary, in her twirling burgundy satin skirts, was more than able to keep up with the youth. At the end, each bowed deeply to the other, and the relatives clapped and shouted for more. Mary declined graciously and returned to her husband Henry, who was seated on the sidelines. She was flushed with pride and happiness.

William turned to his aunt, Barbara Sidney— formerly Gamage— his uncle, Robert's, wife. She was a particular favourite of his. A well-endowed woman, both financially and physically, she had at this date borne seven children, and still had a twinkle in her eye and an energy that he had always found entertaining and surprising as a young boy. She tweaked his cheek and kissed him on the forehead, then bowed in unison with her nephew. They danced the slightly more subdued pavane and she teased him with her wide brown eyes unmercifully, accompanied by the laughter of the crowd.

At the end of the dance, he again bowed and as she left the dance floor he looked directly at his young ten-year-old cousin, Mary Sidney, and said "Who dares dance the courante with me?"

Mary jumped with delight and ran to him and he lifted her off her feet. Her pale green velvet dress brought out the dark chocolate of her eyes and she squealed in delight as he twirled her about. The music began, he again indicated the musicians should speed up the tempo, and they proceeded to amaze the onlookers. "Surely, they have practiced for days!" one woman exclaimed. Mary watched as they moved in perfect unison, admiring her young niece's agility. William feigned tiredness, but Mary kept right on, dancing alone at one point as her cousin marvelled at her poise and energy. The music came to an end, he gestured for it to begin again, and most of the people in the circle joined in the dance, but to a slightly slower pace. Henry and his wife sat on the sidelines, gazing in wonder at the beauty of the swirling skirts of the women and leaping movements of the young and older men.

"Go and join them, my dear. Don't sit here with your old man of a husband! Life is short and you must dance!"

"No, she replied, laying her head on his boney shoulder. "I want to be beside you, the wonderful father of our beautiful son and watch him shine, just as you did in your youth."

"I was hardly a youth when you knew me, my Mary! Though many a time I wish I had been." But his smile was wide and he reached for her hand. She squeezed his hand as a small tear fell from her cheek.

The next day young Mary Sidney was beside herself. She had had such fun the night before, dancing with her grown up cousin, eight years her senior. Oh, how she had longed for this day to come! She was becoming a young beauty and she knew it. She saw how the young men of London looked at her as she drove by in her father's open carriage. She also saw how her mother watched her for signs of budding womanhood and the proud look on her face when she surveyed her daughter in a lovely dress, or combed out her long waist-length dark hair. Barbara had reddish-brown hair and Robert Sidney was red-headed. Somehow, Mary had grown into a young woman with dark hair and olive skin, inherited from her mother's Welsh father, John Gamage of Coity Castle, who had Norman ancestry. Mary was proud of her unique beauty but knew enough not to show it, as it would be considered conceit. She was a girl who knew what was expected of her.

Mary Sidney was also highly intelligent and talented in whatever she attempted. This made her quite ambitious and she sometimes found herself dreaming of what it would be like to be able to have the freedom of the boys in her circle. Her father, Robert, sensing from a young age her curiosity and eagerness to learn, had been determined not to allow this to be stifled, as he was a man of letters as well. She was his favourite; everyone knew that. He gave into her every whim and from afar, he ensured she was well educated. In fact, though his wife was not herself an educated woman, he insisted that Mary be taught alongside her brothers, at home, by the same tutor. His wife had been reluctant at first, thinking this would set her daughter apart from her peers, or cause her to be haughty. But the girl's boredom with the household routines at Penshurst and the trouble she got herself into, finally convinced her mother that Mary needed a challenge. While the other daughters were content to sit with Barbara and embroider, Mary insisted on reading to them all, or acting out a piece of poetry or singing and dancing in front of them. She was energetic to the extreme! Her mother gladly agreed to send her off to the tutor with her brothers, if only to have a few moments peace.

Mary Sidney sat outside Wilton House, under an oak tree far removed from the property where she could watch without being seen. Her-ten-year old heart had such a longing to be in the company of her uncles, William and his brother, Philip. Of the two, William was kinder to her, allowing her to tag along or ride the horses with him. Philip was a monster. He had a short temper and he was constantly criticizing everyone: his brother, his mother, his father, the servants. She grew tired of him very easily. She could have spent all day with William and took to calling him *Will*, which he allowed with a smile. Of the two, Will was much quieter, more pensive, and bookish. The two cousins could often be found, sitting side-by-side in Aunt Mary's library, reading in front of the fire all afternoon and having to be reminded to come to dinner. Their parents teased them with the threat of banning them from all books for the duration of the holiday.

The day came when William was to leave for Court. Everyone lined up outside to wish him a good journey. Mary was at the end of the line. William bent low, on one knee, to wipe a small tear from her eye and he whispered gently, "Write to me and I will to you!"

And then he was off. She envied his excitement, his adventure, and she wished there was something like that for herself and her sisters. But she knew that was an impossible wish. Girls did not get the same life as the boys.

Aunt Mary saw her face as she turned away from the group and ran to her oak tree. After everyone had gone inside, Aunt Mary slowly walked to the old tree and sat down beside her niece. Mary could not look at her aunt and buried her face in her knees. Aunt Mary simply leaned over and held her by the shoulders as she cried.

Finally, her tears spent, her aunt lifted Mary's chin.

"They have an exciting life, these boys, do you think?"

Mary stamped the earth with her foot, like a wild filly.

"Yes, I agree they do," said her aunt. "But so can we, my dear. So can we. I am going to show you how to follow your dreams, if you will let me. What do you say to exploring my laboratory? Would that interest you, my dear? We can start by making a new supply of invisible ink!"

And so, young Mary Sidney's education in everything exciting, continued that spring at Wilton House. She was so enthralled with the many different things her aunt taught her, that she begged her parents to be able to stay the whole year. Her mother agreed, on the condition she learned how to behave like a young lady because, "My dear girl, you will soon be a young woman and you will need those skills to have a family of your own one day."

Her aunt, who by this time was her heroine, agreed with a wink. As her own life had proven, one could be a lady of a manor and still have a *very* interesting— even exciting— life. One secret she knew was worth its weight in gold was this: to go ahead and take a risk, and *that* she intended to instill in her protégée and favourite niece.

For the next two years, Mary Sidney entertained the new courtier, William Herbert with what she called their "secret letters." He would receive a very ordinary day-to-day account of everything going on in her young life, but underneath that, written in invisible ink, were her fondest hopes and dreams, her big questions, and her inner fears. Before William left for Court, his mother, her Aunt Mary, had shown both youngsters how to create invisible ink, from a formula she had concocted in her laboratory. William and Mary Sidney had tried the formula and found it to be simple and sound, so they had agreed to use it in their correspondence. How William loved receiving these letters because they were so different from the swirling world of intrigue at Court. He was not a man who appreciated drama, unless it was in the theatre. He found himself admired and sought-after by most woman, and even by other men, because he had dashing good looks combined with a depth of silence that intrigued everyone at Court. No one ever knew what he was thinking. He kept his opinions to himself, unless he trusted the listener completely. And trust was a scarce thing in the aura Elizabeth wove about her. The Queen seemed to encourage mistrust amongst her courtiers. William realized quickly that she kept everyone else off-balance to keep her own power secure.

Every time he received a secret letter from Mary, he would steal away and simply enjoy himself reading about her little world and all the news about family. Then he would use the same formula his mother had taught him, in order to make the invisible ink legible.

Mary's young heart and mind always brought him joy. Her words brought him right back to his childhood at Wilton House, a happy place and a nurturing one. Gone for a little while were the overwhelming responsibilities of being a courtier, trying to please and be pleasing. He was thankful that Mary was more faithful a writer than even his own mother, and certainly than himself. He wrote back one letter to every four of hers, but he was a busy man and an ambitious one. His time was daily spent observing all the ins and outs of Court life, learning whatever he could to forward himself and keeping an eye out for an opening in which to advertise his talents. It was all very exhausting.

He was home at Wilton House for Christmas in 1600. His father was not well at all and rarely left his bed to join the family at dinner. The doctor was summoned several times, once during the early morning hours. His mother was beside herself with worry and it seemed nothing could alleviate his father's pain and illness. Several times when he stole into Henry's bedchamber to sit with his father for awhile, the elder Herbert slept fitfully through his visits. But one evening, after he relieved his mother at the bedside, his father opened his eyes and smiled weakly.

"William, my boy, how you have grown and changed these past years," he whispered. "I am so proud of your accomplishments, son, and I pray you will continue to please the Queen, as I have heard you do. Dear boy, I am not long for this world, I fear, and you will be my successor. Your mother will need you for a short while, but she is more than capable of managing this estate, along with the others. Please, do not feel you must leave Court to live here after I am gone. Your place is at Court and my hope is that you will secure a place for Philip there when his time comes. Your beautiful mother is much younger than I, and I believe being in charge of things here will be good for her, though at first she may not agree. Give her time, see her often and support her in every way financially. The property will be yours but she and your sister must be looked after well. I can trust you to do this, William?"

"Certainly, Papa!" he croaked through his tears.

"I have had a good life, William, and I pray you will have the same and your siblings too. Remember to make your mother and I proud. That is all I ask now." He laid his head back on the pillow, dropped his hand from his son's arm and closed his eyes.

The effort had cost him dearly. William sat longer until his father was asleep and breathing regularly. He cried quietly as was his way. Then he slipped from the room and descended the stairs.

His mother was waiting for him in her library. She had been crying too and her worst fears were confirmed when she saw the grim look on her son's face. Henry was dying.

The two sat silently in front of the fire for a good long time. There were no words to say.

Mary rose to go to bed. She placed a hand on her son's shoulder and leaned down to kiss his cheek. He held her hand and said:

"Before you go, Mother, there is something I need to say. Please sit by the fire for a moment?" he smiled encouragingly at her. "When Papa is gone, I hope you will know this is your home and that I want you to stay. It will be mine in name only. I have absolutely no interest in taking charge of father's properties! My place is at Court and Philip's will be too. Anne needs you. Please, do not think of anything else now but to have time with Father, for his time is short. I am so, so sorry, Mama!"

Mary began to cry softly and looked him in the eyes. "You are so like your father and you have both our hearts. I am sincerely thankful that you are who you are and that you are our son."

And then she broke down and he rose to hold her in his arms until she was able to stop.

William returned to Court on January 2, 1601. On January 18th he received urgent word to return home. By the time he reached Wilton House in the early morning hours of the nineteenth, his father had already passed away.

He came through the great doorway and was met in the hall by a tearful Mary Sidney, who was there to support his mother. She shook her head slowly from side to side and ran to embrace her cousin. The two cried together for several minutes and then she led William up the stairs, holding his hand gently in hers.

At the bedside sat his mother, Mary, his brother, Philip, and his sister, Anne. The expression on his dear father's face was one of peace. All his suffering, all the strife, was now over. He ran to his mother and held her, stroking her hair. "Mama, I am so sorry!" Then in turn, he hugged each sibling and knelt by his father's bed, taking Henry's hand in his. "He was the best of men and the best of fathers," he declared, his voice wavering. "May we imitate him in all we do."

The funeral was held in Salisbury Cathedral a fortnight late. All the Sidneys, Herberts and members of Court, including the Queen, were present. Henry had been a good and faithful servant to the realm and he was much honoured that day. He was buried in the family vault under the steps of the choir loft. As Mary watched his burial, she thought that one day she and all her children would rest there and her heart broke in two. Henry had been such a loving and faithful husband and she was not ready to lose him or to be a widow. Everything had happened too soon! She remembered the early days of her marriage when the future had seemed so bright. "All is vanity!" she whispered to herself. William and Philip were holding her by the elbows on either side and beside them stood Anne and Mary.

If I must die, I will encounter darkness as a bride, and hug it in mine arms, she thought and let herself be led away.

By the final month of 1602, Philip, now eighteen, had been welcomed to Court by Queen Elizabeth, herself now very frail, sometimes confused, even paranoid, and often ill. He was given a very brief audience with her with his brother William present. The Queen studied him for some minutes, and declared rather severely, "You are not your father, I see." His face blanched but he said nothing. She then stated, "See that you live up to him." And with that, the brothers were dismissed.

Philip took the incident as a rebuff, which doubtless it was. His reputation had preceded him. The Queen had relied on her spies and knew everything about everyone in her Court. Philip's temper, at times uncontrolled, would be the end of him if not curbed. William looked sideways at his brother, noticing the scowl. "Cheer up!" he said, slapping Philip on the back. "Come, let us celebrate with the others!"

If Philip supposed the Queen was to be a roadblock to him, he needn't have worried. Not long after this incident, she took ill again, and was unable to leave her chambers. This had been happening frequently and it was apparent by their frowns and the tightness of lips, that her advisors were worried. Philip, in his self-centred youth, was relieved, to say the least. He even began to believe it was her constant state of poor health that had led to her severity with him. William's raised eyebrows betrayed his surprise.

"Do not let your guard down around Her Majesty, Philip! You must always be on best behaviour at Court."

After a month's time, Elizabeth insisted on leaving Westminster Palace and travelling in the frigid weather of February 1603, to Richmond Palace, her favourite residence, in Surrey County, about ten miles down the Thames. The day was bitterly cold and her ladies-in-waiting scurried about supplying her with blankets and furs for the journey.

By early March, the Queen was deathly ill, with what seemed to be a pneumonia, probably contracted on her last trip. She was bereft, lonely and angry with everyone around her. Her ladies watched over her night and day, and by March 20, Elizabeth had become very paranoid and would let no one near her. She was unwashed and unkempt. She stood all night in one spot by a window gazing out and shedding tears over all who had died before her. Then her weakened body collapsed onto the floor. The ladies-in-waiting were weeping constantly, fearing for her and her safety. They tried to persuade her to lie in bed, but the Queen seemed afraid to lie down. She kept whispering about the death of Mary, Queen of Scots, her half-sister. A few minutes later she would ring her hands and call for her courtier, Robert

Devereux. Both had been executed for treason. This went on for several days and the Queen's doctor spent many sleepless nights by her bedside. "Robert was like a son to me!" she wailed one evening. "Why did he betray me? I loved him!"

"She is so sad!" cried one lady-in-waiting. "I cannot stand to see her thus mortified!" "Our Queen is near death," wailed another. "What will we do?" They were inconsolable and felt helpless. None of the doctor's potions worked to relieve her and eventually Elizabeth refused the care of her physician. The following evening the great Queen lost her power of speech.

Everyone in the palace and those still at Court were devastated. All royal business came to a standstill.

A day later there was a shocking turn of events. Elizabeth nodded when asked if the archbishop could visit. He was able to console her with his talk of Heaven. The ladies then knew their Queen had given up the fight.

The following day, March 24, their great Queen, she of the forty-four year reign, passed away.

With a hand signal, it was said, she indicated that James VI of Scotland would ascend to the throne of England, perhaps because he was her closest Tudor relative. All through her reign, Elizabeth had refused to nominate, or even discuss the notion of, a successor.

The news reached Wilton House a day later, and Mary was alone to receive it. All her family had retired for the evening. The fire burned low in her library grate that night. She sat up all night, recalling memories of Elizabeth: as a young Queen, in love, dancing and laughing with Uncle Robert; as a ferocious woman who once sent a new kitchen servant to the Tower because the meat on her plate was cold; as the sly inquisitor of everyone she met, always watchful for a slip of the tongue or false move. Mary thought back to the day her own mother, the dear soul, the Queen's favourite lady-in-waiting, had taken her young four-year-old daughter to meet the Queen. Mary had looked up at the young Elizabeth's face, had seen a halo of red curls framing it, and had thought she was an angel. *But she was no angel*, Mary admitted to herself that evening. *She caused a great deal of grief to my family, to dear Philip and many others, and try as we did, we could never please her. Ah me, it is all over, now. There is nothing more to say or do. James will be King, England will go on and it is late. I must away to my bed.*

Since her husband's death, Mary was unable to feel grief for anyone else. She had become resigned to the sorrow in her heart and accepted it as a matter of course now. Gone was the lively young mother and wife she had been. She had her sons, her daughter Anne, niece Mary, and her books and writings to comfort her now. She worried over her family, and used the written word to relieve and purge this worry. That was all she had left. Like Elizabeth I, life had stripped her of her fighting spirit.

She penned a special entry into her daily diary that night, heading it as *The Death of a Queen:*

> *To-morrow, and to-morrow, and to-morrow,*
> *Creeps in this petty pace from day to day,*
> *To the last syllable of recorded time;*
> *And all our yesterdays have lighted fools*
> *The way to dusty death. Out, out, brief candle!*
> *Life's but a walking shadow, a poor player,*
> *That struts and frets his hour upon the stage,*
> *And then is heard no more. It is a tale*
> *Told by an idiot, full of sound and fury,*
> *Signifying nothing.*

"Rest in peace, poor Queen. Your time, too, has come. As it will to us all."

CHAPTER SEVENTEEN

Sarah and Janek returned home, more exhausted than they had felt in days. They both realized the search for Mary's writings was at an impasse. They shared a bottle of wine and a bag of crisps and had another early night.

Poppy spent the evening with Crik and his brother Jack and thoroughly enjoyed herself. Jack entertained them with jokes and silly actions, all the while teasing his brother and telling Poppy stories about Crik's coloured youth. Crik was an amazing cook and the supper was a culinary masterpiece. The evening was full of laughter. After Jack left them to return to his computer games, Poppy and Crik put their feet up on the coffee table, listened to Johnny Clegg on the CD player and relaxed with their own wine.

"This is so nice!" Poppy exclaimed, looking around the small apartment. "You are quite the host. I haven't felt this calm in a long time."

"Well, thanks, Poppy!" Crik's red face may have been the effect of the merlot. "I'm happy you like it here. Jack likes you, otherwise he wouldn't have acted so goofy tonight. I could tell."

"I like him too. He really loves you, Crik. He looks up to you, wants to be like you. I was like that with my big sister too."

"That's a bit of a pity, ain't it, 'cause I'm not the best one for him to emulate. I'm not very proud of what I've done, the thieving of my earlier days and all, and even now... well, this job, you know... It's not exactly an upstanding thing to be doing. And with the likes of our Boss, it may get a little rough before we're through, Poppy. How do you feel about that?"

"I can't afford to think too far ahead, or I'd quit. I met Sarah, you know, and I have to admit, I really liked her. She's so innocent. Thinks well of everyone. It irks me that she's gotten hurt, and I knew it was going to happen. She really didn't come here to research the Shakespeare authorship question at all, in fact she just kind of fell into it after she met that Janek fellow. I think she kinda fell in love with him."

"Really? That fast?"

"It can happen that fast, yes. Her research was about the same two people he focuses on and they're both nerds, so it's not surprising to me."

"Yeah, I guess like attracts like," he said, looking sideways at her. Poppy was staring straight ahead into the fire Crik had made in the small fireplace across the room. She had a faraway look in her eyes and a sad expression on her face. He thought she was beautiful in that moment, with her crazily curled red hair and her upturned nose. He knew her to be a fighter, but right now, she seemed vulnerable.

"Listen, Poppy, I'll take the couch and you can have my room. Don't go back to your hotel tonight. Stay awhile and we can watch a movie, or play a game, or something. You can have breakfast with me and that ruffian I live with... what do you say?"

Poppy shook herself out of her reverie and looked at him, gratefully. "That would be wonderful! I'm so tired but I'd like to phone Samantha first, hear her little voice and then, yeah, let's watch a movie."

He beamed at her. She went to get her phone and he lay back against the couch cushions and closed his eyes. Like her, Crik was weary, but he hadn't felt this relaxed in years.

Janek had made breakfast and brought it on a tray into bed so Sarah could have a relaxing morning. She smiled at him and thought she had the best boyfriend in the world.

DEATH STALKS THE HOUSE OF HERBERT

When they had finished eating and were enjoying coffee, he asked, "Why don't we take a break and just be tourists today? I think you deserve to have some free time, away from all the work and worry of the last few days, and after all, you haven't had time to see much of London!"

"Sounds wonderful!" They got out the city maps, poured over the attractions, and decided to make a day of it.

An hour later, they were on the road, headed for Portobello Market. It was about eleven when they arrived and there were crowds of people milling about. It was such a beautiful day that everyone was taking their time and enjoying the sunshine, strolling along leisurely, and looking carefully at the vendors' wares set up in the middle of the street, under bright awnings.

Sarah had never seen anything as colourful as this place. Everything— the houses and businesses on the street— was painted in bright reds, pinks, greens, and blues. Vintage and antique cutlery, china, glassware, cameras, eyeglasses, jewelry, and knick-knacks of all kinds were piled high on tables and there were fruit and food stalls every few feet. The smells were rich, ranging from spicy, to flowery, to sugary. She snapped pictures and marvelled at the age of some of the goods. "We think something from the early twentieth century is old where I come from, but here, look at these plates from the late seventeenth century!"

Janek smiled at her enthusiasm. She was such a delight to be with, and he couldn't help comparing time with Sarah to that of his past. Sybil had frequented only the high-end antique shops and would never venture into Portobello Market, even for the fun of it. He knew in his heart he had made the best choice in Sarah and felt a wave of gratitude for her in his life. He couldn't believe how easily one day flowed into the next and how contented he felt all the time.

Unbeknownst to the happy pair, they were again being followed, albeit at a distance, by Crik and Poppy, she sporting the blond wig again and a large hat that shielded her eyes. They were having fun too, joking over some of the outrageous 1960s outfits that hung on a rack beside Crik. He tried on a furry lambswool vest and a tie-dyed, embroidered bandana, while Poppy giggled. Crik's brother Jack had come along and now stood scowling at the two of them, embarrassed, but even he started to smile when Crik put his big feet into a pair of platform shoes and began to strut around. Had anyone seen the three of them, they'd have thought it was a family out for a Saturday stroll through the market. In his mind, Crik was imagining exactly that, and thinking how great it would be to spend more normal time with Poppy. She had a way with his brother, who seemed to respect the tiny redhead and who freely gave her all his attention. *The poor kid is longing for a mum, I can see that. This time together has been good for both of us*, he thought, watching Poppy slip on a pair of cat's eye sunglasses and a necklace in the shape of a large peace sign. Jack donned a corduroy navy cap with a visor, with *Give Peace a Chance* scrolled across the front and turned to make a face at them, jiggling the pom-pom on the top of the hat. All three burst out laughing again.

Poppy whispered to Crik, "Let's just have fun and forget about surveillance today. Those two nerds are taking a break, I can assure you. Why shouldn't we? It's the weekend!"

Crik whispered back, "I'm in, but what about the Boss?" making quotation marks in the air.

"I'll handle him," she retorted and pulled out her phone, moving some distance away to send a text. Jack came over and Crik put his arm around his shoulders. "You getting hungry?" he asked.

"Yeah, I'm always hungry," replied the boy with a grin.

"Whaddaya say to a giant burger, chips, and a milkshake?" Crik asked.

Jack smiled up at him. "What about Poppy?" and looking around he spotted her a few feet away, talking on her cell. His eyes softened and then he teased his brother with a wicked grin. "She's something, that one!"

Crik's eyes softened, too, as he said absentmindedly, "She *is* beautiful, ain't she?" His brother grinned and turned away, blushing.

After a time, Janek and Sarah left the market with Chelsea buns and coffee and walked down to a nearby park to enjoy the sun and the sounds of children playing nearby.

"This is wonderful, Janek, just relaxing and sightseeing. But you know I can't seem to take my mind off Shakespeare. I keep going over all the clues we've discovered, or I should say, *you've* discovered and introduced to me. I feel like a detective on the case, who can't really let go 'til it's solved. Mind in one place, body in another."

"I know what you mean. It's like going through the motions, but your brain is on hypercharge, in another realm entirely," Janek said laughing. "Sarah, I'm so glad you came into my life! I've never felt freer to be myself. Being with you is like breathing deeply and sighing. I love you so much."

He turned towards her, tipped her chin up, and kissed her. She was completely lost in him.

Poppy and Crik stood on the sidewalk and watched the lovers embrace. "They sure look thrilled with each other," was all Crik could muster. In truth he envied them.

He stole another look at Poppy and thought to himself, I wonder what she'd do if I sauntered over, pulled her to me, did an abrupt bend and dip and kissed her passionately, like the photo of the sailor and the nurse kissing in Times Square at the end of the War. She'd probably flip me over her back and have her boot on my chest in five seconds flat. He chuckled.

"What's so funny about a romantic kiss?" she asked, smacking his arm.

"Yeah, bro, what are you laughin' at? Jealous.....?" Jack teased.

"You two think you're funny! Come on, let's get that burger. We're burning daylight, here," Crik shot back.

For a few hours, Janek and Sarah toured London, having tea in Soho, taking a double decker bus for a few blocks so Sarah could say she did, getting their photo taken squished into a red phone box. By the time they returned to their flat, both were ready for a nap.

The break was good for Crik and Poppy as well and Jack seemed to relax. By nine, the Watchers, as they'd taken to calling themselves, were flaked out in front of the TV, each with a glass of beer, Jack having left earlier to meet up with friends.

"Don't you wish this assignment was over? I admit it's wearing me down," Poppy said quietly.

"Are you sayin' I'm boring to work with? Is that it?" Crik reached over and tickled her side.

"Be serious! You've got to admit, we aren't getting very far. The more I observe Janek and Sarah, the better I like them. I don't think they are going to find anything earth-shattering, either, but, unless they do, we're in for trouble from our employer."

"I know. I feel the same way. Just trying to lighten the mood a little. You have a right to be worried and I know you want to quit after this gig. I think you should apply for the force— the police, that is. You have a natural talent for this kind of thing. And your heart seems to be more on their side than on the other," Crik observed.

His voice had gone all soft and Poppy looked up in surprise.

"Hey, you, don't go all serious on me! I like your humour. It has kept me going these last few days. You're not such a bad sleuth, yourself. Pity we can't join forces with those two nerds and help them on this quest of theirs. That would take the Boss down a peg or two, wouldn't it? Fancy us pulling a little double blind kind of thing!"

"Are you serious?"

"Somewhat. I'd rather be working with them, than for that creep! Wouldn't you?" she asked.

"This is some sort of a test, is it?" Crik eyed her with some caution.

"No. I really am serious. The Boss scares me." Poppy looked frightened.

Crik leaned forward, his elbows on his knees, his eyes closed, deep in thought.

"I've been around a lot of bad guys in my life and I can handle myself. But I'll admit that the guy scares me too. There's something creepy about him." Crik finally stated. He looked at Poppy. He saw her eyes grow wider with fear and he leaned towards her then and reached for her.

"Come here. Let me hold you for a minute," he said. "No pressure, just a little reassuring hug, that's all."

She looked wary but a tear of frustration had escaped and coursed down her cheek. As Crik put his arm around her shoulders, she shivered and said,

"I feel like punching my fists through the wall. I'm that angry with myself for taking on this assignment. The longer I'm in it, the more I sense danger and I can't afford to either be arrested— or worse, injured in any way. Samantha is depending on me and I can't let her down! I *won't* let her down!" She was now gulping back tears.

Crik held her ever so gently as she cried into his shoulder. He put his chin on the top of her head and breathed in the wonderful scent of her hair. His heart went out to Poppy. She was so brave and had tried so hard to hide her fears and feelings to appear tough. He had no doubt that she *was* tough, but at this moment the fact that she had allowed herself to be vulnerable with him brought out a tenderness and respect that he hadn't felt towards someone for quite some time.

We are both so needy, he thought. And so responsible, in a twisted sort of way. Both of us have someone depending on us, and here we are risking losing those relationships by getting involved in stuff that's on the wrong side of the law. What are we thinking? We aren't thinking! We're desperate for the money! He was now as angry at their shared situation as Poppy was, and he could feel the pent-up frustration she had talked about.

"Life really sucks!" was all he could say. "We have choices, but they are so limited! Nobody understands that, do they? People like you and me can never catch a break, you know. These rich dudes have all kinds of schemes and the money to invest in them and always end up on top. They don't even pay their bloody taxes, but we are expected to, from whatever meagre savings we get to put aside. I hate feeling this way! I hate being trapped as much as you do! We have to believe we are not stuck in this shitty life, or we'll never get us and the kids out of it!" and he looked at her with such a pleading look that Poppy smiled and squeezed his hand.

"I can't believe I'm saying this, but you are my witness, Crik. If there is some way of redeeming ourselves through this assignment, I'm up for it. 'Cause if my parents ever discover what my real life is like, they'll disown me and I'll lose my little girl. And I won't let anyone take her from me! I can't go to jail over this stupid Shakespeare thing."

"You won't, if I can help it!" Crik vowed, holding her a little tighter.

The next afternoon found Janek and Sarah deep in conversation, notes strewn about the kitchen table and their computers fired up.

"I think we have to take a different tack, Sarah: switch our focus, do something to break through this impasse," Janek was saying.

"I agree," she replied, "but I admit I am stumped as to where to go next. I have been trying to put myself in Mary's shoes, wondering where she'd hide the notes and scripts she and Philip had worked on once she was no longer Mistress of Wilton House. I'm sure while she was at Wilton House, she'd keep them locked up in a hidden place in the library. But once William took over and she moved out, what happened to them then? Where would she feel safe hiding them? I think she'd feel sure enough of Matthew to let him in on the secret, but would there be anyone else, Janek?"

"Great train of thought, Sarah! You are quite right about William eventually residing at Wilton House. He and his mother had a 'falling out' of sorts and barely spoke for several years, over a combination of events, one of them probably his lack of commitment to his relationship with his cousin Mary Wroth. It was well known that he could be quite the cad with ladies. His mother Mary did go to live in London at various residences once he was married as well as travelling to The Spa in Europe with her Dr. Matthew Lister."

"But one thing I haven't mentioned is her friendship in Wiltshire with a woman not from her class. This lady had come from France, and her father was a Huguenot scholar and writer, struggling alongside Phillippe Du Plessis Mornay and his wife, during the St. Bartholomew's Day Massacre. When her father died, she went to live with a close friend of his who was the pastor of St. Mary's Church, in Wilton itself, not far from the grounds of Wilton House. Mary Sidney Herbert and her family attended that chapel and often prayed there. The pastor was named Jasper Meredith and her name was Jeanne Trefusis, and though she was his ward, and much younger, they eventually fell in love and married. Jeanne's father had ensured she was highly educated, and she and Mary were intellectual equals. Both spoke several languages, were adept at translation, and were highly skilled in music. They became fast friends and it could be likely that Mary eventually shared her secret writings with Jeanne and her husband."

"What do you know about this St. Mary's Church, Janek?" Sarah asked.

"It was built over six hundred years ago, but is now another redundant church, like the one we just visited. There is a monument to William Herbert's servant in the church. The building itself is in ruins, except for the chancel and the first section of the nave of the Old Church, as it is called. The arches of the entranceway remain outside as does half a wall of the bell tower. We can visit it if you like."

"Do you think we can find out more about Jeanne and her husband there?"

"Probably not there, but in the Wiltshire Archives, and for that we'll need to consult the unfriendly Mr. Branscombe again. There is also a book written about Mary and Jeanne's friendship which I have read. It was published in

1906 and is entitled *His Most Dear Ladye: A Story of Mary, Countess of Pembroke, Sister of Sir Philip Sidney*, by Beatrice Marshall. I have not been able yet to find out anything about Marshall's sources for her book but it tells Jeanne's story as well as Mary's and is a fascinating look at Mary's time in history. It may be entirely fictional, but many of the characters represent real people."

"Let's check the Salisbury Library and the Wiltshire Archives to find out about Jeanne and Jasper Meredith!" Sarah was excited now.

The two spent over an hour on their computers. At one point Sarah found a reference to a Captain Samuel Meredith, the first person to be appointed to the Wiltshire Constabulary, in the first third of the nineteenth century, but he was originally from London. Then she discovered a record of the marriage of one Mary Meredith to the antiquary Thomas Gore during 1656, in the Wiltshire and Swindon Archives.

"We should check that reference, Janek. He collected antiquities, and they were born in the early half of the century. Mary Meredith could be a daughter or a granddaughter of the pair. Unfortunately they lived about three hours away from Wilton, by car. I don't know..." her voice trailed off.

"Yes, and I have found a reference to the Grange which was mentioned in Marshall's book, an old barn that is still standing on the Wilton House Estate. Most of the other structures surrounding it were torn down and renovated, but there was a home there where Jeanne and Jasper apparently lived, according to the book. We would have to gain special permission to look at the old barn itself, and that would mean contacting the family of the present Earl of Pembroke." Janek whistled. "I'll fire off an email. It's becoming more complicated isn't it?" he asked.

He had sensed by the slump of her shoulders that she was discouraged. He shuffled his chair along the floor to be beside her and turned her face towards him.

"I know this is really painstaking work. Do you want to take a break, go for a bite to eat, or to hear some music at the pub up the street?"

She smiled up at him. With a suppressed sigh, she admitted she was feeling like they were going in circles and that maybe a break would help.

"Let's just take a stroll around the neighbourhood and get some fresh air, maybe stop for a drink somewhere close by?" she suggested.

When they left the apartment, they didn't notice a parked car a block away. Inside were Crik and Poppy, who today sported a brown wig and the cat's eye sunglasses she had bought at Portobello Market.

"Duck down and pretend to be asleep!" she whispered, as Crik pulled his cap down over his eyes. Janek and Sarah passed right by their car but were oblivious to them. Poppy and Crik heard a snippet of conversation as they walked past, hand in hand.

"... great to get some air and sun... go to Wiltshire tomorrow?" And then they could hear no more.

"Oh no, *another* road trip!" Poppy exclaimed once they were gone. Let's go back to our places and prepare. No point waiting for them to return."

"Why don't I get in and bug their place? That way we could sit at home and listen in, instead of being cramped up all day in the car?" Crik asked.

They discussed the pros and cons. Poppy thought it was too risky. She was afraid he'd get caught if the couple returned in a few minutes and they couldn't risk him being seen so close to the apartment. She wanted to go back to her hotel, get some rest and prepare for a trip.

"What if they decide to leave tonight?" Crik asked.

"Not likely. It's four o'clock, already and it's a bit of a drive. No let's go our separate ways and meet back here really early to tail them tomorrow morning. That will give you time to set up care for Jack, OK?"

She was insistent and didn't envy Crik's responsibilities. She was fond of Jack now, and worried he might get into trouble again. Crik nodded resolutely, admitting he had wanted to bring Jack with them, but knew that was not a good idea. He drove Poppy to her hotel, smiled at her and wished her a good night. "Don't get into any trouble without me, now!" She raised her eyebrows at him and said "I could say the same for you." As she walked away, he watched her until she was out of sight, wishing he had asked her to stay with him and Jack. But it wouldn't do to let too much familiarity scare her away. He sighed and put the rental car in reverse.

After their walk, Sarah and Janek returned home. As they sat talking, Sarah asked, "If we don't find the lost papers, Janek, I was wondering if there are lost books that belonged to the Sidney Family, or the Herberts, which would have samples of the handwriting of Mary or Philip, as well as notes they may have written in the margins, say of history books used in research before writing the plays?"

"Another wonderful idea, Sarah! In fact, there was a copy of *Hall's Chronicles*, found in 1940 by a researcher named Alan Keen. There were, in fact, handwritten notes in the margins, and it looked like the notes were in reference to one of the historical plays of Shakespeare. So, Keen followed the lead from the name of the owner of the book, Richard Newport. A man by that name had sold a property to the Shakespeare family in Stratford-upon-Avon, so he posited that the book had been Shakespeare's. But there were no books in Shakespeare's home, according to his will, when he died. So many scholars did not think this was proof of ownership by William Shaksper."

"However, there was a Richard Newport who lived in Eyton on Severn at the same time, who was a knight. Philip Sidney's father had sent his son often to visit this Richard and his wife Lady Newport. Eyton is about 60 kilometres from Stratford-upon-Avon. It was about 1565, so Philip was young, ten or eleven at the time, and he was asked to represent his father there, many times, so was often a guest. There is one story in which the young Philip represented his father as godparent of one of the Newports' friends' new babies, alongside Lady Newport. Philip and several schoolmates even spent sick time at their home one season and took a long time to recover. The young Philip was like part of their family. So, it is far likelier that it was Philip or one of his classmate's handwriting found in Newport's book than it was Shakespeare's."

"Janek, where do you find all these tidbits of information?" Sarah exclaimed.

"I have been doing this for quite some time, Sarah. Working in a library, it's easy to find books to reference!"

She looked at him with admiration. Her boyfriend was an accomplished scholar and just the right man for this job. She reached over and hugged him tightly, planting a kiss on his cheek.

"Many of Philip's books were willed to his best friend, Fulke Greville, who kept them at his estate library at Warwick Castle until his death. He was stabbed by his valet, and he suffered greatly from complications, and then died six weeks later."

"There is a bizarre true story about his arrangements for burial: years before, he had planned a huge monument made of marble at St. Mary's Church. It was built, but his body is not there. He is buried with his family in their vault below the church. The marble sarcophagus consists of a large double bed on a huge rectangular platform. Fulke wrote his own epitaph and had it inscribed. The epitaph mentions Greville's relationship with Queen Elizabeth and Philip Sidney."

"Fulke had asked that specific documents be buried inside this marble monument, and whether or not that occurred is still unknown. In the late 1800s, Fulke was recognized as a candidate for Shakespeare Authorship. The Fifth Earl of Warwick, Francis Richard Greville, had the entire monument opened up around 1901. There is not a lot of documentation about the excavation, but apparently he employed a man named Elliot as a contractor— I believe he was also the Warwick Castle mason— to open and take out any contents he found inside the rectangular platform. Anything that was there was removed and unfortunately, whatever Elliot discovered has disappeared. After the repairs were made to the sarcophagus, the Earl handed the monument's responsibility over to those responsible for St.

Mary's Church, on the strict orders that it never be opened up again."

"Based on Fulke's secretive words about certain papers, there was speculation that they contained a revelation about the real Shakespeare. We do know there was a tribute by Greville to his best friend Philip Sidney, revealing details of their relationship, another tribute to Queen Elisabeth I, the play *Anthony and Cleopatra* which Fulke claimed was written by Philip Sidney and himself, as well as writings posing accusations towards King James I, (who also retained the name James VI, of Scotland), with whom Fulke had a difficult relationship. Perhaps there were sensitive details in the documents that were deemed too dangerous to be leaked to the public, but the Earl at the time either claimed the sarcophagus had previously been looted of all its contents, or kept the discovered papers hidden. It was a great disappointment to the scholars and researchers of the day."

"So, fast forwarding to the present, between the years 2009 and 2010, radar x-rays and an architectural endoscopy were made of the inside of the monument. The x-rays indicated the presence of what appeared to be boxes, but the endoscopy confirmed that there were only large rocks and stones inside the sarcophagus. So the entire search was shut down."

Sarah looked shocked. "What a story!" was all she could manage to respond.

Janek was disappointed that the Earl of Warwick at the turn of the twentieth century had decided that the contents and documents buried in the platform should not be seen. He felt like this could indicate a cover-up, and he thought it was weird that the monument had been filled with stones.

"We could visit Warwick Castle, Sarah! It was sold by the last Earl to Tussaud Group, who then passed it on to Merlin Group, who have made it something of an attraction, though they at present only run the place, as it was flipped again to Prestbury Group, co-owned by Nick Leslau, a wealthy British investor. I have met him at an event that Syb organized several years ago. The castle is beautiful, and only about one-and-a-half hours from

London."

"I don't know, Janek. Would it be worth our while? That is, could we find something there that would help our research?"

"Most likely not," he replied. Then he laughed. "You are *so* the girl for me!"

He gave her a hug and continued. "There's another lead I've explored in the past. It's a long shot. As you know, Mary and Matthew Lister travelled to the village called 'The Spa' in Belgium. They actually lived there for a couple of years between 1614 and 1616. A lot can happen in that amount of time. The area was very popular with wealthy tourists. It was a party place for the rich and famous. There was theatre, music, shooting ranges, the baths, much culture, good food, and all kinds of merriment."

" Mary was known as a vivacious woman, who loved to have fun. It would have been just her kind of place! I am sure, given how much she loved to write, that she would have organized a like-minded group around her in Belgium, just as she had with the Wilton Circle. In fact, she probably wrote plays or closet dramas for their entertainment. It was what she did!"

"So I began to research if there were extant records of the couple having lived there, maybe even marriage records. So far I have found only one reference under Matthew's name, and have written to the appropriate source, the State Archives in Ghent, Belgium. I have sent another request to the Musée de la Vie, Walloone, for information about a book called *Four Centuries of Parish Life in Spa: 1574-1974,* which concerns the parish of Saint Remaclus. It is about one-and-a-half hours from the village of Spa. It has been about a week since I contacted both of these sources. So the question now is..." He paused for effect.

Sarah gasped in delight. "You want to visit Spa!" she blurted out.

He smiled at her enthusiasm. It would be such a fun trip and Sarah deserved a holiday.

"Yes!" he laughed. "That's why I didn't share the research with you. I wanted it to be a surprise!"

"When can we go?" she asked, throwing her arms around his neck. They kissed and he replied, a twinkle in his eye, "Right away, if you like!"

It was now 10 p.m. and they poured themselves coffee and sat down to plan the trip. Janek suggested they leave as early as possible the next morning, and that they take the train to the south of England and cross to Calais. There they could rent a car. He was a little concerned as to the health of their present car. Sarah agreed. They planned everything, and went to bed early.

The next morning they arrived at the St. Pancras International train station at 5:15 a.m. Both were sleepy, but very excited. Sarah had packed her swimsuit and lots of sunscreen, as she had pale enough skin to burn easily. She felt like this was the closest she would get to a European holiday and she was so thrilled to be able to combine the healing baths with more research. Janek purchased their tickets and the two sat side-by-side on a bench at the station, Sarah's head resting on his shoulder. She was mesmerised by the Gothic arched ceilings of the station and surprised by how many people were rushing about at this early hour. In her sleepiness it all felt a little overwhelming. London was a place one had to get used to, coming from Ottawa. Life was not quite so hectic there. Being a bookish person, Sarah appreciated silence. She thought of Janek. He had come from farming country to the great metropolis. He had admitted he had felt the same way years ago, and maybe even now, once in awhile. She snuggled into his shoulder and breathed in the soapy scent of his plaid shirt. She felt such love at that moment. He kissed the top of her head. "Sleep Sarah, I've got this," he whispered.

At 5:45 a.m. that morning, Poppy and Crik were again parked down the

street from Janek's apartment. It was a cloudy, overcast day, and the pair took turns sleeping as the day progressed to rain and then a small thunderstorm.

"Blasted weather!" Poppy complained.

"Looks like the lovebirds are staying put today. Can't they take a little downpour?" Crik smiled at Poppy.

She was in no mood for joking today. He saw her shrug and he leaned over and put an arm around her shoulders. "Are you cold? You can have my jacket," he offered. That got a smile out of her, but she pushed her seat back and said she was fine and would sleep for another hour. She set the alarm on her phone and soon drifted off. He gazed at Poppy as she slept, thinking she was one of the prettiest women he had ever seen. In sleep, her expression softened and there was no frown to discourage him from trying to pierce the wall she had built against the world at large. Some of her fortress had crumbled around him, but she always resurrected the ramparts. She was a tough one, was Poppy. But she made him smile and life with her was always changing. *She keeps me on my toes!* Crik thought, his smile reaching his eyes.

By 4:00 p.m., there was still no sign of Janek or Sarah. Their car remained parked in the driveway. Crik commented, "It's not unusual for new couples to spend a rainy day in bed I guess," as he looked over at Poppy.

"Humph!" was all she could muster. By 5:00 p.m., both began to think there was something wrong.

"I have an idea. I'll call one of me mates and get him to knock on their door with some excuse that he has the wrong apartment. That way they won't suspect us."

His friend came, entered the building and soon returned. "There's no sound from inside and no answer," the young man declared. Crik handed him 20 quid for his trouble. He leaned in the window, took one look at Poppy, winked at Crik and said, "Anything I can get your young lady?"

She answered, "No. Thanks, though."

"What was that about?" she quipped as he rode off on his motorcycle.

"I've never seen him act so polite before," Crik frowned, his face red, then added with a wink of his own. "He thought you were a looker! And you are, Poppy, you really are."

She stared at him for a moment, noticing how gently he said the last sentence. She blushed and Crik noticed. Then she fidgeted in her seat and burst out:

"So, they've done a runner, those two sly ones! They must have left before we got here this morning. I told you they were smart. Now we are in big trouble. If the Boss finds out we've lost them, he'll punish us, you can be sure. We'd better have our story ready when we do our daily report. Get your thinking cap on. And I'm starving!" The last sentence came out loudly as she pounded her fist on the side of the car door.

Crik sat looking straight ahead. He knew Poppy was raging at herself and him. Wisely, he chose to just close his eyes and wait out the storm. Arguing with Poppy would do no good. He focused on a solution to their problem, letting his mind go very still, as he had learned in a meditation class offered at reform school when he had been fifteen years old. He concentrated on his breathing. In seconds a thought came to him.

"Poppy, didn't you tell me you and Sarah had exchanged emails?"

There was a long moment of silence. He shifted to look at her. A smile was slowly making its way from cheek to cheek and her eyes were lit up when she turned to him.

"You, my lad, are brilliant!" and she threw her arms around him across the car, pulling him into a rambunctious embrace. She knocked his baseball cap off his head and the smile on his face could have melted an iceberg.

Whipping out her cell, Poppy searched her contacts list, found Sarah's email address, and began to type, while reciting the text to Crik.

Hi my friend. Guess who this is? Remember me? – it's Poppy - who met you at the Bed and Breakfast while we were both in London? Sorry I did a "runner"- when last we saw each other, I had given you pain medication after the attack you went through on the Subway. Well, I hope you are recovered and happily going about your research?

My poor daughter got sick and I just panicked and returned to Manchester asap! I meant to contact you sooner but she had measles and needed my constant care..."Here Poppy blushed and stopped typing, and Crik noticed it cost her to lie.

"You really liked her didn't you Poppy?" Crik asked.

A tear escaped her eye. "I did Crik! I do! I feel bad 'cause I gave her something to make her sleep, so I could search her B&B for evidence. How horrible was that?"

"Now don't you go gettin' soft on me, Missy!" Crik joked, giving her arm a playful soft punch. "Carry on typing!"

"Whatcha up to?" Poppy typed as she recited. "Would you be interested in meeting up in London? That is if you are still there? Let me know OK? Happy we met...hope we can be "Pen Pals?"

"So now we wait," Poppy slumped in the seat.

Sarah's cell pinged while she and Janek sat side by side in the train to Calais.

"Why, it's from Poppy!" she said excitedly to Janek. "The young Mom I met at the B&B in London when I first met you. She's asking how I am, what I'm up to. I suppose it wouldn't hurt to tell her where we're headed?"

Janek wasn't sure what to say. Part of him thought it could be harmless but he wasn't sure who they could trust. He looked conflicted.

"How about I just say I've left London to continue my research on the Continent and I'll contact her when I get back?" Sarah suggested.

Janek agreed, seeing no harm in that.

Ten minutes later, Poppy's phone now pinged.

"They are on their way to "the Continent" of all places! I wonder what lead they are tracking. Time to call in the "big guns." I'll text Sybil Merryweather, Janek's old girlfriend, and get her to text him. He has no idea she knows me! BINGO!" she exclaimed.

Sybil was at home waiting to go to dinner with a new "friend". She agreed to send a text to Janek, saying that her father had decided on the amount Janek owed him for the damage to Sybil's car, so she had meant to talk to him anyway.

A half hour passed and Poppy was visibly agitated.

"That girl is sure taking her sweet time!" she complained. And then her phone pinged.

"So they are going to The Spa, in Belgium! But not for a holiday. Of course not! Janek is much too studious for that!" Sybil spoke with venom in her voice. "Always the bloody researcher! Never far from his thoughts is the lovely Mary Sidney! What a jerk! They are tracing her stay there, in Spa, way back in the early years of 1600, in the hopes of finding some missing manuscripts! Can you believe it? You or I would be there for the wine, the healing waters and the men….."

Before she could continue, Poppy blurted out, "Thanks a million Syb. I owe you one. When we return from The Spa, we'll go out on the town, OK?" She rang off.

"I hope you intend to take me with you?" Crik joked, as he reversed the car and sped off. "But right now, we have a trip to plan!"

Dear Reader,

I hope you have enjoyed the second installment of *To Pluck a Crow*. Yes, once again, I have left you on a cliff. But please know, this is not the end of the story.

Janek, Sarah, and now their watchers, Poppy and Crik, are about to start out on a new adventure, this time across France and Belgium, in their pursuit of clues to the authorship of the Shakespeare Canon.

You will see them all again, in just a little while.

Please stay with me, on this journey, as we *pluck a crow together?*

ACKNOWLEDGEMENTS

I continue to be so grateful for all the many people who have supported this effort. First, thanks go to my patient and encouraging husband, Bob. Many times I felt like I was stumped and he never gave up hope in me and in this story. He has given me time to think and write, food for the journey and wonderful encouragement.

Thanks to:

All the staff of Presses Renaissance Press, their editors who went over this book with a competent fine toothed comb, the Executive Committee, including the wonderful encouraging Nathan Frechette, illustrator extraordinaire, Marjolaine Lafreniere, ever calm and competent, and to Marie-Claude Goulet, whose enthusiasm is infectious; to all the authors, truly they are talented! This Renaissance family of ours is one in a million;

To my family, Bob, again, Matt and Kate, Mary and David and Jonah and Frankie; my sister Sharon who never stops promoting me; Jessica, Kris, Gavin and Ava and to Brendon, Kylie, Cayden and Isla (born during the last year), Shauna, Dylan and Harriet, who bring me so much joy all the time; my siblings and their families Dave, Dan and Brenda, who could not be a better more fantastic family; Nadia Hately;

To my beautiful kind Mom, who passed away shortly after the release of the first book, and my Dad and relatives "way up there" whose support I feel;

to my Aunt Joan Aubrey, my mentor, her daughter Chris Graham, and my cousin Carol Wicker, who came to the first launch and encouraged others to read Book One, and all my cousins far and wide; to Aunt Helen, Uncle Lorne and Tim, who also attended the first launch; to Sr. Anne Taylor and the Grey Sisters of the Immaculate Conception of Pembroke, who read my book and have been so encouraging; the Maloney clans in Ottawa, Kemptville and in the USA; Paul, Deb, Michael M in UK; Christine Graveline in Fort Coulonge; the Davy sisters, Linda, Sarah and Nancy;

To Mr. Fitzpatrick and his dear wife, both such wonderfully kind people...Mr. Fitz, I could not and would not have attempted this without you...you are my very BEST editor ever and to you I owe a great debt. Your unflinchingly honest comments and amazing encouragement have so touched my heart.

To friends and neighbours, especially Bridget C., who has been my greatest support, along with Anne K. who sat with me at book fairs, Tom L., Janice M., Ray C., Betty-Jean Bone, whose call of encouragement came at a time when I really needed it, Alexis and Mark Mongeau, Gale Thirlwall, Cathryn D., Susan J.-D. And Catherine M. both Moms extraordinaire, Jelena, Cynthia, Anne H. and Kevin Q., Barb F., Carole J., Gloria M., Bobbi Florio-Graham, writing mentor extraordinaire, Nancy and Colleen, Suzanne, the Stripinis family; To Margaret and Bob Nelson, who were my best "cheerers on" and helped promote my book and gave me encouragement; to Lisa Sadler, Nancy MacPherson, Janet Lemoine, Sandra Weedmark, Judy Pare, Audrey Henry, and Lois Presley and all my friends at Rideau Park United Church, and at the Ottawa Public Library, Bridget Carriere (again), Joanne Seguin, Kristina, Belinda, Sarah Lawrence, Evelyn Housch, Michael Houry, Lucy Bedard, and many more (so sorry if I missed your name!), who listened to my historical presentations on the Shakespeare

Authorship Debate and the Sidney Herbert families; to John Bond and his daughter Siobhan, the artistic Gabbie, and her talented mother, Thoma, Carolyn Stewart, musician extraordinaire and such a ray of sunlight, to the "Magoos" and Heather, and all my Blue Skies friends; and to anyone I have missed, I am so sorry!;

To my "Family away from home" Marie-France; Natalie, Ian, Rick, Diane, Linda, Eugene, Tony, Carolyn, Chris, and many more. And to my Serenity Renewal for Families Family who have been so much fun, so supportive and so giving to everyone they meet...Michelle T., Genna C., Donna C.-N., Jill E., Ed, Eleanor, Ann, Diane, Lynda and so many other kind people...especially Sister Louise Dunn, Father Harry McNeil, and John Robertson, whose help to me and my family was beyond words....blessings on this organization and all the hope it brings.

To my Coady Co-op friends, who listened to my presentation, especially my dear friend, Nancy Kelly, Carol Evoy, Diane D'A and her lovely daughter, Anna R., Catherine B., herself a poet, Carol C., Gail, Anne H. again and Kevin Q. and their families.....

Oh if I forgot anyone I really am sorry....and to anyone who bought or enjoyed my book at the first launch and since!

Renaissance. Diverse Canadian Voices

Renaissance was founded in May 2013 by a group of friends who wanted to publish and market those stories which don't always fit neatly in a genre, or a niche, or a demographic.

This is still the type of story we are drawn to; however, we've also noticed another interesting trend in what we tend to publish. It turns out that we are naturally drawn to the voices of those who are members of a marginalized group (especially people with disabilities and LGBTQIAPP2+ people), and these are the voices we want to continue to uplift. Our team is the same; we seem to naturally surround ourselves with people who are, like us, people with marginalized identities.

To us, Renaissance isn't just a business; it's a found family. Being authors and artists ourselves, wecare as much about our authors enjoying the publishing process as we do about our readers enjoying a great story and seeing a new perspective.

pressesrenaissancepress.ca
pressesrenaissancepress@gmail.com

TO PLUCK A CROW
Book one: The hands behind
Shakespeare's pen
SUE TAYLOR DAVIDSON

Do we truly know who Shakespeare was? Could the plays and sonnets have been written by more than one person? This historical mystery revolves around two possible candidates, Mary Sidney Herbert and her famous brother, Sir Philip Sidney, poet and courtier, in the court of Elizabeth I. Born in the same era as William Shakespeare, their lives were as real as his, and the three may even have met. Their story interweaves with the modern tale of Sarah and Janek, as they explore modern day London and the British countryside, searching for clues to prove Mary and Philip Sidney's contributions to the works of Shakespeare, a thesis one of them very much believes in. They are not alone. Two unidentified "watchers" are following them, hoping to discourage their search or to steal whatever information they find.

pressesrenaissancepress.ca

Journey of a Thousand Steps
Death by Association

Madona Skaff-Koren

Naya had the perfect life. Co-owner of a fast growing security software company, she ran marathons in her spare time. Suddenly everything changed when she developed multiple sclerosis, and now she can barely climb a flight of stairs. Hiding at home, her computer the only contact with the outside world, she reconnects with her childhood best friend.

But when her friend disappears and the police dismiss her concerns, Naya leaves the safety of her home to find her. She ignores her physical limitations to follow a convoluted trail from high tech suspects to drug dealers, all while becoming an irritant to the police.

pressesrenaissancepress.ca

Nothing Without Us

Edited by Cait Gordon
and Talia C. Johnson

"Can you recommend fiction that has main characters who are like us?" This is a question we who are disabled, Deaf, neurodiverse, Spoonie, and/or who manage mental illness ask way too often. Typically, we're faced with stories about us crafted by people who really don't get us. We're turned into pathetic, tragic souls; we merely exist to inspire the abled main characters to thrive; or even worse, we're to overcome "what's wrong with us" and be cured.

Nothing Without Us combines both realistic and speculative fiction, starring protagonists who are written "by us and for us." From hospital halls to jungle villages, from within the fantastical plane to deep into outer space, our heroes take us on a journey, make us think, and prompt us to cheer them on.

These are bold tales, told in our voices, which are important for everyone to experience.

pressesrenaissancepress.ca

The Baker City Mysteries

Éric Desmarais

Elizabeth Coderre has always known that there was something strange about her home town, Baker Ontario, but it isn't until her English teacher disappears that she starts to find out how strange. Getting through classes, killer kitten swarms, and bullies are going to be the easy parts of surviving at Sir Arthur Conan Doyle High. Elizabeth and her best friends, Jackie and Angela, are up to the challenge... they hope.

pressesrenaissancepress.ca

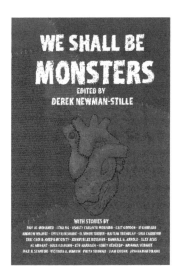

WE SHALL BE MONSTERS

EDITED BY DEREK NEWMAN-STILLE

Mary Shelley's genre-changing book Frankenstein; or, the Modern Prometheus helped to shape the genres of science fiction and horror, and helped to articulate new forms for women's writing. It also helped us to think about the figure of the outsider, to question medical power, to question ideas of "normal," and to think about what we mean by the word "monster." Derek Newman-Stille has teamed up with Renaissance Press to celebrate Frankenstein's 200th birthday by creating a book that explores Frankenstein stories from new and exciting angles and perspectives. We Shall Be Monsters: Mary Shelley's Frankenstein Two Centuries On features a broad range of fiction stories by authors from around the world, ranging from direct interactions with Shelley's texts to explorations of the stitched, assembled body and narrative experiments in monstrous creations. We Shall Be Monsters collects explorations of disability, queer and trans identity, and ideas of race and colonialism.

pressesrenaissancepress@gmail.com

If you enjoyed this book, please consider leaving a review where you purchased it.

Independent authors and publishers rely on those review for visibility.